FALLEN ANGEL

Carson stood over them, watching as they subdued the Seraph, his stomach writhing, bile splashing up into the back of his dry throat. They bound the wings to Zeke's slender torso with the coil of rope, then carried him to the van. Carson followed, ice inside, but sweating, his clothes glued by perspiration to his body.

They put Zeke in the back on the floor. They'd stuffed a handkerchief into his mouth, and Carson heard him wheezing, struggling to breathe. As they moved away to shut the doors, the Seraph's gray gaze locked onto his own. His eyes were dull, like iron, but they held Carson with magnetic intensity. Two words formed in the vacuum of his mind, soundless, clearer than sound.

The white enamel door of the Toyota slammed.

He still heard them. . . .

Elisabeth DeVos

THE SERAPHIM RISING

A ROC BOOK

ROC
Published by the Penguin Group
Penguin Putnam Inc., 375 Hudson Street,
New York, New York 10014, U.S.A.
Penguin Books Ltd, 27 Wrights Lane,
London W8 5TZ, England
Penguin Books Australia Ltd, Ringwood,
Victoria, Australia
Penguin Books Canada Ltd, 10 Alcorn Avenue,
Toronto, Ontario, Canada M4V 3B2
Penguin Books (N.Z.) Ltd, 182–190 Wairau Road,
Auckland 10, New Zealand

Penguin Books Ltd, Registered Offices:
Harmondsworth, Middlesex, England

First published by Roc, an imprint of Dutton Signet,
a member of Penguin Putnam Inc.

First Printing, October, 1997
10 9 8 7 6 5 4 3 2 1

Material used on pages 137–38 is from Peter Gorman, "Making Magic,"
Omni 15:9 (July 1993), 64–67, 86–90.

ROC REGISTERED TRADEMARK—MARCA REGISTRADA

Printed in the United States of America

To my husband, Steve DeVos
with love and thanks for making it possible

ACKNOWLEDGMENTS

My most heartfelt thanks to the following:

Jack Remick, writing guru, for the superb training, his patience, understanding, and generosity, and for the R&R writing circles;

Don McQuinn, the best mentor in this or any other world, for his expert guidance, ongoing encouragement, and immense generosity;

a terrific group of writers whose fellowship, feedback, and support made this a better book and/or the journey a lot more fun: Jackie Owens, Chris Parsons, Yvonne McCord, Cynthia Staehlin, and especially Lisa Kraft (who keeps helping me jump the hurdles), Andy Hazzard, and Dave Rispoli;

my father, Stanley Fenwick Rosenberg, for his Don Quixotean belief in me, his sanity-saving advice, and for literally seeing me through to the end;

my family and friends, for their enthusiasm, encouragement, and support, with special thanks to my mother and stepfather, Madeline Landing Pots and Robert Massaro, for turning off the TV and turning me on to science fiction; to my siblings, Dr. Jonathan Bear, Ph.D., Debi Rosenberg, M.A., and Rebecca Rosenberg, R.N., for sharing their professional expertise; and to Tom Gruver, for being so interested in an unfinished manuscript;

Irene Kraas and Jennifer Smith, my literary agent and editor respectively, for helping me to refine the story, and for their belief in me and my writing, which is why you are holding this book;

and to Ursula Le Guin, William Gibson, and the many other writers whose work served as inspiration and example, and whose stories left stars in my eyes.

Prologue

A Minotaur 2000 dwelled at the heart of the subterranean labyrinth that Destiny World used for operations control. The crew of young technicians manning the ultracomputer's command space worked in a virtual free fall, tethered to the real world by coffee, a control pad, and the air exchanger's perpetual hum.

Above the techs, above ground, in the balm of a spring evening, fifty thousand tourists swayed to the hymns of The True Believers, a neon rainbow coloring their upturned faces as lasers reflected off low clouds over Earth's largest amusement park.

The Destiny World Easter Spectacular was precisely on schedule.

"Cue Seraph," said a voice in operations control. Keys clicked at one of the workstations, opening a hidden door on the roof of Neptune's Castle, through which Ezekiel ascended, unnoticed by the tourists in the pandemonium of light and sound. As The True Believers launched into one last, rousing chorus of "Lord, We Will Follow," the beams converged to form a giant red cross. Inside the projection hovered the robed angel, his wings washed crimson in the laser glow, silken hair cascading over his shoulders, arms reaching toward the throng below.

The crowd roared its approval and appreciation, then continued to roar as the Seraph launched himself upward. He receded into the dark gray evening sky, a lonely figure clad in white.

From his seat in the VIP booth, Carson McCullough watched with disbelief as the angel went AWOL.

One

The Destiny Ambassador's smile was fading. Carson faced her in the living room of his suite at the new Herald Resort, waiting for the next appeal.

She said, "I'm certain Ezekiel has very good reasons for his absence, but I've got six hundred guests who were expecting to meet him tonight."

Her tact infuriated him. As Zeke's personal liaison, he knew the importance of the Seraph's appearance at the Herald Party fund-raiser. He just didn't know where the angel *was*.

He watched the ambassador tuck an errant blond wisp into her chignon. She wore a black velvet sheath, which he imagined peeling like a banana to expose soft, creamy flesh. The fantasy sparked a hot backlash of anger and shame.

"This is difficult, isn't it?" he asked, gazing into her green eyes. They glittered, reflecting the twenty candles of the chandelier. "But we're doing our best, all of us, and I'm sure your guests will understand the delay." Behind her, Juan Perez emerged from one of the suite's bedrooms. He was a sharp man, perpetually frowning, dressed in khaki slacks and a white mesh shirt.

The ambassador pressed her pink lips into a resigned smile. "Of course. Please join us as soon as you can." She left, trailing cinnamon and gardenia.

The bodyguard's Cuban accent abraded his words. "Won't be soon enough for Alden," Juan said, after the suite's door had closed behind the ambassador. "He's on the vid, for you."

Carson sank into a striped armchair and flipped the screen on. The British priest's digitized image peered at him. Age had creased the pale skin around the Herald Party leader's eyes and mouth; now anxiety deepened the lines. His thin white halo of hair stuck out in tufts. It occurred to Carson that Ocean City, floating in the mid-Atlantic, was three time zones ahead of Florida.

"How could he do this?" Alden asked, in his stately English. "There's less than two weeks till the UN vote." He ran a hand over the halo. The tufts sprang back.

"Maybe he had a pressing appointment with God."

The priest winced. "Carson, please."

"Well, they say the messiah's coming any day now." He checked his watch. "Two hours until Easter. You'd think if he's going to show—"

"He will," Alden said, sternly. "Hold on."

The screen blipped and Vance Torrington, the Party's sallow chief of security, appeared in a window at the bottom right corner. Over the sat-con, Torrie sounded like he was barking. "No press, no press!"

Carson muttered, "Give me a break." Then, "It's quiet, okay? Destiny's people are tight. Everyone else thought it was part of the grand finale. They loved it."

"Just make sure it stays that way," the security chief said. "So where is he?"

Carson said, "*I don't know.* Which of those three words can't you understand?"

Alden winced.

Torrie snarled, "Cut the lip, McCullough. I'll ask the questions. Did he say anything?"

"No."

"Was he drinking again?"

He lied, "No." The suite was complimentary; the Party wouldn't see a bar bill.

"What did he do today?"

Carson thought back to before the seamlessly orchestrated Easter Spectacular. "He took a shower. He ordered room service. He watched *Freak Follies* on virtual."

Alden gasped. "He was watching that filth?"

Carson shrugged. "He said it was good distraction. He told you he didn't want to do the spectacle. Maybe he's just—"

Torrie cut him off. "Forget it. We'll ask the other 'Phim. Meanwhile, tell Perez to get his team ready." Torrie and Alden were replaced by a pair of cherubs waving a banner that read WAIT PLEASE.

The Cuban was leaning over a desk at the far end of the living room, staring intently at the screen of his laptop. Carson crossed to him and peered at the scrolling lines of amber text. "You scanning emergency response?" When Juan nodded, he scoffed, "Why don't we just try the missed connections on LoveNet?"

The corners of Juan's thin mouth twisted, deepening his scowl. "You're the liaison. Isn't it your job—"

"Right, right." Carson swung around. "I'm the liaison," he said, introducing himself to his reflection in a floor-to-ceiling window. "So when some angel decides to go on a joyride, it's my fault. Just who does he think he is, anyway?" He pointed at Juan. "Wasn't it your job to shoot him down or something?"

The Cuban was one of two bodyguards permanently assigned to Zeke. Carson had worked with him for three years, and in that time he had never heard the tone the man used now. "Don't push it too far," Juan said.

Carson detected concern and danger in the warning, both genuine. "What's that supposed to mean?" He caught the Cuban's dark gaze.

Juan shrugged. "Just be careful, Carson. You've been on the edge lately. I'm not the only one to notice." His tone mellowed. "Usually we check known associates and hangouts. Of course, in Ezekiel's case . . ."

He decided to ignore Juan's comments. "Yeah. He never goes anywhere or sees anyone unless we're with him."

"You two talked a lot. Maybe he said something?"

Carson snapped, "Torrie asked me that."

"Okay. Now I'm asking."

He went to the window, cupping his hands against the glass. A full moon lit the flat green landscape punctuated by man-made ponds, clustered palm trees, and the distant spire of Neptune's Castle. "No." It was the truth.

"You grew up here, didn't you? Where would you go?"

A seagull glided past.

Carson said, "Where all Florida escapists go: the beach."

Juan actually smiled. Then the vid beeped.

When Carson answered it, Torrie appeared on the screen. "Gabriel's linked from Tokyo. He's gonna tell us what he sees."

The Seraphim had an extrasensory awareness of each other. Zeke once described it to Carson: "It's similar to memories, but they didn't happen to you, so there's no particular reason to recall them, and when you do, they don't necessarily make sense."

"Can you talk to one another?"

Zeke smiled, his silver eyes narrowing in amusement. "What would we say?"

Carson wanted to ask what the voice of God sounded like, but the question seemed irreverent.

Three years before, Earth Militia terrorists had kidnapped Uriel. That memory had been vivid for the other five Seraphim and had led to their brother's rescue. As the self-appointed steward of the angels, the Herald Party had milked it, stating that evildoers couldn't hide from the sight of God.

Omniscience, however, presented its own data-retrieval problems. How, Carson wondered, would Gabriel pick out the memories belonging to Zeke? He asked Torrie.

The security chief said, "Destiny World. It's pretty hard to forget. Now tell Gabe about that shindig today."

Gabriel listened patiently as he described the Easter Spectacular. The Seraph was taller than Zeke, with pale skin, gray-blue eyes, and white hair that blended into the wings peaking over his shoulders—striking, as were they all. But he lacked Zeke's air of vulnerability, and Carson always perceived a coldness about him. It was a small relief when Gabe shut his eyes to concentrate.

"Yes, this is familiar," he said. "I see the crowd. Many lights. I am rising up. In the distance is the city, but I avoid it, rejoining the highway on the other side." He continued to describe what Zeke saw as he took flight. The Seraph had made good time; Gabe's last images were of the beach.

"Recognize anything?" Torrie asked, every fifteen seconds, as Carson listened to Gabriel's account.

He ignored the question until the Seraph was fin-

ished. Then he shook his head. "Sand, hotels—he
could be anywhere along the Florida coast."

"No. He is at Daytona," Gabriel said, fixing Carson
with his cool gaze.

"How do you know that?"

"God sees all." He added, "You will find him."

Carson wasn't sure if it was an order or a statement
of fact, but the Seraph had disconnected, leaving Torrie's dour face to fill the screen.

The security chief nodded to Juan and said, "Give
us a minute here, McCullough. Then you can go col-
lect Zeke."

Carson wondered what orders Torrie wanted to im-
part to the Cuban out of his earshot. The security
chief and his subordinates were all agents of ICARUS,
the international military-industrial consortium responsible for relations with Earth's Special Visitors.
Their presence was a necessary evil the Party endured,
a provision of the United Nations Planetary Security
Council resolution that gave the Seraphim their autonomy, and the relationship between ICARUS and the
Heralds was one of cooperation based on underlying
mutual distrust. After all, the Party existed solely to
spread God's word as witnessed by His host of Seraphim, in person and through their testimony, *The Seraphic Revelations.* ICARUS, on the other hand, had
come into being to save the world from invasion by
aliens that turned out to be angels.

"I'll be downstairs," Carson said, grabbing his windbreaker off the suite's sofa. He let himself out into
the hall. A cloud-puff motif in blue and white papered
the walls and ceiling, and repeated on the tightly
looped carpet, giving him the odd sensation, as he
walked to the elevator, of passing through a tunnel
of sky.

The lobby furnishings were upholstered in a peach

damask woven with more grinning cherubim. He sat and contemplated the main decorative feature, a two-story, idealized depiction of the Rising of the Seraphim from the Atlantic, nearly a decade before. Zeke rose first, so he was shown at the center and largest, arms reaching toward the viewer, a beatific smile on his handsome face. Small silver-green fish leapt from the waves around his feet. Behind him, his five brothers were in various stages of birth. Some drifted between rosy clouds; others, still partially encapsulated by their floating eggs, stretched their winged torsos skyward.

A sunburned young mother sat down next to Carson on a gilded settee. She lifted a pudgy little boy to her lap and pointed at the mural.

"Angels!" the child said.

"That's right," she cooed. "God sent his angels down in shooting stars, and they stayed in the ocean for a long time. Then, when it was time for them to tell us that Jesus was coming, they hatched, like chicks. Do you remember when you saw the chicks hatch at Aunt Mary's?"

Carson spied Juan approaching from the elevators. He met him in front of the mural.

The Cuban said, "Team's ready. We'll take the resort's helijet."

Carson was staring up at the oversize image of Zeke.

"You coming?" Juan asked.

"Yeah." He stabbed his finger toward the drape of white cloth across the Seraph's hips. "You know, as I recall, he was butt naked with a hard-on."

The Cuban scowled. "This is what I mean," he said, as they left the lobby. The shuttle that would take them to the landing pad waited at the curb. "Why are you jeopardizing your position with these remarks?"

Carson shrugged. "What do you care? You're just here to guard the aliens, right?"

"The aliens?" Juan turned his words on him. "I thought you believe they are angels. Or are you losing faith?"

Carson didn't answer. He couldn't.

The eggs had arrived three decades prior to the Rising. News reports of the unexpected meteor shower and its accompanying starburst phenomenon were sporadic. Rumors of a shocking find by a French astronomical survey team boiled to the surface of the media, then plunged back into the murky depths of obscurity. Had it not been for Déjà Vu, the world might have slumbered in blissful ignorance during the thirty years it took the Seraphim to gestate.

Vu was the darling of tabloid video, an amalgam of sexual ambiguity, psychic prowess, and theatrical flair—just the right feather to titillate the dulled sensitivities of a jaded audience. When the androgyne appeared on *Hot Topics* in a gold lamé space suit and announced that aliens had arrived, the story exploded. After one of the show's hackers pilfered the survey team's logs off the net, reporters schooled to the ocean site like sharks drawn by fresh blood. Shortly thereafter, the truth was made public: Earth had unhatched extraterrestrial visitors.

Carson had been born in the wake of that first, infamous tidal wave of hysteria.

As time passed and the eggs didn't hatch, the hysteria subsided, but the fear remained, the specter of alien invasion hanging over the planet like an invisible cloud, a nascent storm that gave rise to periodic gusts of panic and destruction.

The summer of his eighth year, one of those gusts carried his father away. Through the remainder of his childhood, through the invasion drills and endless videos warning of a poisoned, lifeless world, his mother told him to have faith in God.

And he had tried. Tried and failed.

"That's why you have big ears," she'd said. "So you can hear the Lord calling. You hear him, don't you, Carson?" And, oh, how he'd wanted to hear, had waited for that call, had known it would come; for when it did, the fear that seemed to have entered him at birth, as if through a psychic umbilical cord, would drain from him, drain from everyone.

But the call never came.

He went to the seminary anyway, sure that he'd hear it if he spent enough time on his knees, not intending to spend most of it underneath the coconut palms outside the refectory, vomiting bourbon into Brother Todd's impatiens bed.

He'd wanted to save the world, but he hadn't been able to stay saved himself.

So he left, got married, exhausted the patience of a good woman, and drifted, ever seeking.

Then, the Seraphim rose.

The day of the Rising, martial law had been in effect for almost seventy hours, part of the panic-prevention measures the government had had thirty years—Carson's entire life—to perfect. It didn't matter to him; he could telecommute to his job at the International Refugee Alliance. But the thought of displaced Zairean children held little poignancy for him when they might *all* be refugees soon.

Kara had gone to be with her folks. The marriage was over, just not the formalities. He didn't bother to dress that morning, sat around in boxers, drinking whiskey out of the bottle and watching NewsNet. They split the screen between the eggs floating on the Atlantic's surface, the Planetary Security Council updates coming out of Geneva, and the running odds in the prediction lotteries. Payout was four hundred to one for anyone lucky enough to guess the exact moment the first egg cracked.

At 11:02:43 Greenwich time, betting stopped.

The heart attacks and suicides attributed to that moment never saw the alien that emerged. For months afterward, as every possible angle of the "where were you when" report was exhausted, people described reactions ranging from hysteria to euphoria to relief.

Carson had laughed. He had watched Zeke rise on his vid screen, watched the unnamed alien, with his massive wings and engorged penis and exquisite smile, rise above the Earth, and he had laughed until his face was streaked with tears, thinking his problem solved.

Faith was no longer necessary because proof had arrived.

He wasn't surprised when he learned that the aliens introduced themselves in perfect English, insisting they were angels, and after two years of quarantine, the Planetary Security Council had given in to the campaign, spearheaded by the newly formed Herald Party, to let them assume their rightful place.

The Seraphim promised the emergence of a messiah and the salvation of man. It was a prophecy that Carson embraced, freeing him as it did from the need to do the job himself. A significant percentage of the world embraced it as well, and under the Herald Party's leadership, prepared themselves spiritually for the coming of their savior and the new Jerusalem.

Unfortunately, the Israelis liked the old Jerusalem. The closing of their borders three months prior to the Easter Spectacular was, at the very least, inconvenient, especially with the messiah due to arrive any day. And so the Heralds had requested a UN mandate for universal access to the holy city. As the first-risen, Zeke's appearances were crucial in raising the support needed to win the vote on that mandate, less than two weeks away.

And now, Zeke had disappeared.

As the shuttle parked in front of the landing pad, Carson remembered Gabriel's flat assertion, "You will find him."

He hoped Gabe was right. He hoped he was right about that—and everything else.

Destiny World was the spider at the center of a very big web of RTV tracks called the Link. Strands radiated north to Orlando, west to Tampa, east to the Space Coast and Port Canaveral, and south to Miami. From the air, Carson saw the trains speeding along their routes as frantic, noctilucent bugs.

They landed in Daytona, on a pad adjacent to the airport Link station, terminal point for the Dolphin line, where Spring Break Specials disgorged the annual influx of college students.

Juan called Torrie for an update while they drove to the city in a rented Toyota minivan.

"Gabriel has nothing more to tell us, except that he thinks Ezekiel is holed up somewhere," the Cuban announced as he put away his phone. "No reported sightings. He's probably waiting until everyone is asleep or too drunk to notice. I want to start searching; the Hyatt will hold our rooms."

They parked the Toyota and split up, the five of them sectioning off the main drags of the city. Carson wandered aimlessly at first, thinking: This is not what I signed up for. But already the Seraph's desertion was a given, something he accepted as part of his reality, just as mankind had accepted aliens, and then angels.

He bought a Coke and headed toward the ocean. He couldn't hear the water, only the crescendo of traffic moving through the gauntlet of stoplights on Atlantic Boulevard. Sunburned bodies swarmed out of the hamburger joints and T-shirt shops closing for the night, but there was no real darkness here: The city dispelled it with holographic beacons, flickering from every billboard and rooftop.

He kept walking. A fitful breeze stirred trash littering the sidewalk. The crowds dwindled. Around two, a prostitute emerged from a doorway between barred storefronts. "Lookin' for somethin'?" she asked, running painted nails along the curves of her red spandex dress.

He watched with an odd mixture of pity and lust. It had been that long.

She draped a hand on his shoulder, seeing as she did the silver crossed-wing insignia pinned to his jacket. "Herald? Huh. Baby, *I* can take you to heaven."

When he said no, she shrugged and moved off.

He looked for Zeke in the alleyways, on the rooftops under the garish projections, behind the chain fences. Eventually everything closed except the bars. They were all the same, gaping mouths exhaling smoke and the aroma of stale beer, sickening him in his exhaustion.

A block from the beach he passed a low-slung building. Beautiful men clustered around the entrance, their muscular bodies cased in black leather. Two of them mounted a Harley, the machine springing to life like a sleek chromed jaguar and roaring off into the night. He tried to muster the requisite indignation. They were sinners, after all, standing between mankind and its salvation.

He found a concrete ramp, buckled and cracked from the relentless sun, and skidded down the incline

to the wet sand. Hotels crowded the waterfront, their
UV canopies rippling with the breeze. Stumbling along
the beach, he wove between stacks of chaise lounges,
past the big luxury resorts to a stretch of smaller ones
with names like The Sand Dollar and Pirate's Inn.
He'd forgotten the old pier, but there it was, reaching
over the water on crusted pylons. It was darker underneath, and the air seemed liquid, tasting more strongly
of salt. He looked around. A giant concrete drainpipe
protruded from the seawall, spewing a stream of de-
cayed garbage into the surf.

Enough was enough. Climbing up the beach, Carson
sat down in the sand, leaning against the pipe's cold,
rough surface, and folded his arms across his knees,
resting his forehead against them.

He'd stay here, for a little while.

Dawn. The sun rising, leaving a fiery afterburn
across the seamless gray vista of sea and sky. Behind
him, he heard condensation dripping within the concrete chamber. Then there was another sound, familiar, and a soft breath of air from inside the pipe. It
carried with it an odor of seaweed, rot, and gasoline.

He knew without looking. Pulling himself up onto
stiff legs, he brushed the sand from his pants and got
out his phone.

Juan's voice rasped in his ear. "Carson? Have
something?"

"Yeah." He stooped and looked into the pipe. "I
found Zeke."

Juan and the others arrived in the Toyota. They
drove it down onto the beach, stopping a dozen meters
short of the pier. Carson watched them climb out,
holding a hand up to shield his eyes from sunlight
ricocheting off the van's polished surface. They

marched toward him. One of the guards carried a coil of rope.

Carson ducked his head to check on the Seraph. Zeke was still asleep, crumpled within the cylindrical interior of the drainpipe. He'd used his white robe from the Spectacular as a pillow and wore only the matching pants. One wing was tucked against his body; the other extended over his torso, sheltering him.

They reached the pipe, and Carson moved out of the way so the others could see. Crouched before the opening, they looked inside, then glanced at each other and shook their heads.

Juan stood up. "Wake him," he told Carson.

They made way. He climbed into the conduit and squatted beside the sleeping form. The air within the pipe was damp, cooler, but pungent.

"Zeke." The Seraph didn't stir. "Zeke." He reached out. Zeke's shoulder was covered by the wing. Carson grabbed his knee instead and shook him.

The Seraph moaned and the wing retracted. He clutched a whiskey bottle in his long, slender fingers.

Carson frowned and shook harder. "Come on, wake up."

The Seraph's eyes opened. They were silver-gray, matching his hair. The pupils were dilated and the whites veined with red. Zeke turned his head and focused on Carson.

"Come on, Zeke. Get up."

Zeke's gaze moved past him, to the opening. Something flashed across his face. He yawned and propped himself up on a bony elbow. "Reporters out there?" His voice was low and graveled.

"No, just us. Come on, let's get you to a hotel. We'll talk later."

The Seraph lifted his other hand, which still clutched the bottle. He stared at it, considering.

Carson took it from him gently.

Zeke groaned, then folded his legs underneath him and shifted to a kneeling position. "Why did you come with them, Carson?"

"What did you expect me to do?" He reached out a hand, but the Seraph shook his head.

"Go on," he told him.

Carson obliged, scooting backward out of the pipe. Zeke grabbed the robe and followed on hands and knees. They emerged into the semicircle of guards. One had moved beyond the shadow of the pier, stationing himself as lookout.

Zeke straightened, the wings spreading involuntarily to steady him. He turned to Juan. "You're here to take me back?"

The Cuban's face was impassive. He said, "That's right."

"Then let's go."

Juan stepped aside. "Bring the van over," he told one of the others. The man walked toward the vehicle.

Zeke sighed and unfolded the robe, shaking it out. Then, in one smooth movement, he tossed it over Juan's head and shoulders and broke into a run.

The Seraph charged toward the open air, wings spreading with each step. The other guard took off after him, shouting to the lookout and knocking Carson out of the way. As Carson reeled backward against the pipe, he saw Zeke launch himself. Not soon enough. The lookout reacted, leaping upward and catching him by the ankle. They hung there for an instant, suspended, as the powerful wings beat at the hazy air. Then both Seraph and his captor tumbled to the sand.

Carson staggered after Juan, toward the fallen angel. Two more guards were already on top of Zeke. Carson saw white wings flashing in the tangle of bodies. There was a spurt of red, and Zeke howled. The sound was unearthly, keening, an animal wail of pain. It sliced into Carson's psyche, severing his connection to the moment, the cry, the men wrestling an angel in the sand. He reached them, shaking. Zeke was still thrashing. The pristine feathers were splattered with red.

"Shit," someone said. Zeke howled again. "Gag him." "I'm trying."

He stood over them, watching as they subdued the Seraph, his stomach writhing, bile splashing up into the back of his dry throat. They bound the wings to Zeke's slender torso with the coil of rope, then carried him to the van. Carson followed, ice inside, but sweating, his clothes moving with him, glued by perspiration to his body.

They put Zeke in the back on the floor. They'd stuffed a handkerchief into his mouth, and Carson heard him wheezing, struggling to breathe. As they moved away to shut the doors, the Seraph's gray gaze locked onto his own. His eyes were dull, like iron, but they held Carson with magnetic intensity. Two words formed in the vacuum of his mind, soundless, clearer than sound.

The white-enameled door of the Toyota slammed.

He still heard them.

And as he walked through the sand, sinking heavily with each step, the words echoed, an inverted echo, louder as they returned again and again.

He climbed into the passenger seat of the van, still hearing, not wanting to hear, but they wouldn't leave him, not as Juan revved the engine, not as the Toyota wheeled up the ramp and onto Atlantic Boulevard, and not as they drove, without speaking, to the hotel.

He put his hands to his ears, but in the absence of outer sound, the inner voice was only clearer.

Two words. Over and over.

Help me.

TWO

Carson was glad when Juan told him to go upstairs and check in. He left them in the dull fluorescence of the Hyatt parking garage, pondering how to smuggle the Toyota's captive passenger into the hotel.

Zeke's plea had finally faded away.

He located his room and slid his plastic key into the lock. The door clicked open. It was cool inside, dim, the floral curtains drawn. A vid sat on a black-lacquered stand opposite the beds.

"You've got to do something," he told the priest, after Alden had listened, without comment, to his account of Zeke's capture.

"I think you're exaggerating, Carson." The corner of Alden's mouth twitched. "Obviously, you're tired. Why don't you—"

"You weren't there. He was howling. They broke his wing—" His voice cracked.

"Get hold of yourself." Alden looked past the screen. "I don't know what happened, but I'm sure Torrington's people did what they thought was best. I need your cooperation and so does Ezekiel. Do you understand?"

Carson clenched his jaw, breathing in through flared nostrils, smelling the sourness of sweat and fatigue. "*I* understand, but I don't think *you* do. They beat up an angel. An *angel,* for God's sake!" He watched the vid, waiting for the words to impact the priest. The twitch accelerated.

In the muffled distance of the hallway, an elevator chimed. He heard a low murmur of voices.

"I know what he is, Carson. And I'm sure . . ."

Torrie appeared behind Alden. "We all know what Zeke is, and I've already talked to Perez. Zeke's got a problem. Seems to me, you had a similar problem yourself." He paused, then, "Now do your job: Cancel his appearance at that Church of the Messiah service and help Perez get him back here." *Blip*. The screen returned to the red Hyatt logo scrawled across a shimmering aqua background.

Carson stared at the vid. He had found the indignation. It floated in the acid pit of his stomach, like a buoy.

The murmur of voices grew louder, then someone rapped on his door. When he opened it, Juan was there with another guard and a large wheeled laundry cart.

"Room service," the Cuban said, without smiling. He guided the cart over to one of the double beds.

Zeke was inside, his eyes half-shut. He was ashen.

"Give us a hand," Juan told Carson.

The three of them lifted the Seraph onto the bed. Carson realized he could have done it himself. They stared down at the winged form, curled on the rose and moss green coverlet. Then Juan removed the gag. Zeke lay still.

The Cuban said, "All right, Ezekiel, I know you hear me. If I untie you, are you going to run again?"

The answer was barely audible. "First chance I get." Zeke closed his eyes.

"That's what I thought." He sighed. "We want to help. Tell us what's going on." There was no answer. Juan looked at Carson, frowning. "Have to get the jet here. It'll take some time. See what you can do about that wing. Someone will be outside." They left.

Carson went into the bathroom and wet a towel. He dabbed at the bloodstained feathers, to little effect.

"Zeke, talk to me."

The Seraph didn't respond.

He looked around. On the opposite wall was a lacquered desk, matching the vid stand. Beside it, a small opaque door and touchpad were set into the pastelstriped wallpaper. An autobutler. He punched for coffee and donuts.

Zeke wouldn't drink. Carson put the cup of coffee back on the tray. "Do you want something else?" he asked.

The Seraph whispered, "Help me."

He was squatting beside the bed, on eye level with Zeke. "I heard you the first time."

The gray eyes opened.

Carson looked away.

"You're not going to do it, are you, Carson?"

He didn't answer.

"Fuck you."

He shot his gaze back to the Seraph, but Zeke's eyes were closed.

"Right," Carson told him. "Fuck me." He straightened. "I gotta take a leak."

He stayed in the bathroom for ten minutes, rinsing his face with cold water, hiding from the pathetic sight on the other side of the mirrored door. When he emerged, Zeke was snoring softly.

He called the Church of the Messiah in Orlando and, apologizing profusely, explained that the Seraph would be unable to attend the noon Easter service. Then he took a donut and the coffee out onto the narrow balcony. The city steamed from heat and the exhaust vents of the fast-food joints. The coffee was cold.

He went back inside, stripped to his underwear, and lay down on the other bed, listening, for a while, to the roar of traffic, like waves breaking on an asphalt shore.

Then there was silence.

Sun, slicing into the room around the edges of the floral drapes.

Carson groaned, rolled over, and looked at Zeke's bed. It was empty. He jerked upright, catching his breath. Then he saw him. Zeke was on the floor, on his side, in front of the lacquered desk and the auto-butler. Tiny glass bottles littered the rose carpet.

Carson dragged his hands down his cheeks, then he climbed out of bed and knelt beside the Seraph.

Zeke gave him a lopsided grimace. "Just reach," he said, lifting a hand to his mouth and making a drinking gesture. The rope didn't bind his lower arms.

Carson leaned toward him. "What in God's name are you doing?"

"Getting drunk."

"I can see that, Zeke. What about the drainpipe? What about that Destiny stunt?"

"Stunt?" He spit the word out. "I wasn't aware that I was a prisoner. At least, not until . . ." He shrugged at the ropes.

"They think they're helping you. If you hadn't taken off like you did—" The Seraph's expression silenced him.

"I expect more from you, Carson, I really do."

Carson winced. His cheeks tingled, and he knew they were coloring underneath his freckles. "They're uptight about the vote, Zeke."

"I don't care about the vote. Now are you going to help me or not?"

Carson saw himself in the leaden pupils, receding as he pulled away. "Why don't you help yourself? You're the angel."

"Just what is it you expect me to do, Carson?"

He held out his hands, as if he could pluck words from the air. "I don't know. Something. Anything. Bring down the wrath of God. Isn't that the sort of thing you angels do?"

Zeke's next words were spoken evenly. "I am tired of being the puppet of your wrathful god."

Carson froze, hands still outstretched, caught in the unblinking gaze, the words. Then he heard himself demanding shrilly, "Is that it? You've decided you're not an angel after all? The Infidels are right, and you're just some winged alien that rode in on a meteor shower? Is that it?"

"I don't know."

Carson dropped his hands and stared at them. Then he shook his head. "I need a drink." He reached over and punched for a double shot of Cavaliers bourbon.

"Make it two," Zeke said.

"Fuck you."

He took the shot bottles from behind the door and fumbled with the caps, cursing to himself. He could feel the magnetic gaze, but he didn't look back at the Seraph until he'd emptied the first one. "So, you're having an identity crisis." Carson raised the second bottle in salute and tossed back its contents.

"I understand why you started drinking at the seminary."

His esophagus burned from the whiskey. "How'd you know about that?"

"You told me . . . last time you were drunk."

Carson considered. "So I did."

"And you told me how you couldn't believe. Remember?"

He held up the empty bottle, catching a glint of sun on the curve of the glass. "Yeah."

"You needed proof, so you left."

Carson turned his head to look at the Seraph. Zeke's face was drawn. He appeared frail and decidedly uncelestial in his grungy white pants. More like a dirty seagull. "Yeah, I needed proof. Then you showed up and you said, 'The messiah is here. Cast the devil out. Salvation is coming.' " He looked away.

The words touched his mind: *And you believed.*

"Stop that shit," he snapped, turning on the Seraph.

Zeke gazed up at him. "You don't like it, do you?"

Carson didn't respond.

Zeke went on anyway. "Neither do I. I don't like this voice of your god that's in my head. I don't even know that it is your god, but whoever it is, I want him to shut up." He clawed at one of the empty bottles. "And this is the only quiet I've found."

"How can you say that when—" Carson's phone beeped. "When for all these years—" The phone beeped again. He got up and snatched it from the nightstand.

Alden sounded breathless. "Ezekiel has told you the glorious news?"

Glancing at the Seraph, he answered, "No."

The priest almost choked out the words. "He is come, Carson. The messiah is come and is asking for you."

Carson sank onto the bed.

"I don't understand," Alden told him. "The others relayed the message . . . Carson?"

"I'm here," he managed.

"The others relayed the message. I have an address in Orlando, of all places. You are to go there, as quickly as you can, but alone. *He* does not wish ICARUS to be involved. Tell Juan you have orders on the highest authority and don't explain. Here— take this down."

Carson's hand shook. The pen wobbled across the Hyatt notepad as Alden dictated the address. Carson stared at what he'd written, gasping when the recognition hit.

"Are you sure?" he asked the priest.

Alden said, "Sure? Of course I'm sure. The other five all called with the same message."

Carson shook his head, bewildered. "No . . ."

"Yes!" the priest said jubilantly. "Oh yes!"

He ran for the two o'clock to Orlando, lodging an arm in the automatic doors of the train as they slid shut. A synthesized voice chided him for the delay while he found a seat. The other passengers looked damp and uncomfortable despite the cold, stale air blowing from gills underneath the windows flanking the car. He could feel his own back adhering to the thinly padded vinyl. He wasn't used to public transit, but he didn't have a driver's license, and the Link was fast.

They eased out of the station. Carson rested his forehead against the window, watching until the strip malls and storm-shuttered houses faded to sand and empty sky. Then his fingers slid tentatively into his pants pocket and found the slip of paper.

It was real.

He pulled it out, checked the address again. Harry's house. He could see the scrolled black numbers over the arched wooden door. Why did the Seraphim think the messiah was at his house? Harry Chen, who had parodied them in his virtual-reality show. Alden had called the *Freak Follies* filth. He was right. Chen was a freak.

But it *was* Easter Sunday. What if He really was there?

Then we've been gypped, Carson decided. The Son of God was supposed to assume his throne in a new Jerusalem, not phone from a friend's house.

Maybe this is Chen's idea of a joke, he thought. After all, Chen had been the weird little kid who'd grown up and gotten weirder, the one who Carson stayed in touch with only because he was the closest thing to a brother he'd ever had, and while Carson went about his business of saving the world, Chen did his best to escape from it. The spacers called him "King of the Realm." What was the King of the Angels doing at his house?

Carson didn't have the patience for any more surprises. He checked the ETA on the car's display. The Seraphim said when God returned, the illusory veil of space-time would be lifted. Perhaps the messiah had yet to come; the distance between him and the truth seemed very real indeed.

Thirty minutes later he was at the Orlando transit center, riding an escalator to the lower level. She appeared beside him in the jostling crowd, touched his arm. He looked down into paisley-shaped reflective lenses, rimmed by rhinestone-studded turquoise plastic. Her light brown skin set off full dark lips. Long plaits of coarse blond-streaked hair fell over one shoulder.

"I know the messiah is waiting," she said, "but we need to talk."

He froze mid-step and stared at her, struck dumb. The oncoming tide of humanity parted, rippling with annoyance, and flowed around them.

"Let me give you a ride." She repeated the address on the paper crammed into his pocket. Her eyebrows crested above the curved plastic.

"Who are you?" he managed.

"Miriam. And you're Carson McCullough. How about that ride?"

"I don't think so."

She reached into her canvas bag. "I really wish you'd reconsider."

What good would it do, he wondered, to pull a gun here?

Her hand reemerged. The slender brown fingers clutched a black metal case. She flipped it open. He peered at the video display of the microcorder. Someone was running on the beach, someone with wings.

"We shot this in Daytona, from the old pier."

On the tiny screen, Zeke plummeted to the sand.

Liquid fear trickled down his spine. "What do you want?"

"Just to talk. I'm not going to hurt you, Mr. McCullough." The 'corder disappeared into the bag. "And I promise you won't be late."

She guided him out a side exit, where a small white sedan with tinted windows waited at the curb. A hooded orange sweatshirt and dark glasses concealed the face of the driver, but as Carson climbed into the backseat, he saw thick masculine hands resting on the steering wheel.

They pulled out into traffic. Her left thigh was centimeters from his on the red velour, and his mouth tasted like cotton.

"I thought this only happened in old videos."

The car veered up a ramp and merged onto the interstate.

Miriam nodded. "I followed you from Ocean City. We've heard that you're having some doubts."

"You've obviously heard a lot more than that. And who's 'we'?" Her clothes were young, eclectic. She wore a batiked jumpsuit and maroon patent-leather combat boots. "You're an Infidel, aren't you?" The green movement offshoot had become an active foe of the Herald Party.

Behind her, the Orlando skyline sped by, mirrored buildings reflecting scattered puffs of gray. "Do you still believe they're angels?"

Cold beads of sweat pricked his face. "I know you don't," he said. "I've seen your propaganda on the net. What'd you call them? 'Migratory visitors from another world.' They're not a bunch of astral homing pigeons, that's for sure."

She laughed, her throat rippling like a caterpillar, smooth skin moving over fine ridges of the trachea. "They *are* flesh and bone," she said.

"So was Jesus," Carson pointed out.

"Yes," Miriam conceded. "And over two thousand years later, there's no real proof that he was God—or that he'll ever return."

He finished the litany for her. "So we'd better get busy saving ourselves."

"*Anyway,* we know Ezekiel tried to leave. We know that you're having doubts and—"

"I don't really see where my personal feelings are any of your business." Carson shifted uncomfortably as they exited onto an expressway. He wanted to get out of the car.

She went on, ignoring the remark. "And the way they're treating him, I'm not surprised. You have to wonder what's really going on."

"They're doing their job."

"Are they? If that tape was broadcast on NewsNet, do you think your believers would agree?"

"Is that what you're going to do? Or is this just blackmail?"

"What I'm going to do is ask you to deliver a message: If Ezekiel wants asylum, we'll help him. And in return, he must help us."

"I see," he said, cynicism twisting his tone. "Zeke goes turncoat, we lose the vote, and instead all the money's used to save the Earth."

"Something like that."

"I'm sure you're enjoying this, playing spy."

"We had to act fast. You're taking him back to Ocean City, where he'll be locked in the Herald Tower. And now this messiah . . . If people believe in him, it will be hard for us."

He bit off another acerbic remark, turning away. He was angry and afraid, but somehow he didn't want her to hate him. "And if I don't deliver your message?" he asked, staring out the window. Beyond the palm trees, precise rows of pastel houses blurred into a picture of suburban banality, Florida-style.

"We'll do what we have to do." They pulled off onto Tropican Boulevard.

"You can't prove they aren't angels, even if Zeke helps you."

"Maybe not. But perhaps we can find out the truth. Doesn't truth matter to you, Mr. McCullough?"

He let the question go unanswered.

When they skidded to a halt in front of a gated private drive, Miriam pressed a card into his hand. "Think about it. Leave a message at this number if you change your mind. It can't be traced, of course." She reached across him, her thin brown arm brushing his chest, and opened the door.

"Thanks for the ride," he said, and climbed out. Watching the sedan speed off down the street, he tasted whiskey and bile.

A vidcom was mounted on one of the brick pillars supporting the massive wrought-iron gates. Carson hit the red call button.

A synthesized voice said, "Identify yourself, please."

"Carson McCullough."

"One moment."

The glare lessened. Soot-colored clouds were gathering overhead.

"Please enter," the voice invited him, and the gates swung open.

The house was at least fifty meters from the street, at the end of a gravel drive. Carson crunched his way toward the two-story Spanish colonial. The orange groves had died out, and now the yard was reverting to native scrub, a dense tangle of palmetto and clumped live oak. The trees were spindly and silver moss threatened to defoliate them. Little had changed since his last visit. The familiarity reassured him. He tried to remember how long it had been. Two years? Maybe three. He tried not to think about what Miriam had said.

The arched door was open and Harry Chen stood in its place, looking like a character from his own VR show. He was dressed in white, except for round purple glasses, which were nonprescription and, Carson suspected, a vanity intended to distract from the epicanthic folds over his eyes. His black hair was twisted into a topknot, he hadn't shaved in fifteen years, and he wore his mustache and goatee braided together in a long rat's tail that flicked when he spoke. As Carson reached the stoop, Chen smiled, showing square yellowish teeth.

Anger overcame his anxiety. "You didn't answer your phone, Harry. I had to come all the way here. Now what the hell is going on?"

A soundless voice in his mind said, *Chill, man. Is that how you greet your god?*

He stared, confused. Then he looked back, up, trying to find the Seraph that must have sent the words. There was no one except Chen, leering from behind purple shades.

"Who was that?" he demanded, acid washing up over the question. He knew the answer before it was given.

Me. Harry.

The sound that wasn't triggered an uncontrollable wave of nausea. Carson lurched forward, doubling over, and vomited on the messiah's bare feet.

Three

Harry Chen's living room was a shrine to Armageddon. Aside from a few minimalist pieces in black leather, the large space contained only artifacts of mankind's thirty-year obsession with its own impending doom. Multiple vid screens ran invasion-preparedness ads, a small forest of poles topped by successive versions of the envirohazard helmet sprouted in one corner like some space-age headhunter's trophies, and an entire wall was dedicated to various speculative images of the unhatched aliens. There was even a scale model of a Seapod personal survival craft suspended from the ceiling.

Carson had never understood Chen's fascination with the Dark Ages, as he liked to call the years of their youth. It was a time Carson preferred to forget, although that was difficult when surrounded by its memorabilia. He focused on the room's view through cypress to Lake Minneola. A pool of molten gold leached from the sun onto its rusty surface.

Chen emerged from the bathroom. The cuffs of his white pants were damp where he'd swabbed the vomit. "Didn't know you'd heave, man. I mean, I sent the message. Thought you'd—"

"Message? Every Seraphim on this planet, except one, suddenly calls up Alden and says, 'The messiah

wants you to send Carson over to Harry Chen's place.'
I didn't know that meant—"

"Except one?" Chen's eyes were bright behind the
tinted lenses. He sat, barely, on the corner of a bench.

"Never mind. Harry, we've known each other a long
time. I don't know how you did what you did, but
you're not God. Now tell me what's going on."

Chen opened his left hand and extended it to Carson, palm up. In the center was a small vial of black
powder. His forearm was branded with zigzags composed of tiny dots. Burns.

He's wired, Carson realized. Burnt. "Space? This is
about drugs?"

"Hey, I'm impressed. You know what it is. Haven't
been realming yourself? But you should, Carson. You
might understand then. You know what this does?"

"Opens new frontiers, or so I've heard. But I want
an answer, Harry."

"Yes—I've prepared a special show, just for you.
Come." Chen sprang up, walking briskly to the room's
far corner, where a circular stair ascended to his studio. Large drops splattered against the lakeside
window.

"I'm not watching a show, Harry. Not until you tell
me what's going on."

Chen's mouth twisted in disappointment. "But Carson, I want you to *experience*." He took the stairs, two
at a time, calling, "It'll answer your questions,
promise."

Grudgingly, Carson joined him.

"The womb of my evil stepchild," Chen said, as
they entered the windowless studio. Carson had heard
him refer to *Freak Follies* that way before. It was irreverent, obscure virtual reality, but the cult following
had made him rich. "Sit, sit," Chen said, gesturing to

the reclining lounge he'd ordered years before from a dental supply catalogue.

Carson sat without leaning back and put on the VR headset. Computers were stacked around the perimeter of the room, red and green power indicators winking at him from their status panels. Three control pads were mounted on a steel stand next to the lounge. Chen typed something on the center one.

And the room was gone.

Carson's eyes strained against the emptiness. Then he heard a familiar sound: the movement of volumes of air. Wings flapping.

Red, the host of the *Follies,* alighted beside Carson. He was a satanic angel, a cruel caricature of the Seraphim, with a crimson Mohawk that trailed between black chrome wings. His upper lip was curled into a perpetual snarl, and his nose was threaded with a brass hoop attached by a small chain to its mate in his right ear. He wore a studded black leather vest and leather pants that bulged with an enormous erection. A cockney accent thickened his words. "Bloody 'ell, then, let's go." The Seraph grabbed him by the wrist, black talons closing viselike.

They were suddenly on the roof of a very tall building. Traffic crawled in the street below, but the cars were antennaed bugs with shiny metallic shells. Two collided. A green geyser spurted into the air.

Red jumped, dragging Carson over the edge. Perspective of falling and once again he tasted bile. Then Red spread his wings and they swooped upward, over the dark cityscape, toward a giant moon.

As it loomed larger, the abstract surface patterns of the moon rippled and swirled, heaving into features, shimmering into flesh tone. Silken black hair sprouted. The features grew recognizable. It filled Carson's field of vision, the giant face of Harry Chen.

The Chen face smiled, opening its mouth. A long purple tongue flicked out and wrapped around him. He saw Red waving, then yellowed teeth overhead.

"Here's lookin' at you," said Chen's voice.

He stood in front of a gilded mirror. He was Harry Chen. The mirror cracked.

Red kicked the broken glass out of the way and stepped through the frame.

"Yer first inspiration was dreams." He snapped his fingers and a cigarette materialized between them. The Seraph stuck it in the corner of his mouth, then scraped a talon across the bottom of one of his spurred boots. It burst into blue flame. Lighting the cigarette, he drew in, then exhaled a cloud of white smoke that billowed until he was no longer visible.

The smoke compressed into a vertical sheet, which flew at Carson, covering him. A clawed hand indented the whiteness and pulled it away from his face. He seemed to be lying on his back, in bed, with Red hovering above.

"Problem is, ya wake up, and they're gone." The bed disappeared, and he was upright again. "Not to worry though, 'cause next thing ya know, the dreams start to come whether y'asleep or not." As he spoke the words, two-dimensional black-and-white images flashed in the space around them at subliminal speed.

Red held a remote control. "Slow it down a bit, shall we?"

The images blinked on, lingering seconds, long enough for their subjects to be recognized. An eclectic collection, like random frames clipped from media archives. Aerial view of Ocean City. Deformed nuke babies in a hospital ward. Parliament. An antigay demonstration. Himself, Carson, smiling.

"Hold it," Red said. The image held.

The Seraph planted his fists on his hips and stared

up into Carson's grin. "Our old friend Carson. We grew up together. Now what's 'e doing 'ere?"

Life-size projections, like publicity hologens, appeared in increasing number, until there were so many they receded into the blank distance as if multiplied by trick mirrors. Different clothing, different poses, but every one was himself.

"Seems ya can't get rid of the bugger."

One of the Carsons walked over to him, lifted a glass of red wine, and they were in a restaurant that he recognized from a visit to Orlando years before. He'd dined there with Chen. The Carson leaned forward conspiratorially across his plate of linguine.

"Well, they get these memories from each other, Harry. All the time. But it's so much information that mostly they just ignore it."

A bow-tied waiter approached, bearing a covered silver platter, and lifted the domed lid to present a small glass vial of black powder resting on a cut-paper doily.

He saw his own hand reaching. As his fingers closed around it, the vial exploded into gold flame that spurted between them, taking the form of serpents, their backs ridged with fire. The restaurant scene fractured into wedge-shaped sections, each in turn devoured by a set of golden jaws. Then the snakes wriggled off into the darkness.

A black-taloned hand punched through nothing and pulled down, rending the dark as if it were a sheet of paper, exposing gray static on the other side. Red climbed through the tear. He held up a long gold key shaped like a serpent. A giant padlock floated before them.

"Just like Sherlock 'olmes, ya started to piece it together. The images were comin' from *them.* That's why good old Carson was in there. Ya asked yerself,

'What does this mean?' And then ya found the key!"
Red opened the padlock.

And he was in the desert, under a purple sky. Sil-
houetted against the twilight was a hill, and on top of
the hill, a crucifix. He was moving toward it, climbing
up through the wiry brush. The sky darkened at an
impossible rate. When he reached the base of the
cross, the man on it was a shadow, suspended above
him. Then a pale moon raced up from the horizon
and stopped dead overhead. It blinked on, extending
a solitary beam to light the man's face. Harry Chen.

The crucified Chen opened his eyes. "Carson," said
Chen's voice, "thanks, man. If you hadn't been there,
I might never have figured it out."

Red sat on the cross, one knee pulled up against
his chest, the other leg dangling. Chen's eyes shut, and
his head lolled.

Red grabbed him by the topknot and cried, "All
'ail the King!"

The moon switched off.

He was back in Harry's studio. Carson ripped away
the headset, feeling as if someone had wired his rib
cage shut. Pictures from the VR show reeled in front
of his mind's eye, superimposed over the studio, Chen
smiling beside him.

"Memories—you're getting memories from the Seraphim, and you saw me in them, and that's how you
figured out what they were—" He stopped and gasped
in air. "And you're burning some drug, so now you
can talk in my head, and that—that makes you *God*?"

And talk to angels, too, the soundless voice reminded him.

"Stop that shit," he said, raising his voice. "You
and Zeke—"

Chen mused aloud, "Ah, Ezekiel. I told Gabe he
was in Daytona. Knew they wouldn't recognize it."

Carson grabbed him by the shoulders, shaking. The rat tail quivered. "Harry, how did this happen?"

"My birth mother. She's the one who'll know. Maybe it was immaculate conception." He stifled a laugh, snorting instead. "It must have been."

Carson let go. His chest was going to explode. "Why me? Why'd you call me here?"

Chen's eyes focused on him through the twin disks of purple glass. "Well, someone has to be the first disciple, Carson." He snorted again. "This is going to be totally weird. Where should we start? Rousing the dead? Zombies?" He snapped his fingers. "Your father! You'd like to see him, wouldn't you?"

"No!" Carson yelled. *"You are not God!"*

Chen jerked as if he'd been struck. Then his face melted into a smile, and he reached out, clasping Carson's hand. "I understand. I was pretty whacked myself. But you'll get used to it." He leaned forward, vibrating with suppressed laughter. "You're destined for sainthood, Carson. Always thought so."

Carson wrenched his hand free. "Harry . . . go to hell." He was out of the studio, descending the spiral steps in pairs, momentum carrying him across the tiled living-room floor. The weight of the oak door slowed him. Pulling against the black iron handle, he lost place and time for an instant. Memory conjured up another aged and heavy door, another house of the Lord, another departure made in haste and fear.

Carson fled then as he had fled from the seminary years before, breaking into a run when his feet hit gravel. Sheets of rain billowed around him, like curtains lifting on the stage of his life. He leaned into the wind and kept going. White-hot fingers of electricity snatched at the twisted trees, but he kept running, undeterred by the storm of some angry god.

*   *   *

Sixteen years since he left the New Franciscan Theological Retreat, sixteen years since he fled into a humid August night. He'd spent the previous months lapsing in and out of secret drunken stupors, but it had taken a night of sobriety for him to arrive at the truth and finally depart. And then leave he had, like an animal running for its life, the last vestiges of devout resolve pulverized beneath his pounding feet.

It was a disappointing epiphany, at that. After waiting most of his life for such a moment, to have it come while taking a whiz . . .

He'd been standing in the john, watching an amber stream splash against the white tile, wondering how the aliens would urinate. Then an image sprang into his mind from a cartoon he'd seen, a picture of three bathroom doors labeled Men, Women, and Other. It had meant to remark on the increasing social acceptance of nonheterosexuals, but Carson, standing in his scrubbed white stall, thought of his celibacy. Suddenly he saw himself walking through that "Other" door, in the company of transvestites, androgynes, and spindly aliens with oversize heads and huge almond-shaped eyes.

As he jiggled himself back into his pants, it struck him, a sense of absolute certainty that he had walked through the wrong door. It was an unsanitary thought, and he left the bathroom, hoping it would stay behind and seep into the drain with his urine. But striding down the hall, over the tiles of pale Mexican clay, a little voice reverberated through the inner corridors of his mind, calling, *Go, go, go.*

And when he found himself heaving open the oak door of the chapel, the voice, the certainty, was all there was. Like a jet engine, it drowned other sound and propelled him out, across the loosely cultivated grounds, toward the road below.

*   *   *

Carson stopped running when he turned the corner onto Tropican Boulevard. He was soaked, warm water dripping from his clothes and hair, his breath coming in ragged gasps. Thunder rolled and clapped to the west, but the lightning had abated.

There was a traffic light, swinging across the silver lines of rain, and a convenience store, its fogged windows lit by the bright auras of neon beer signs. He took shelter under the red awning. It was hard to think, but he managed to key on his phone for a cab company and give the dispatcher his location.

By the time the battered yellow Chevrolet pulled into the parking lot, the rain had thinned to a sporadic drizzle, and he knew where he was going.

"Airport," he said, slamming the door.

Waiting in line at Orlando International to buy a ticket for the next Atlanta shuttle, he called to find out if Tao would see him. When his phone beeped a few minutes later, the display showed Alden's code. He hesitated. The priest no doubt wanted a report on the visit with Chen, and he definitely wouldn't approve of where Carson was heading next.

Clenching his teeth, Carson pressed the disconnect. Alden's questions would have to wait until he got some answers of his own.

It was spring in Atlanta. Floodlights illuminated drifts of daffodils under pink-flowered trees as the cab traversed an upscale shopping district on its way to Tao's apartment. She lived at the edge of downtown, where the Easter colors dwindled into blocks of narrow gray tenements. The city had been hit hard by the pre-Rising unrest—especially during the Temley era—and it had rebuilt its razed slums with grim determination. Maybe that was why the concrete buildings reminded him of tombstones.

The setting matched his mood, and he almost regretted coming. A private meeting was no guarantee. He could imagine the headline: "Ezekiel's liaison seen with aide to radical, anti-ICARUS Senator." It wasn't fair to her, even if three whiskeys en route had desensitized him to the consequences. But he'd come anyway, and in the elevator to her third-floor unit, he acknowledged why: Tao was the only person who might know what had happened to Harry Chen.

She'd met him three years before the Rising, in his pre-cult-hero days, when she was a shy émigré studying information science at the university, and Chen was just a struggling video artist who'd sloughed off his religious upbringing in his early twenties, and who liked, when he wasn't stoned or tripping, to pontificate about the "doomsday dementia" of the government and society in general. For a while he'd even insisted that the eggs were a fraud, the centerpiece of an international conspiracy.

"Just look at what happened, man," Carson remembered him saying. "The world was advancin', headin' onto a higher level, and the righters were losin' their grip. They needed a way to hold us back. Then, *splash!* And all of a sudden we got martial law and inquisitions to uncover alien sympathizers, and the military-industrial beast that was wheezing for life is resuscitated at a cost of about a trillion dollars." The considerably shorter rat tail had twitched. "Not a coincidence, man, I'm tellin' you. We're being snowballed in a big-ass sort of way."

Of course, the Rising disproved his fraud theory, giving a whole new meaning to the term "right wing," as well as providing the conservative factions a half-dozen advocates with unprecedented credentials.

Chen had regrouped and come up with a bevy of new opinions, but it was Tao who translated rhetoric into action and got politically involved. Although his contacts with Chen had grown fewer and farther between, they were enough for Carson to see the requisite balance: As his lover advanced into the outer world, Chen retreated into his inner one.

The *Follies* were in their second season, and the royalties were adding up. They'd just bought the Spanish colonial, but she'd walked out. Chen's bewilderment and rage had been that of a director whose star actress refused to say her lines. And that was when Carson realized that for his longtime friend, the boundary separating real and virtual wasn't completely intact.

Tao Diredawa opened the apartment door before he knocked. She was almost six feet tall, with licorice-colored skin that set off a dazzling white smile. Her speech was musical, the accent distilled from the hybrid tongue of her Central African homeland. "So what is up with you, Carson? You look like *merde*."

"Feel like it, too," he said, wrapping his arms around her tiny waist. "Listen, I'm sorry about all this." She had a pleasant, musky smell. He thought again that Harry had been a fool.

"Not t' worry. Come on in."

The dismal view outside contrasted almost surreally with her living room. She'd painted the walls bright primary colors, then decorated them with black lines and dots that formed intricate geometric patterns. Modular seating upholstered in red and yellow surrounded a spun-aluminum table. She sat him down and poured aromatic tea from a raku pot.

"So tell me what you're doin' in the enemy camp," she said, passing him a small, handleless cup.

The tea was spiked with pepper and ginger. Its warmth helped. "Can this be confidential?" he asked. "I know you're committed to your boss, but—"

"You're my friend," she assured him. "I keep my word."

He took a deep breath. "It's Harry. He thinks he's God."

She sang her laughter. "I knew that."

"So do most of the Seraphim," he added.

The song stopped. "What do you mean, Carson?"

He told her about his visit to Chen, skipping the encounter with Miriam. Then he said, "I ran, Tao. I left Zeke, I left the Party." He shook his head, amazed at his own rashness. "I wanted this, you know? I wanted it for so long, but not if it means—"

"Harry Chen? If anyone but you told me, I wouldn't believe it." Her eyes were big and round. "He talked in your head?"

"Zeke did, too, but that's another story. Look, Tao, I know I probably shouldn't have come, but you're the only person I thought might understand."

"Because I slept with the man for eight years? Believe me, he wasn't God then." The smile flashed.

He needed an explanation. He needed it desperately. "What about space?"

She shrugged, bony shoulders lifting under a tan sweater. "I've burned it. Good for long nights on the net. But I didn't hear any angels." She gave him a meaningful look. "Though Harry's different, t' be sure. Even has a dog tag, a subcutaneous microchip, ID coded."

"How'd you find that out?"

"We went to a shelter and got Vesper—that gray cat? They scanned the cat and picked up Harry. He was mad, yappin' like a jackal 'cause he'd been 'serialized.' Never could figure it out. Wasn't his folks. They wouldn't even have his genetics done. Hmm." She ran long, spidery fingers over her cropped hair. "That's probably the first thing ICARUS will want to do. Bet Harry didn't think about that."

Carson shook his head. "It just doesn't make sense. He's ridiculed us on a weekly basis for years, but now he wants to play savior."

"But you know Harry," she pointed out. "Everything's *merde* till he says it's not." She poured more tea. "You really think the Heralds will take him? They wanted his show banned; can't see them bowin' down now. And the Seraphim? You said most of them think he's God. What about the others?"

His expression must have given it away.

"Something you're not sayin', eh, Carson?"

He'd omitted the events leading up to Chen's summons, but considering that he'd already revealed the messiah's secret identity . . .

He told her about Zeke's disappearance and capture.

She clucked her tongue. "Oh, I wish I hadn't given you my word. Senator Bloom would kill for this one."

"Yeah, I know. Believe me, I'm not crazy about ICARUS either."

"But it makes sense, no?" she asked. "Harry could drive anyone to drink."

He stared at her, wondering why he hadn't seen it: *Chen was the god that Zeke wanted to shut up.* Zeke knew it was wrong. Zeke would tell them, except—

"Zeke tried to fly away," he said.

Tao pointed out, "So did you."

She was right. "I shouldn't have left," he said. "I shouldn't have left Zeke."

"Then go back, Carson. Tell them Harry isn't God." Her tone was very serious. "But remember: If they don't listen, Bloom will. And you can tell 'Zekiel that, too." She got a card from her purse, jotted a number on the back, and handed it to him. "This line's as secure as they come."

Pocketing the day's second ticket to damnation, he gave thanks that Tao didn't have anything on video. The Party always faced opposition, but he was feeling besieged. The Infidels, Senator Bloom, ICARUS—all of them waited like vultures, ready to tear away the promise of salvation, leaving a bare skeleton of scientific theories. No wonder his anxiety and doubt had been mounting these last few months. On the Link to Chen's, he'd been right: The messiah had still to come. But he sensed a catalysis, the attainment of some cosmic critical mass, and now it was only a matter of that most beguiling scientific theory, time. Then the debate would be over, and the truth would prevail.

That, he knew, was inevitable.

Four

The gold club at the airport was deserted except for a uniformed hostess and two Brazilian businessmen hunched over their laptops. Carson fortified himself with another whiskey before calling Alden from one of the soundproofed booths.

Irritation clipped the Herald Party chairman's speech. "Why didn't you answer your phone? And what are you doing in Atlanta?"

He hadn't mentioned where he was, but ICARUS had the resources to find out just about anything except the one thing they wanted to know most: the origins of the Seraphim.

Carson apologized, telling Alden, "I'm at the airport and I'm taking the next shuttle to Orlando. I'd rather explain from someplace a little more private." The lie bought him a chance to talk to Zeke.

"You can explain in person. Torrington and I will be at the Herald Resort shortly. Ezekiel is already there. You have the benefit of the doubt until then, but I am most perturbed by your actions, Carson."

"How is he?"

"As well as can be expected when his liaison runs off. This has been a most trying weekend. I trust you haven't done anything to make it more so?"

"No." The slip of paper with Chen's address was in

his wallet, folded around Miriam's and Tao's cards. "Alden, the message. Have you talked to—"

"Yes," the priest interrupted. "I spoke with him myself. But we'll discuss that when you arrive. Check in with Torrington's people and have someone pick you up. I don't want any more disappearances."

Maartens, the other bodyguard permanently assigned to Zeke, met him at the gate. He was a quiet, stocky man in his early thirties with a ruddy complexion and faded blue eyes. Carson had never liked him or his cool professionalism. Sometimes he wondered how anyone could spend the majority of his waking hours with an angel and be so passionless. But then, his job wasn't to be passionate, or to believe, just protect.

Their limousine arrived at the Herald Resort, and Maartens ushered him into the private elevator for the concierge level, then down the cloud-puff hall to his suite. Juan opened the door.

"Making things difficult again?" he said, by way of a greeting.

"I had a bad day," Carson retorted, meeting the Cuban's dark gaze. "But I'm back. Where's Zeke?"

Juan nodded, indicating one of the bedroom doors as it swung open and a thickset man in a rumpled twill suit emerged, pulling it shut behind himself. Torrie.

The security chief stopped a meter away and glared at Carson with watery brown eyes set in a fleshy face underneath a high forehead capped by slick black hair. Day-old stubble peppered his chin.

"I want to make one thing clear," he said. "I know who you know in Atlanta, and if there are any leaks, you'll be answering to a Geneva tribunal so fast you'll think we figured out a way to exceed lightspeed after all. Understood?"

Carson kept his tone neutral. "Whatever you say."

"Alden's waiting in his suite. We're both real anxious to hear about your bad day."

"Yeah, well, I need to talk to Zeke first." He stepped toward the bedroom door, but Torrie blocked him with a hand against his chest.

"I said Alden was waiting. Besides, Zeke doesn't feel like talking right now."

"Gee, I wonder why." Carson reciprocated the glare. "Unless you've got some more rope you're planning on using, I'm talking to him. Alone." He pushed past.

The Seraph was at the bedroom window, beyond the subdued light cast by a nightstand lamp. Carson saw that he still wore the dirty white pants. His right wing was bound to his torso with an elastic bandage, bloodstained feathers sticking out at odd angles.

"Zeke . . ."

The Seraph turned. He held a soda can in his left hand. "Welcome back."

"Zeke, I'm sorry. I truly am. How's your wing?"

"Probably fractured. Imogene is coming to treat it. There isn't a balcony anyway." He raised his drink. "And they put the kiddy control on our autobutler."

Carson smiled with nervous relief. "Alden and Torrie are waiting for my report, but I needed to talk to you. It's Harry Chen, the guy who does the *Follies*. That's who the others think is the messiah."

"Yes, I know."

He dropped his voice to a whisper. "Zeke, please forgive what I said in Daytona. I understand now why you left. When I found out, I had the same reaction. So I went to visit an old friend. Harry's ex, actually. She helped me realize that it was all a mistake."

The Seraph regarded him with mild curiosity. "And why do you say that, Carson?"

"Well, it's obvious, isn't it? I know he's linked to you somehow, and he talked in my head like you did, but that doesn't make him God. I grew up with the guy, Zeke. He's always been pretty freaky. There's an explanation for this, and I'm sure ICARUS will find it. They'd love to discredit a messiah." He glanced at the bandage. "So let them do some good for a change. It's probably the drugs, and rumor's always been that ICARUS developed space. Anyway, they'll get it straightened out. I just thought it would be better if you told them."

Zeke's lips curved in a faint, wistful smile. "Carson, I do not want to tell them anything. I told you because I thought you might understand. You taught me silence, the silence of whiskey. You use it to mute your doubts, and now I use it to mute these voices, your god and your devil, that clamor for—"

"Our devil?" His cheeks burned. It didn't help that he could still taste that last shot. "What's he got to do with this? You always said you ignored him, that he was the prince of lies—"

"Have you never listened to your doubts, Carson?"

Raising his voice, he said, "I'm not an angel, Zeke. I'm *supposed* to have doubts."

The Seraph spoke calmly. "And that is exactly why I fled. I am trapped in these definitions you cling to, and I want to be free."

Carson felt nauseous again. He gazed out the window at the full moon above Mars Mountain, thinking: I've led an angel astray. That'll go down real well on Judgment Day.

"Do not blame yourself," Zeke said, as if he'd heard the self-reprobation. "Perhaps it is we who have misguided you."

"No offense, but that's not much comfort." He

looked at him sidelong. "So what are you going to do? Tell ICARUS they were right?"

"So I can be their alien? No. When this wing heals, I will leave."

Carson wanted to hold him. "They'll find you. Harry said that he told Gabriel where you were. If he did it once, he can do it again."

"That will not happen," Zeke said quietly. "I am shielded from his sight."

"How?" he asked, and then before the Seraph could answer, added, "No, don't tell me anything else." He shook his head. "Ignorance might just be bliss."

Zeke nodded in understanding.

"What do you want me to say? Should I tell them the truth?"

The Seraph's gray eyes glinted moonlight. "I could still use your help."

"I was afraid of that." He hadn't delivered Miriam's and Tao's messages, and he wasn't going to, not yet. There's time, Carson assured himself.

He left Zeke cloaked in shadow and went to make his report.

They didn't like it. If he'd mentioned his encounter with Miriam, they would have liked it even less.

"I didn't use good judgment," Carson acknowledged of his visit to Tao. "But I was shocked. I didn't tell her anything except that I'd had a strange message from Harry. I thought she might know something that would help explain."

"It has been quite a surprise," Alden said. He sat opposite Carson in a striped armchair. Torrie was pacing. "But your response was not acceptable. Especially in light of the difficulties Ezekiel is having. He has been very uncommunicative. I apologized for the damage to his wing. It certainly shouldn't have happened, and Torrington has spoken to his people about their overzealousness."

"They had no right. He's not our prisoner."

"No one said he was, Carson. But we do have a responsibility to Ezekiel. He needs our protection." The priest looked ethereal, his washed-out skin and hair contrasting with the black clerical shirt.

"What'd he say during your little chat?" Torrie interjected. He stopped behind Alden, thick fingers curling over the armchair's wood trim.

Carson fidgeted on the couch. Its cushions were soft, but he couldn't get comfortable. The chandelier seemed too bright. "I think he needs some time by himself."

"Well, a culvert is not the place to take it." The priest sighed, exasperated. "His schedule has been cleared for the next few days, and perhaps it's just as well. He's behaving erratically."

"Alden, if Harry Chen was in your head, wouldn't you behave erratically? Zeke just wanted a little peace, and he didn't know how to get it. I think the best way to help him is to figure out why Harry is linked to them, and to straighten this whole thing out before the situation gets any worse."

Torrie commented, "And so you decided to fly up to Atlanta and do a little investigating of your own."

"What are *you* going to do?" he countered.

The priest said, "Dr. Berthold is coming tomorrow. She and Torrington will interview Mr. Chen, but we must remember their limitations. The Seraphim speak with a higher authority."

He stared. "Are you saying you'd accept Harry Chen as the messiah?"

"I'm saying that it is not our place to question the divine, Carson. Only to have faith in its ultimate wisdom." Alden's eyes were sapphires embedded behind tired lids. "We all need some rest. I'm sure the morning will bring a fresh perspective."

"What about Zeke?"

"You must do what you can to help him," the priest said, standing. "After all, that is your job."

Personal liaison to an angel. It wasn't something that he'd grown up expecting to be.

The position itself, along with the attendant rituals—from amusement park pageants to Sea Station baptisms—was an invention of man. The Seraphim had called themselves "heralds sent to enlighten the world as to the coming of its savior." Carson's role was to help them, but the exact manner in which he was to do that had been defined by Alden and the Party's board of directors, who had tasked themselves with compiling *The Seraphic Revelations,* and with forming an independent organization to serve the disseminators of the Lord's word.

Zeke and the others had gladly stepped to the pulpit provided by the Heralds, and had done their best to answer the thousand questions asked of them. Their responses, though, were often frustratingly vague, and left the Party with little choice but to make it up as they went along, creating dogma and organizational charts where there was only a message. But that message had broad appeal, especially since Alden kept the door wide-open so that anyone, regardless of denomination, could climb aboard the glory train. All it took was professed belief to join the Party, and those who joined could donate. And the donations were used to spread the word.

That was the whole point, after all, or so Carson had thought. He'd performed many duties in his eight years at Zeke's side, some unexpected, but serving the angel had always been synonymous with that point.

Until now.

*   *   *

Carson looked up from his breakfast at their suite's glass dining table and told Zeke, "Imogene's on her way."

The Seraph had showered and put on his casual uniform, a pair of tapered, cream linen pants and a specially cut, matching tunic. Most of the dried blood had washed off the lame wing. He stretched his good one and flicked it. Tiny beads of moisture shimmered in the midmorning sun.

"How did your report go?" he asked.

Carson tossed his napkin onto the table. "I told them that you wanted some peace and quiet. Alden said a drainpipe wasn't the right place to find it."

"Thank you."

The sincerity of Zeke's words pained him. He'd lain awake brooding and come up with no better course of action than to wait, but he still felt like a Judas.

"They're going to investigate Harry," he added, as a knock came from the hall.

Carson opened the suite's door, and Dr. Imogene Berthold, personal physician to the Seraphim and ICARUS's chief biological scientist, breezed by with a curt nod. She was a tall, imposing woman of about fifty with silver-blond hair cut to chin length. This morning she was dressed in a short-sleeved navy turtleneck and narrow pants, and carrying an old-fashioned black medical case.

Zeke let her examine the wing.

"Some pain, yah?" she asked, as she manipulated the pinion. "I have made arrangements with Destiny to take images at their center for rare birds." She smiled at the Seraph, then turned to Carson, the humor gone. Her contact lenses were an unnatural shade of violet. "And when we finish, you'll be accompanying me to Mr. Harry Chen's."

                         *   *   *

Zeke's prognosis was for a slow but complete recovery from a fractured metacarpal. Imogene had splinted the wing, then they'd dropped the Seraph at the resort.

Now Carson sat in the back of the limo, across from Torrie and the physician. The security chief opened up his laptop and swiveled it to face him. The record function was enabled.

Imogene crossed her long legs. "Tell us about this voice you heard when you visited Chen."

His first thought was of Zeke's plea on the beach. The Seraph had never done that before, and he wasn't sure if Zeke wanted them to know that he could. "It was only a couple of words. You should ask the Seraphim."

"We're asking you, McCullough," the security chief said.

The physician added, "How would you describe it, other than as a voice in your head? Was it akin to an auditory memory or hallucination? That is to say, did you recognize the voice?"

Carson wanted to answer: I don't know; I was too busy puking. Instead, he told them, "I guess I did, but it was more a feeling of knowing the voice . . . like when the vid beeps and you know who it is before you answer."

"And you're certain there was no audible sound?"

"Look, it wasn't a particularly pleasant experience, and we're going to be there soon. Why don't you just ask him for a demonstration?"

Torrie scowled, but said, "All right." He turned the laptop around, telling Imogene, "We've got a few meg on him so far—adoption, school, medical records, plus everything on his VR show. Here's the brief." He read from his screen, "Thirty-seven-year-old Chinese male, raised in the States following adoption at age six by an American family. Found wandering around Xiaoping after the revolution. No relatives, not even a name. So the relief workers called him Harry Chen, their idea of an oriental John Doe. Thought he might be autistic. Adoptive parents wanted a 'special' child, placed him in alternative ed, due to early history of emotional and cognitive difficulty. Graduated high school, dropped out of community college. Extensive drug use for the last sixteen years, including space." He looked up. "We're working on the standard profiles. Should have them this afternoon." He asked Carson, "You've known him how long?"

"Since I was about nine. They lived down the street."

"And they were religious?"

"Very. Very strict, too. No TV, no VR, nothing. Thought it was evil." He told Imogene, "They didn't believe in genetic scans either. Harry's never had one and he hates doctors. He's not going to cooperate."

"And that," Torrie said, as they stopped in front of the wrought-iron gates, "is exactly why you're here."

"Absofuckinglutely not." Chen stood in the middle of his pre-Rising museum, glaring at them through purple glasses. He had on the same clothes he'd worn the day before. Carson recognized the vomit stains on the pants cuff.

Imogene tried again. "Please, Mr. Chen, this will not be painful. Just a simple blood test. You understand that the results will be kept in strictest confidence."

"I'm not your lab rat," he said, belying the braided goatee that twitched with his words. "I'm the messiah." He asked Carson, "What are you doing with these guys? Where's Zeke?"

"ICARUS has jurisdiction over anything involving the 'Phim," Torrie said. "Now why don't you just—"

Chen cut him off. "You don't have jurisdiction over me. I have jurisdiction over you. All of you. Only reason I let you in is 'cause you've got my angels."

"Then let's not worry about tests right now," Imogene said, snapping shut her medical case. "Mr. Chen, I was wondering if you would do us a favor. We would like to experience this ability you have to communicate via telepathy."

Chen peered at her. "Lady, are you for real? You're like asking God for a demo? What do you think I am, some sort of beta version?"

Torrie shot Carson a look.

"Harry, can we talk a minute?"

Chen didn't take his eyes off the others. "Yeah, if they wait outside."

Carson nodded to Torrie. The security chief and the physician left by the front door.

He faced Chen. "Harry, they're not going to let you anywhere near the Seraphim until they get their tests, and they're not going to let the Seraphim anywhere near you. That's just the way it is. And you're lucky they didn't pull some sort of planetary security crap and bust in here. Then you'd be a lab rat for real, and there wouldn't be a damn thing you could do."

Chen said, "I already thought of that, man. I told that priest Alden if anything happened, the Seraphim would know. Those ICARUS bastards won't risk it 'cause they're just along for the ride, still hoping they'll find some spaceship hiding on the dark side of the moon. And your Party doesn't want the bad press." He snorted with disdain. "They ain't gonna do shit, man."

Carson rubbed the base of his skull, where a headache was kindling. "What is it you want, Harry? Huh?"

Chen scratched his chin through the beard, pensive. "I'm the messiah, you know? I mean, I haven't worked out the details, but you Heralds've been gearing up for me, and now here I am. I gotta assume my rightful place and all that other shit."

Great, Carson thought. God's just as unprepared as the rest of us. To Chen, he said, "In the meantime, ICARUS isn't going to back off. I know you hate doctors, but they want some sort of proof and—"

Chen snorted. "Proof? You can't prove God."

"Fine. But they've got the angels. And even if you get them to come to you, you won't be assuming any rightful places, because the minute you do, ICARUS will be beating down the door." He shrugged. "So until you turn omnipotent, it's a standoff."

Chen glowered. "You're being an asshole, Carson."

"No, I'm just pointing out the obvious. It's your call, Harry." He strolled across the room and interested himself in a video montage on Déjà Vu. The androgyne appeared in a succession of elaborate costumes, executing his trademark court bow, followed by early segments from his psychic/sex net, Foreskin & Foresight.

The montage had progressed to news clips of Vu's presumed death in a shipwreck a few days before the Rising, when Chen appeared at his side.

He said peevishly, "Ain't no communion, man, but tell them they can have their blood."

Tuesday afternoon. Carson floated on his back in the resort's pool, eyes shut, watching a golden orb pulse in the sanguine darkness. It dimmed, and his wet body chilled as a giant shadow shifted across it. He opened his eyes. A swollen gray cloud obscured the sun. In a response drilled into him since childhood, he twisted onto his stomach, kicking to the side, and hoisted himself out of the water. No one else seemed to have noticed the impending storm. The tourists still splashed in the free-form pool. It was huge, at least forty meters long, with a sand beach. A fountain of patinated Seraphim rose from the aqua surface, the sculpted fish at their feet spurting little jets of water.

The swim had not been as diverting as he'd hoped. Over an hour until Imogene and Torrie made their preliminary report. He stared at the fountain, remembering the lobby mural, and thought: This is limbo, my own private limbo. Then, skirting the supine bodies, he made his way to the locker room, and after rinsing off the smell of chlorine, got dressed.

Walking to the elevator, Carson passed the arcade. On impulse, he veered through its arched entryway. Quiet inside. It was all virtual reality now, the kids strapped into spring-loaded seats that provided kinetic effects, microcosms flickering in their fixed stares.

He climbed into one of the vacant games titled JUDGMENT DAY. Small script under the name stated that it was officially licensed from the Herald Party. Carson put on the headset and pressed PLAY.

A booming voice said, "Welcome to the end of the world!"

His vantage was an aerial view of a smoldering volcano. It was night, but the volcano lit everything with an eerie red glow. He was one of a circle of white-winged Seraphim that hovered around the mountain. The other six were sheathed in armored combat suits, their eyes covered by reflective visors. Each had a crossbow and a quiver of silver-tipped arrows.

A star fell from the midnight sky into the rock cauldron. Black smoke boiled over the jagged lip. Then, with teeth-chattering vibration, it blew.

Out of the crimson lava fountain rose a demonic giant. The devil laughed maniacally and scooped up a huge ball of flame. Molten rock dripped from his black claws.

"Will good triumph over evil on Judgment Day?" the voice boomed. "It's up to you!"

The devil hurled the firebomb at him. It widened as it approached, flame blocking out the scene, until there was only static and the receding sound of demented laughter.

Carson pulled off the headset, deciding, as he left the arcade, that it was a very good thing the bounds between real and virtual were breached only in the minds of people like Harry Chen.

"The common term is UGO. Unidentified genetic object." Imogene stood at the end of a long oak table in one of the resort's meeting rooms, using a pointer to enlarge a section of the complex pattern on the wall screen. "This extra sequence from Mr. Chen's gen-scan is totally unique. Components have been found in an extraordinarily small percentage of humans, but the entire sequence is unprecedented in our species. So we compared it to other genomes." She used the pointer to bring up another pattern and drag it until it perfectly overlaid Chen's. "And as you can see, we found a match."

"A match to what?" Alden asked, leaning forward to peer at the screen.

Carson thought: Maybe Harry *is* a rat.

"This sequence," she said, "is from the Seraph genome."

Carson stared at her. "Are you saying they're related?"

"That's a rather imprecise term." The physician clicked off the screen. "To our knowledge, this DNA was not on the planet until the eggs arrived, and Mr. Chen was born a few years after. That makes common ancestry unlikely."

The priest asked, "What else have you found?"

"So far, this is the only anomaly. Mr. Chen refused to demonstrate his alleged telepathic abilities. We have only Carson's account, and the assertion of the Seraphim that he is in contact with them." She glanced at Torrie, who stood by the door, arms crossed. "Ezekiel was not forthcoming. We'd like to interview the others. It is possible they have information which we lack."

The priest's blue eyes hardened. "I'm certain if they had anything they wanted to tell you, they would do so. And that applies to Ezekiel as well."

Torrie came to the table. The sleeves of his yellow oxford shirt were rolled up over thick, hairy forearms. "We have a mandated responsibility, Alden. We can't let you turn the Seraphim over to this guy just because he says he's the messiah."

For once, Carson was with the security chief, but the priest answered sternly, "I agreed to this delay so that you might assure yourselves you had fulfilled that responsibility. But that same mandate gives the Seraphim autonomy. It is they who bear witness to the messiah." Carson cringed, remembering Zeke's dissent, as the priest continued, "Your own findings confirm that Mr. Chen has sprung from divine seed."

"That's one view," Imogene commented. "There are other possibilities: mutation, recombination."

Alden said, "Gene-splicing? The only gene-splicing that's been done is by the Lord."

The skin around her violet eyes crinkled with disdain. "We've had the technology for years." She added hastily, "Of course, ICARUS and its predecessors did not perform experiments of that nature, but any sufficiently advanced race could have—"

Alden cut her off. "And fortunately, ICARUS and its predecessors safeguarded the eggs." He sighed. "This is a tired debate, Dr. Berthold, and one that I am loath to pursue. Please share your findings with the Strategic Planning Office. There is much to be done, and they are most anxious to begin."

Torrie said, "These results are classified."

"It is not your decision, Torrington, and I do not need your approval. It is Mr. Chen's scan. If you do not provide the information, then we shall just ask him to have another one performed."

The security chief's jaw tensed, and he cracked his knuckles. "It has to be done right, Alden. All hell will break loose if you announce the messiah's come, and none of the governments have been put on alert. We need time to brief the Planetary Security Council, and while that's happening, we might as well talk to the other 'Phim."

"You had two years to interrogate them," the priest said, his tone abrupt. "If ICARUS wishes to indulge in paranoid fantasies of alien plots, that is your business. But I will not permit the Seraphim to be harassed. Like it or not, they have delivered the salvation which your science failed to provide. As for the PSC, I am quite certain you have already apprised them of the situation. They have until tomorrow morning. With their global alert network, that should be more than adequate." He stood. "Now if you'll excuse us, we have a press conference to arrange."

When Torrie and Imogene had left, Alden said, "I would very much like Ezekiel to make the announcement."

Carson poured himself a glass of water from a plastic canister on the table and drank half of it, stalling. He couldn't find the right words.

The priest watched him. "I know this is difficult, Carson, perhaps most of all for you, having known Harry Chen these many years. But the Lord works in mysterious ways. Do not falter just because the path is unclear."

He put down his water and said, "Harry's a drug addict, Alden. He's burning space."

The priest nodded. "Yes, I am aware of his drug use. But sometimes those who have fallen into darkness are best able to find their way to the light. It is not our place to judge. Now about Ezekiel—"

He looked away. "I don't think Zeke feels like doing any press conferences."

The priest came around the table to perch beside him, age-spotted hands clasped in his lap. "Is there something you're not telling me, Carson?"

ICARUS didn't have an explanation for Harry. This one time he'd put his faith in science, and as Alden had said, science failed. Carson looked up at him, defeated. "Zeke wants to go off and find himself. That's why he left. He's confused. He doesn't accept Harry; he just wants him to shut up, him and the devil."

"What are you saying, Carson?"

He shrugged. "Just what he told me. He didn't want ICARUS to know. Especially after what they did to him in Daytona."

Alden shook his head. "No, this cannot be." For a moment, he stooped forward, bent under the implications, then he straightened. "Come, let us speak with Ezekiel."

"You just made me look like a fool," Carson said, as the suite's door closed behind the priest. "Alden comes up here to find out what's wrong, and you say,

'Nothing. I'd be happy to do the press conference.' What about wanting to be free? What about your doubts?"

The Seraph brushed silver hair from his face, tucking the long strands behind his ear. "As I told Alden, I have laid those doubts aside."

Carson was too stunned to show the proper respect. "Is that the truth, or did you just tell him what he wanted to hear?"

"Truth is relative, Carson." Zeke busied himself adjusting the bandage that circled his chest.

"Sure. And that's why you asked him to take the kiddy control off our autobutler." He went to the window. The sun's glare obscured Destiny. He didn't believe the Seraph, but he didn't believe much these days. That made it hard to determine where his loyalties should lie. "The problem, Zeke, is that I'm supposed to be doing this job, except I'm not really sure what it is anymore." He turned around.

Zeke was still fiddling with the bandage. "Your job hasn't changed," he said. "And in the future, I hope you will exercise greater discretion." Looking up, he repeated the familiar maxim. "The glory train is coming, Carson. Faith is the ticket that lets you on board."

The vid beeped. Scowling, Carson answered it.

The Destiny Ambassador smiled from the screen and said warmly, "Mr. McCullough, I'm so glad to reach you. I hope the facilities at the Rare Bird Center were adequate and that Ezekiel will make a full recovery."

"Yes," Carson said, composing himself. "It does seem that way."

During dinner in their suite, Alden announced, "The Strategic Planning Office has rescheduled with the Church of the Messiah. They'll be holding a special service on Sunday."

Carson was aware that several members of the SPO had flown in from Ocean City.

"The other Seraphim will be present, as well as a number of dignitaries who have been sympathetic to our cause. I've already discussed it with Mr. Chen. I trust you have no objections, Ezekiel?"

The Seraph finished chewing a bite of pasta primavera before answering, "Not at all." Behind him, reflected white feathers curved around the coppery metal of a wall sconce.

"Good. This particular church has first-rate multimedia capabilities. I'm afraid we have a certain stigma to overcome. With the UN vote a few short days after the service, we must ensure that the right impression is created."

Harry's debut, Carson thought sourly. You can dress him up, but you can't take him out in public. He picked at his noodles. The Seraphim couldn't tolerate meat, and the Party forbade the consumption of animal products in their presence.

The priest continued, "The others inform me they are most anxious to be with him. I explained the importance of their engagements to Mr. Chen, especially in light of his coming forward, and he agreed to let us bring them on Saturday. If you need to see him before then—"

Zeke said, "No. That's not necessary."

"What about Harry?" Carson asked. "What's he going to be doing?"

"Staying at home. Obviously we can't have him here; he would be sighted, and his identity exposed." Alden's pale forehead creased. "I must admit I am perplexed by the lack of direction, Ezekiel. He has not indicated his desires."

"He doesn't know what his desires are," Carson said. "I asked."

The priest reproved him. "Mr. Chen values your allegiance highly, Carson. You were the first one summoned, and I know he is looking forward to your presence on Sunday." He turned his attention back to the Seraph.

Zeke pushed his plate away. "He seems to be . . . adjusting."

Alden nodded. "Yes, how foolish of me not to realize." He glanced at Carson. "I think we all should keep in mind how difficult this must be. I'm sure Mr. Chen is reevaluating his life, the misjudgments he made in his ignorance."

"Is that it?" Carson asked Zeke, feigning innocent curiosity.

The Seraph looked away. "More or less."

After the meal, Carson sneaked out, telling Zeke and Maartens, who was posted in the hall, that he was going for a swim. There were three bars in the resort, but he couldn't take the chance. Pocketing his telltale silver-wing insignia, he went downstairs and boarded the Destiny Express to the Link station at Orlando International.

In the lobby of the Airport Hilton, he spied a rank of pay phones and thought of calling Tao. The futility of it prevented him. Nothing would change; Harry Chen would still be God. Alden had made his decision, and Zeke had recanted his doubts. The optimism Carson felt when he departed Atlanta was lost in a roiling cloud of uncertainty.

He needed a drink.

The bar was a crowded, wedge-shaped room on the top floor of the hotel. He found a leather swivel chair next to a semicircular wall of glass and ordered his whiskey.

"Keep 'em coming," he told the too-cheerful waitress, pointing out the window at the distant wing lights dotting the Florida night. "Just like those."

She laughed, and wiggled off across the room.

Carson watched her, watched the tight curves under black hot pants. Her swaying pelvis moved, beckoning him, the polyestered outline of her ass a dark beacon, flashing in the monochrome of the bar. Through the fog of his confused anger, sex pulsed from her hips, a primal semaphore, the code that would lead him back to a place where the world was okay.

She returned with his drink, put it down with fuchsia nails, the color pulled like saltwater taffy in the cut crystal, her tanned cleavage like—

"Thanks," he said, averting his gaze.

"Order you another?" she asked.

He could have another. He could keep going until he crash-landed, and that would finish it. They'd fire him for sure.

He said, "No, I can't."

Then he drained the glass, paid with cash, and left.

Five

For the press conference, Zeke dressed in his formal uniform of white pants and a matching double-breasted tunic with silver tab closures. Imogene had temporarily removed the bandage and splint; his injured wing drooped.

Carson affixed the insignia to the lapel of his own somber suit. No one had commented on his temporary absence from the resort the previous night. He'd been testing himself, standing on the edge of a cliff, daring himself to jump. And, of course, he hadn't. It would take more than fancy lasergraphics for Carson to accept Harry Chen as his savior, but he couldn't leave Zeke. And maybe that was the real reason he'd come back from Atlanta: The ignominy of it—abandoning an angel—was more than he could bear.

That's shame, not faith, Carson reproached himself, feeling grateful that the only blinding light and intense scrutiny he faced today would come from an international press corps.

Zeke's statement was brief: He was honored to announce that the living messiah had revealed himself to the Seraphim and would address the world via satellite on Sunday.

Almost in unison, the reporters shouted, "What's his name?"

Zeke stepped aside to let Alden field the questions.

"Out of deference to his wishes, the messiah's earthly identity cannot be divulged at this time," the priest responded.

"So the messiah's definitely male? Is he biologically normal?"

"Yes, the Son of God is once again among us."

"What about his daughter?" a female voice yelled. Carson recognized the questioner as an antagonistic reporter from QueerNews. The network was always badgering the Party for their moral stance against homosexuality.

Alden ignored her, gesturing to an aide, who distributed packets that bore the Party's insignia. "To use the corporeal as a measure of the divine is human folly," the priest chided them. "However, the Lord recognizes our preoccupation with such measures and in his wisdom has made the information which you are being given available. Its essence is that the messiah has come as a human being who shares certain genetic characteristics with the Seraphim."

The reporters didn't miss the obvious question. They asked, "Does he have wings?"

Alden smiled, then answered, "No," and called on NewsNet's regular correspondent, who asked if the Heralds were asserting the end of the world, and if so, what cataclysm was to come.

"This is a beginning," Alden said, "the dawn of a new age in which we shall be reunited with our God. That is the Lord's promise, and as the Seraphim's very presence here attests, it may be relied upon. Although we do not always understand *how* something can be, we may nonetheless feel assured that it *will* be."

"What does that mean for the average individual?" the reporter pressed. "Are you saying we should stay home from work tomorrow because life as we know it is over?"

The priest hesitated before answering, "The messiah has not yet revealed the details of his plan for our salvation. And I want to emphasize that everyone remain calm. Rejoicing is in order; rash actions are not. No assumptions should be made at this point, except that the Lord will make his will known." He took a question from a GlobeNet reporter.

"The Seraphim haven't done anything except talk. They said when the messiah came a gateway to paradise would open. So where is it? Where's the evidence for their claims?"

Alden cleared his throat. "The Seraphim stated that the gateway to paradise would open when their work here was done, and the fact that our savior has come may be taken as evidence." He pointed to someone else.

"Have you conferred with the Planetary Security Council? How will this affect the proposed mandate?"

"It is our hope that the Israelis will reconsider their border policy. We will continue to pursue the mandate. Obviously it is more imperative than ever. I will let Mr. Torrington address your first question."

The security chief stepped to the microphones. "The Planetary Security Council will be releasing a statement shortly. It's my understanding that their position is neutral on this issue."

"So there isn't a perceived threat?"

"Not at this time, no."

The rest of the conference was interminable for Carson, standing at attention while the priest circumvented the requests for detail. If some cosmic critical mass had truly been attained, an explosion was imminent. He felt it like a hot breath on the back of his neck.

"I think that went fairly well," Alden told them, after it was over.

He stared at the priest. "What about Sunday, when they find out who it is?"

Alden patted his arm. "Faith, Carson. Miracles abound. I'm sure on Sunday Mr. Chen will surprise us all."

And how many lives will the charade have cost by then, he wondered. The conference had lasted an hour, but Carson knew only too well that instantaneous worldwide communications eliminated the delay between cause and effect—and whatever grace might be granted by that delay.

They adjourned to the meeting room, where the wall screen showed NewsNet coverage of a massacre at a population-control center in Dublin.

"Sinners must be purged! He is come; they must all be purged!" screamed the surviving gunman, as he was dragged from the clinic.

The broadcast switched to a stampede in the Hong Kong banking district, then to Dr. Kir Rasputin, author of a recent best-selling cyberbook *The End of the World and Other Disasters.*

"The Seraphim have always failed to provide *instructions,*" the sociologist said. His head was shaved and tattooed with a pair of wings that curved around his skull from either temple. "They should have sent e-mail to the human-race *alias,* something with a subject line like 'Salvation in Ten Easy Steps.' The angels of old were very explicit and now we see why."

Next to Carson, Alden muttered a prayer. Then he said, "Torrington, why were precautions not taken? The Planetary Security Council had three days."

The security chief responded, "What'd you expect? Extremists will always find a way. That's why I wanted to go slow, diffuse the bomb—"

NewsNet was airing the PSC's statement. A haggard-looking Chairman Tepanov asked for an end to the violence, then described the Party's announcement as having "as yet undetermined ramifications," and stated that the PSC would deal judiciously with the situation.

Right, Carson thought, as around-the-globe coverage resumed. Just wait until he meets the situation. He glanced at Zeke. The Seraph was inert.

Eventually a Strategic Planning Office staffer, who Carson remembered as the golden boy from the last presidential campaign, came and whispered to the priest.

"Yes," Alden said. "We should get started."

~ Someone turned off the wall screen, and the staffer began running through a list of clarifications to be issued at the noon press briefing. Carson tried to concentrate, but cold swells of panic lifted him out of the room. When each subsided, he found himself immersed again in the business of salvation.

The discussion turned from the likelihood of the golden boy's former boss attending on Sunday to the appearances and video audiences planned for Zeke.

"We'd like him on *Candice* tomorrow, if it can be cleared," an SPO scheduler said, with a questioning glance at Torrie.

"We'll work it," he answered. "Sneak him out through the service alley. But keep in mind security's tight, and it's only gonna get tighter. As it was, we had a bunch of believers camped in the lobby this morning, singing His praises. Destiny people had to move 'em on out."

The golden boy nodded, his handsome face expressionless. "Now about the *Freak Follies* . . ."

Carson shivered as another swell rolled in.

"I will convey your request, Minister Bola," Zeke told the earnest brown face on their suite's wall screen. "I know your people have suffered greatly from this plague. It may be that the Lord visited it upon them in his fury, and if so, it will be by their fervent prayers, not my intervention, that they are redeemed."

The Seraph accepted the man's tearful thanks. When the call terminated, he relaxed his soldierly posture.

"You said you were tired of being the puppet of a wrathful god," Carson blurted. The medical crisis in the Central African Republic was nothing new, but with the riot images fresh in his mind, he'd barely maintained his composure. Thankfully, Bola was the last of Zeke's audiences. That afternoon, he'd delivered celestial reassurance to three heads of state, and eight clergymen in six countries.

"People are dying," Carson added, knowing it was out of line.

The Seraph looked pained, but Carson wasn't sure if it was his words or the splinted wing. Zeke said, "I disappoint you."

"I'm disappointed, yeah." He hit a key on his laptop, filing a record of the audiences, then looked back at the wan face. The Seraph's eyes were dull iron, as they'd been in Daytona. "You said you expected more from me; well, sometimes I expect more from you, too." He bit his lip. It was the unbeliever's criticism, that angels ought to do something besides herald the coming of the savior.

Zeke said only, "I understand how you feel," which made him feel worse about wishing God could have sent a more proactive corps.

He went back to his work. Although security concerns kept them in Orlando for the rest of the week, doing most of the appearances over the net, the Strategic Planning Office was writing a tight schedule for

Zeke. He might have to tell them to loosen it. If talking on the vid drained the Seraph this much, he'd be down for the count by Sunday. Imagining Zeke out sick on Chen's big day gave Carson some small, momentary satisfaction. The cloud of angst blotted it out. Whether Chen was the conductor of Zeke's glory train was one thing, whether Carson had a ticket was another.

He was glad that night for the stepped-up security: It made a surreptitious drink impossible.

"Can I do anything else for you before I go to sleep?" he asked Zeke. The guilt over his outburst had set in quickly; his deference to the Seraph had yet to appease it.

"No, thank you." Zeke continued to cycle through entertainment channels on the living-room wall screen.

"GodNet went down," Carson offered.

The Seraph looked up from the vid.

"Five million users tried to access the PrayerLine, and Testimonies is totally hung."

Zeke's countenance was inscrutable.

Carson said, "Well, anyway, good night."

Waking from a bad dream sometime later, he heard the Seraph moving restlessly in the dark beyond the door.

Carson stood naked in the cultured-marble interior of the shower. He knew the stone was fake because it wasn't cold, and the swirls, in shades of blue-green, looked too much like waves. More important, he and the marble were perfectly dry. He tried the spigot again—not a drop.

"Our deepest apologies, sir," said the square-jawed young man that answered his call to Guest Services. "There was a malfunction in the reclamation unit, but it will be back on-line shortly."

He was still in his robe when Zeke got up.

"There's no water," the Seraph told him.

"I know; their reclamation unit went down. State ran out of fresh water about twenty years back. It's all recycled these days."

"*All* the water's gone?"

"Maybe not all of it. Used to come from an aquifer, but I think whatever's left is probably carcinogen soup."

The Seraph's eyebrows rose.

Friday night, Alden had a spot on *WorldReport.*

"Mind if we watch?" Carson asked.

"No." Zeke sat backwards on the chair from the living room's desk; it was usually the most comfortable position for him because of his wings. Glancing at the Seraph, Carson saw that he wasn't watching the vid. His face was slack with loneliness, his focus lost somewhere in the expanse of apricot carpeting.

Carson switched channels.

"—when the course of human history was forever altered by the discovery of mysterious capsules floating in the Atlantic Ocean. Now, forty years later, Earth's Special Visitors and their sociopolitical intermediary, the Herald Party, have announced, in typically ambiguous fashion, that they will introduce the world to its savior in less than forty-eight hours. This announcement, coming days before a critical United Nations vote on a mandate for universal access to old Jerusalem, has ramifications that go infinitely beyond the religious issues.

"Later, we'll talk about those ramifications with Alden Xavier, a former Anglican bishop, and chairman of the Herald Party. But first, let's go back to that unforgettable day, ten years ago."

A 3-D graphic of an egg appeared, rendered with

glowing white lines, and inside it, a winged form, kneeling in profile. The egg shattered into fragments, and the Seraph straightened, stretching slowly, like it was moving underwater, swimming almost, as the wings spread and the creature took flight. It disappeared off the top of the screen, the shards meanwhile rearranged themselves, forming words etched in phosphorescence: THE RISING.

The words faded, white evaporating off the screen, segueing into the famous footage . . .

On a silent spring morning, under a sky pale as clear water, the eggs floated to the surface. They bobbed there, among the gilded waves, in a square kilometer of ocean ringed by international forces: French Navy, a new Japanese sub, the USS *Manville,* Scandinavian Alliance, and others, all at the ready, gun turrets manned, radars tuned, missiles sequenced, fingers quivering on *the* button, while their respective presidents and prime ministers, safely squirreled away, were alerted to every rise and fall of the blue Atlantic waters through satellite communiqué.

Three days. Three days of waiting, three days of official observers and Sea Station scientists smelling each other's nervous sweat and stale breath.

And then, a *crack* heard and seen on screens around the globe. A scorched egg rocking in syncopation with the waves. A collective holding of human breath, perhaps the closest to unity the world had ever come.

The rocking slowed, the breath released. Silence. A tern entered the arena from overhead, diving now, its scissored tail pointing up, making the sign for peace—

Crack—

End to end, the egg split open. And awaiting its inhabitant, the epitome of human achievement, the most sophisticated weapons systems that man's imagination could muster and his ingenuity create.

A hand reached up out of the egg, a shockingly human hand, a five-fingered hand, and following the hand, a bowed head, hair slick, as if anointed with some ancient oil. And then, as the combined adrenaline threatened to explode mankind's heart, the *wing.*

The first, the one that would later be called Ezekiel, pushed his torso free of the egg, wings stretching, dipping, awkward over the foiled waves, wobbling as they flapped against Terran air.

A shot buzzed across the water like a metal bee, a rogue shot, stinging the moment and later resulting in life imprisonment for the seaman who fired it.

The creature, blinking up at clouds the color of mourning doves, seemed not to notice. Drying in the southern sun, its wings pulsed stronger by the second. As another egg cracked, sending broadcasters into a schizophrenic frenzy, the firstborn rose up into the salt air, its body, except for the wings, unmistakably human, even unmistakably *male.*

The cameras zoomed for the first time on an alien face that wasn't, on an aquiline nose, and dark lips, and eyes like silver in the clear-water sky. And on that face, an expression that needed no words, no explanation.

The creature, aloft now, its white wings spread in benediction over the waiting world, was smiling.

Cut from the newborn Zeke to the anchor, who was silent for one carefully timed moment, an expression of polite appreciation on his distinguished face.

A voice said, "He's here."

Carson looked away from the screen, confused.

"Harry Chen," Zeke added.

"In the hotel?" Carson asked, as a knock came from the hall.

The Seraph was already up, striding to his bedroom. He shut the door, and Carson heard the lock click.

The knock came again. He answered it to find Torrie and four of his people closed in a tight semicircle around Harry Chen. Chen smiled when he saw Carson.

"Got a visitor," Torrie said, as they pushed en masse into the room.

Chen turned and raised his hands, halting the escort. "Privacy, man, we need some space."

"Why's he here?" Carson asked Torrie.

The security chief said, "I'm not any happier about it than you are."

Chen wandered over to the couch. He was dressed in loose white cottons, a black leather pack slung over one shoulder. "Space. We need some space," he said again.

Torrie snapped, "All right." He told Carson. "We'll be in the hall." They left.

Chen was slumped on the blue damask, the pack next to him.

"What are you doing here, Harry? Do you have any idea—"

"I hadda talk to you," Chen said. "So I got in the car. You should've seen their faces. Wasn't shit they could do either, 'cept follow." He pulled himself to his feet, leaning across Zeke's chair toward Carson. "It's the end, man, the end of the world. That's what this means." He dropped his voice to a whisper. "And you know what, man? I haven't the fuckingest idea what I'm supposed to do."

Carson's fingers dug into the chair back. "I thought this was fun for you, Harry."

Chen shrugged. "I thought I'd get to see the angels by now. Where's Zeke?" He looked around. "In there?" he asked, pointing to the Seraph's bedroom. He went and pounded on the locked door. "Zeke? Zeke, man, come on out."

Carson said, "Leave him alone." When Chen didn't, he grabbed him by the wrist. "Leave him alone, okay? You'll see him tomorrow."

Chen yanked his hand free and pounded again. The door swung away from his fist.

The Seraph's face was ashen, his expression cold.

"Whoa," Chen said, intimidated. He took a step back.

Zeke asked, "What do you want?"

"Hey, man, what's the matter? It's me, you know? Here—"

The Seraph's eyes narrowed, and he said, "Get out of my head."

Chen's tone was injured. "Hey, you can't talk to me like that."

Zeke still had the door by the handle, and he started to push it shut.

"Where you goin'?" Chen shoved the door, knocking the Seraph backward and off-balance. His wings spread involuntarily and he grimaced in pain as the injured pinion strained against its bandages. Chen was advancing, oblivious to Zeke's discomfort. "I'm the messiah! You can't just slam the door in my—"

Smack. Chen's head jerked back and to the side. The rest of him followed, spinning a quarter turn. He teetered for an instant, then crumpled to the floor.

Carson stared down at the limp body, amazed.

Zeke had taken out the messiah with one right cross.

"Shit. What are we supposed to do now?" Carson knelt by Chen, who had opened his eyes when he rolled him over, then groaned and apparently passed out again.

"Let him sleep." When Carson gave the Seraph a

skeptical look, Zeke added, "I could use the peace and quiet." He stepped over the prone messiah.

Carson straightened Chen's glasses. The right side of his mouth was swelling. He got some ice from the autobutler, wrapped it in a hand towel, and held it over the bruise.

Zeke perched on the back of the couch, watching.

"Why did you lie?" Carson asked, without looking up from his ministrations. When the Seraph didn't answer, he added, "Was it because I told Alden what you said about wanting to leave?"

"I asked for your help."

He met the gray gaze. "I didn't abandon you, Zeke; you abandoned me." He stood, leaving the ice. "You wouldn't talk to them; you wouldn't back me up. You went along with this whole thing when we both knew it was wrong."

The Seraph folded his arms. "Carson, I don't know what is right or wrong, and I don't want to be held responsible for making the determination."

"So you just go along with this . . . this bad joke?" He looked at Chen. The messiah was wheezing.

"That's what you've been doing."

"I'm not an angel."

"An excuse which I covet." Zeke nodded at the white wing peaking over his left shoulder. "These do not end wars or banish plagues, Carson. They are good only for flight, and now not even that."

Carson clenched his teeth against the welling emotion. "I stayed because of you, Zeke; that's the only reason."

Chen coughed, lids fluttering. The towel slid onto the apricot carpet. He opened his eyes. "What happened?" he asked, his speech slurred by the swollen lip. He reached a hand to his face, groaning when his fingers found the bruise.

Carson glanced at Zeke, then said, "You tripped, Harry. Remember?" There was a secretary against the wall next to the bedroom door. He added, "You tripped and hit the desk."

Chen's black eyes focused on him. "Don't remember." His gaze moved past Carson, to the Seraph. "Him. I was talking to him." Suspicion tightened his features.

"That's right, Harry. You were talking to Zeke, and you tripped."

"Oh." His face relaxed.

"Come on, let's get you up." Carson helped him to the couch.

Chen saw his pack and started to grin. "Ow." He touched his sore lip.

"I'll get some more ice," Carson said.

"No ice. Glasses." Chen flipped open the pack and pulled out a bottle of red wine.

Zeke appeared beside them, a slow smile spreading across his face.

Chen made a little snort of amusement. "You know, Zeke, for an angel, you're all right."

After Chen left, Alden and Torrie summoned Carson to report on the visit. He lied about everything except Chen's insecurities. Zeke was being honest with him, and he wouldn't betray that trust again, even if it meant they both missed the glory train.

When he returned to the suite, the Seraph's door was shut. He went to sleep feeling less alone, and dreamed of the show Chen had composed for him, of Red pulling the pillow from his face, whispering, "Wake up, wake up."

Carson grabbed for the pillow, but it wasn't there. His eyelids peeled back then, and he saw someone bent over him, silhouette of an arm, faint shafts of light seeping across the room, illuminating feathers—

He yelped, making some unintelligible sound, and pushed back into the padded headboard.

"It's just me." The arm moved toward the night table. He heard fumbling, *click.*

Carson blinked away the sudden brightness, saw Zeke standing there.

"You scared the—"

Zeke shushed him with a finger pressed against his lips. He said softly, "I have to leave, Carson. I can't wait. Will you help me?"

Carson sat up and shook his head, trying to clear it of sleep. "You can't even fly, Zeke."

"I know. That's why I need a ride."

"What do you want me to do, call you a cab?"

"No. But I called Miriam. She can meet me if—"

Cutting off the Seraph, he demanded, "How do you know about Miriam?" He grabbed his wallet from the nightstand and flipped it open. The cards were still there. He looked up at Zeke. "Did you put them back?"

"No." The Seraph knelt, elbows resting on the bed. "Michael told me how to contact her."

"Who the hell is Michael?"

A faint smile played on the dark lips. "As you say it, Carson, he is the devil. One of us. The fallen one."

Carson stared.

"I told you before that I would be shielded from Chen's sight if I left. Who did you expect would shield me?"

He'd been right in thinking he didn't want to know. "So you serve him now, is that it?"

The Seraph shook his head. "I am no more certain of Michael than of Harry Chen. But he has offered these favors, and there are few who will help me."

Voice rising, Carson asked, "You said he was exiled in darkness, that he couldn't come, that he wasn't here, not like the messiah. So what is it he wants for helping you?"

Zeke's tone became bitter. "What he wants is what is always wanted: answers. ICARUS wants the answers of some alien race, the Heralds want the answers of your wrathful god, and Michael wants his answers, perhaps his lies, spread." He added, "I have promised him nothing."

Carson tried to absorb this latest revelation.

"I told you I was drinking to deafen myself to his voice, his and Harry Chen's. Since my capture, I've had no respite. Out of desperation, I listened. Michael told me of this woman and her offer, so not everything he says is untrue. I called. She'll pick me up if I can get out of this hotel." He slid a cardkey from his pants pocket. "This is for the service elevator. I can take it to the laundry, leave by the back, as we did yesterday when we went to the studio."

"Where did you get that?"

"Our maid, Rosita. She heard the voice of God, and it told her to give me her cardkey." The Seraph scowled at his own subterfuge.

"What about the guard in the hall?"

"If you set off the fire alarm, I can hide in the closet by the hall door. When the guard knocks, take him to my room and I'll sneak out."

Carson felt smothered. "I can't do that."

"Please, Carson, you said you came back for me. I need your help."

The Seraph's pose, kneeling in supplication, was too much. He buried his face in his hands. "I can't do it," he repeated.

Help me.

The words sliced through his psyche. How many

times could he ignore the plea of an angel? Carson looked into Zeke's eyes, into the dark wells rimmed with silver. "I hope you'll tell this Michael to go easy on me when I get to hell." He offered his hand and the Seraph took it, his own long fingers closing around Carson's, then slipping away.

Two new words formed in his mind: *Thank you.*

He pulled on his pants while Zeke got in position. Then he took a book of matches into the bathroom. The tiled floor was cold against his bare feet; he needed to piss. Another decorous ending, he thought, as he unzipped his fly.

The smoke detector was set in the ceiling. He climbed on the cultured-marble vanity, struck a match, and reached the small orange flame toward the flat white disk.

It took three matches. When the shrill bell of the alarm finally sounded, he jumped with surprise. Immediately, someone pounded on the hall door. He dropped the matchbook into his toiletry bag, switched off the light, and felt his way across the suite.

It wasn't Maartens or Juan, but another man whose name Carson didn't know. "Where's the Seraph?" he demanded, pushing past him. "Turn on the lights."

"Room on the left," Carson said.

The guard ran to the closed door, cursing as he collided with a chair. Carson stood motionless, not daring to turn his head, delaying, even as the guard yelled again for light. He didn't look toward the closet, but he was almost certain that at the edge of his vision he saw a winged shadow, and then, it was gone.

The guard emerged from Zeke's bedroom, yelling, "He's not in there!"

"He's got to be," Carson protested.

The man already had his phone out, was speaking into it. Carson strained to hear over the alarm. Before he could get close enough, the guard ran out of the suite. Without thinking, he followed.

The corridor of sky blew past, the shrill bell ringing in his ears. The guard yanked open the door to the stairwell. Carson caught the brushed-steel handle as it swung shut. The man was already halfway up the first flight. Above him, Carson thought he saw a flash of white.

Two flights, then they burst out onto the roof. The night air was crisp and cool as he gulped quick lung-fuls. Between the hulking shells of the industrial air conditioners, security lights flooded the gravel surface with ocher.

The guard moved off to the left, staying close to the concrete shed that housed the stairwell. Behind Carson, the dull thud of running feet escaped from the half-shut door, the sound merging with the rattling drone of the AC units and the cycling alarm. The guard was out of sight, around a corner. Quiet foot-steps crunched the gravel in the blackness ahead of him. The winged shadow that had vanished at the edge of his vision reappeared now, moved into the yellow light.

Zeke gestured to the stairwell. Before Carson could shake his head, the door flew open and Juan charged onto the roof. Zeke retreated, but too late; the Cuban saw him.

"Stop," he called, running toward the Seraph. The other guard was suddenly there, behind Zeke, inching forward, nodding to Juan.

"Behind you!" Carson yelled, as the guard lunged forward, arms outstretched. Zeke darted sideways, be-tween two of the steel shells. Juan and the other man ran after him, and Carson saw the gunmetal terrain of the roof careening, realized he was running, too, as sharp gravel nicked his bare feet.

There was nowhere to go. Just beyond the AC units was a short wall topped by white tube railing. Zeke was climbing onto it, one foot wedged precariously under the rail. The guards stopped a meter away.

"Come on, Ezekiel," Juan said. "Don't be a fool."

Zeke placed the other foot, straightened, his good wing extending. The thin wail of a siren carried through the starless night, and Carson remembered Zeke's howl, that unearthly howl on the beach. His connection to the moment severed, cutting him loose, and some still-present part of him knew it was in fearful anticipation of that sound.

Juan stepped toward the Seraph. "You can't fly, remember? Come down."

Zeke's gaze never wavered. Yellow glinted in his dark pupils, and then he stepped off the ledge and fell from view.

Carson heard a scream, his own, as he dived toward the wall, caught himself on the rail, saw Zeke dropping away, the one wing unable to control the fall. His slender body receded, accelerating toward luminous aqua water.

The Seraph was over the hotel pool.

Carson waited two heartbeats, expecting a splash. Instead he heard nothing, then Zeke was tumbling forward into white sand. He somersaulted onto his back, limbs and wings askew.

Carson held his breath, praying sincerely for the first time in months, but the Seraph didn't move again.

Six

Torrie paced the length of the couch, cracking his knuckles compulsively. Alden huddled in the blue damask, looking old and frail. Carson watched them from Zeke's straight-backed chair. He'd waited two hours, under Maartens's cold stare. It was almost four in the morning.

"How is he?" he asked, for the third time.

"It's over for you, McCullough." Torrie said.

"I didn't do anything."

"Cut the bull." The security chief stopped pacing. "We know you set off the alarm. It was a stupid trick; the service elevator locks as soon as the alarm's triggered. We had surveillance on the hall, saw the 'Phim when he broke for the stairs."

The guilt racked him. He tried to keep it out of his face. "How is he, Alden?"

The priest looked up at the sound of his name, digesting the question. He finally answered, "The wing is bad, very bad. Imogene doesn't know if he'll fly again." Alden rubbed his eyes. He seemed bewildered by the turn of events. It was the first time Carson had seen any sort of crack in his Kevlar coating of certainty. "I'm very disappointed, Carson. How could you betray us?"

He countered, "How could you let them do this to Zeke? What's going on here? You didn't believe me when they brutalized him in Daytona. If his wing's ruined, it's their fault."

Torrie barked, "Shut up."

Alden said weakly, "Torrie, Carson, please . . ."

Carson told the priest, "We're supposed to be their servants. Isn't that what our literature says? So if Zeke wants to take off, why don't you just let him go?"

"It's not that simple, Carson."

"Yes it is."

"We're finished here," Torrie said. The priest got up obediently. The security chief opened the hall door, gestured for Maartens to resume his post in the living room. "He gives you any trouble, you have your orders."

"I haven't done anything wrong," Carson said, to the slamming door. They'd taken the bedside phone, taken his personal phone, put a block on the vid's call and mail functions. His incarceration was probably illegal—the UN's Special Visitor Resolution didn't provide criminal penalties for aiding and abetting an angel—but then, so was Zeke's.

He shut himself in his room and lay on the bed, a pillow over his face, thinking about his predicament, wondering if Miriam would go public with the tape of Daytona. It might be his only chance to clear himself of whatever charges ICARUS brought, because Tao had no proof. He regretted that now. Her boss was one of the very few people willing to take on the military-industrial consortium that included virtually every authority to whom he might otherwise make an appeal.

But an appeal against what?

The arrival of the eggs had generated a global single-mindedness, a putting aside of differences in the interests of joint survival, that all preceding causes—famine, plagues, environmental decline—had failed to rally. In one splash, the world shrank, and every member of the human race looked skyward in fear. The certain knowledge of *other* finally drove home that most New Age of clichés: "We are one." ICARUS was the outgrowth of that awareness, the wax wings on which the species hoped to greet—and, if necessary, defeat—the gods.

Shortly after the news hit, the United Nations formed the Planetary Security Council. The PSC, in turn, appointed a multinational task force to study and assess the aliens, then passed the Law of the Species, declaring that humankind should act in unified interest when dealing with extraterrestrials. The enormity of the situation demanded it. Space programs had atrophied during the post–Cold War years, when the hard fact that man might be living in the information age, but virtual reality, no matter how convincing, could not support life, struck home. Those programs needed to be rejuvenated, accelerated, preferably beyond lightspeed. A global defense had to be engineered. And so the task force gradually metamorphosed into ICARUS, a consortium of governments, their militaries, and private industrial concerns, the idea being that after jointly saving Earth, they would jointly reap whatever rewards galactic trade might yield.

The French expedition easily found the eggs submerged just beneath the surface of the Atlantic because they glowed. No one expected to wait thirty years for that glow to subside.

ICARUS's predecessor decided not to risk moving the capsules, a politically agreeable choice, since the high seas were, metaphorically, no-man's-land. As time passed and the protractedness of their incubation became apparent, the Sea Station was built to house the scientists and military observers. Eventually a few support facilities were floated nearby. And then, like schooling fish, the first ocean squatters arrived. After fifteen years of nonhatching, ICARUS made only a token attempt to chase them off. Most people assumed they were glad for the company the fledgling sea-city provided.

Following the Rising, much of the world was willing to cast away its wax wings and their crippling cost. Those that believed in the promise of salvation saw no need for them, and even those that didn't found the Seraphim, because of their relative passivity, of increasingly less concern. Indeed, the fact that the angels *didn't* perform miracles might have been their saving grace, the sole reason ICARUS agreed to let them go.

But had they? It seemed to Carson that what he'd taken for freedom was more an invisible labyrinth.

The Special Visitor Resolution gave the Seraphim autonomy within the broad governance of the Law of the Species. Zeke had committed no interstellar crime, but ICARUS obviously didn't want to let him out of their sight, and that might be it: The walls had been there all along, behind the facade of the Resolution, undetected until Zeke veered from the path and smashed into them. Could it be that simple?

Frustrated, Carson tossed the pillow and his speculation aside. There'd been voices in the hall for the last hour, frequent elevator chimes. Soon the other Seraphim would be arriving, filling the suites the Party had reserved.

He remembered Zeke's face, slack with loneliness, flickering in the blue light of the vid. I failed him, Carson admitted. But that's the story of my life.

He felt a chill along his spine. Fear was seeping in at the edges of his consciousness, a viscous liquid like the gel that leaked from a broken coldpak. He'd dammed the icy flood with the seminary, dammed it with the Party, dammed it with whatever institution seemed sturdy enough to fend off its numbing influx. Once again, the dam had failed. He had failed.

He got out of bed and took a hot shower, watching the water run in rivulets over his white skin and catch in his coarse red body hair, drops netted by a mat of copper pubic curls above his shriveled, impotent self.

He ordered food from the autobutler, ignoring Maartens, and carried it back to his room. Later, he slept, and when he woke, turned on the vid, watching as the lunacy resumed. It had subsided, thanks, presumably, to the combined effect of policing, curfews, and time. More likely, it had just been a lull before the all-out insanity expected on Sunday. ICARUS, Destiny, and the local authorities had done an excellent job of insulating Zeke and his entourage from the fires they'd ignited. Carson felt less guilty about that now that his career with the Party was over.

The afternoon crept by.

Around six o'clock, the door opened. Harry Chen entered with Alden and three guards in tow. His lip was still swollen; the bruise was the color of ripe plums.

"Dress rehearsal, man. You comin'?"

"I don't think so, Harry."

"You promised, man."

"It's not that—" He glanced at the guards.

Chen caught his meaning. "No, no," he said impatiently, "you're comin'. I told them I got to have you there."

The priest asked, "May I speak with Carson for a moment?"

"Sure, papa," Chen said, smirking. He and his escort retreated.

Alden said brusquely, "Consider it probation." The

silver-wing insignia gleamed against his black suit. The crack, apparently, had been sealed.

"From what? You don't have the right to keep me locked up like this."

"Torrington can provide some justification, but that is not my concern. My concern is avoiding scandal. I will not permit you to undermine ten years of the Lord's work. After the UN vote, we will arrange a quiet retirement for you, assuming you are willing to abide by certain terms. The first of those is your cooperation during this service." He went to the open closet and pulled out Carson's ceremonial uniform.

"What about Zeke?"

"Ezekiel is no longer your concern, and I have no intention of discussing this further." He tossed the clothes onto the bed. "Get dressed."

Carson put on the charcoal tunic and pants, then Maartens led him downstairs to the alley, where six limos waited in the moist evening air that smelled like bleach and perfumed soap.

Chen rambled as they merged onto the interstate. "I saw it before, Carson, ya know? When I was a kid."

"No, Harry. What did you see?"

"Armageddon," Chen said, shutting his eyes behind the purple shades, the pressure of his head fluting the black leather seat in a dark halo. "Somethin' blew, bomb maybe. I was in this place, always smelled like ammonia, had a bed, but it was bolted to the floor. Fire came, burning red snakes, slithering down the hall, slithering on the fucking *ceiling*. Next thing I know, I'm under the bed, I'm burnt, I can taste my own burnt skin, kind of a sweet taste, caramel-like, and the building's gone.

"So I started walking, and there were bodies in the street. One man, I remember, his eyes were still open, and he was staring up at me, but I just kept walking, and things blowin' up all around, and *he* was there, man, the devil, he was there with me—" Chen was shaking.

"Take it easy," Carson said.

Chen opened his eyes and whispered, "I've been there, man: I've been to hell. That's why it's me, ya know?"

Twenty minutes later, Chen said, "That's it. Church of the Messiah."

To their right was a corrugated guardrail. Beyond it a grassy bank fell away, then leveled at the base of a giant, domed auditorium, a sort of machine-age Taj Mahal. The massive walls were supported by columns of silver-white metal that reminded Carson of the old space-shuttle fuel tanks. Mirrored glass reflected the deep orange burn of the setting sun. The whole structure looked as if it might lift off.

They exited, turning right onto a residential street. The building was ahead of them now, surrounded by police barricades. Carson remembered the place. "This used to be Holy Cross. It was big before, but—"

"They fed it some nuclear waste."

He craned his neck. "There were cracker cabins around here."

"Yep. Lot of old folks. Then the fags moved in, fixed 'em all up."

"Church buy all those houses?"

Chen smirked. "You should watch my show, man. When the boys didn't want to sell, the church ran 'em out with some help from their buddies in the Klan. I did a King Kong episode, only it's Klanman. He's like this preacher with a little black mustache, and he's chewin' up houses, then he grabs this drag queen—"

The Church of the Messiah held a congregation of thirty-five hundred according to a brass plaque mounted in the three-story lobby. A statuesque blond in a short-skirted lemon suit was waiting to greet them.

"We are so honored to have you here," she said to Chen, her lips sliding back from perfect white teeth to pink gums. "I'm the Reverend Backwater's administrative assistant, Cherie. The Reverend is in the sanctuary with Father Alden and Mr. Torrington. If you'll follow me . . ."

Cherie's round ass swayed down the aisle, and they followed in procession: Chen, Carson, and the guards bringing up the rear. Carson had accompanied Zeke to appearances at some of Europe's largest cathedrals; the square sanctuary was on that scale, with tiered balconies on three sides, and on the fourth, wide steps rising to the altar, a vast semicircular expanse carpeted in midnight blue sprinkled with gold stars. A crucifix fashioned from synthetic crystal was suspended just beneath the scrim-lined dome. It reached almost to the carpet and was flanked by two lifelike Seraphim, clad in white robes. Both were twice their actual size.

"Sit here," Maartens told them, gesturing to the pews. Carson slid onto the padded bench next to Chen. Small debit scanners were set into the polished wood in front of him. Carson read the short messages scrolling across the one-line display: *Give and ye shall receive . . . Don't forget to key your member number . . .*

A bass voice boomed, "Hallelujah!"

A hulk of a man stood in the aisle, beaming ear to ear. He had a dense crew cut of light brown hair and aquamarine eyes. His thick hand was extended, a sculpted chunk of gold emblazoned with some team insignia wrapped around the ring finger. He introduced himself with gusto. "Louis Backwater, pleased to meetcha."

Chen, slouched in his wrinkled white cottons, looked up dreamily and said, "Klanman."

"Beg pahdon?" Backwater drawled. He wore an immaculate brown pin-striped suit, tailored to his linebacker build. Centered on his paisley silk tie was a small gold cross.

Alden stepped around him, clearing his throat. "This is our Lord, Harry Chen, Reverend. And Carson McCullough, Ezekiel's liaison. The Seraphim should be arriving shortly."

Carson shook Backwater's hand. "Impressive place.'

The Reverend beamed. "The pride and joy of our little family. Just wait . . . Ah dare say, only Destiny puts on a better show."

Carson eyed the oversize Seraphim. "I'm sure."

The real Seraphim arrived together. They wore their ceremonial garb: floor-length robes girdled by tasseled silver cords and edged at the sleeves, neck, and hem with bands of silver brocade. The wings folded against the drapes of ivory silk were identical, but the six faces ranged from pale Gabriel, with his white hair, to dark Uriel, whose eyes shone like coals in his smoky skin.

Zeke came limping in after the others, supported by Imogene and Juan. The injured wing was splinted and bound to his chest with lengths of stretch bandage. Carson tried to make eye contact, but the Seraph disappeared into the swirl of robes and rustling wings. He wondered what the others knew, and why Zeke had agreed to come. Perhaps he hadn't.

Carson's colleagues, the liaisons, filed in behind their charges. They shunned him, except for the occasional glance toward Chen, who was slouched in the pew, eyes shut, hands clenched in his lap.

A curl of down settled on the burgundy carpet at Carson's feet. Out of habit, he picked it up. It was one of his duties, as a liaison, to ensure Zeke didn't leave any souvenirs.

"You sleeping, Harry?"

Chen's eyes opened. "No. Watching. Listening." His gaze swept across the milling Seraphim. "They believe in me, man."

"Then why don't they come over?"

"I met 'em all this afternoon."

"Did you see Zeke?"

"Yeah, man." Chen frowned at him. "You know, I'm kinda pissed at you. Papa Alden told me about last night, but I gotta have a full cast for this thing tomorrow. I talked to Zeke; he's cool with it." Chen scratched his chin, mussing the braid. "He wanted to know if I heard the devil. That's what's whacking him out."

"Do you?"

"Sure. Comes with the territory. But I'm real good at ignoring that fucker."

The nonchalance didn't ring true.

Chen asked, "You see the news?" He snickered. "Now everyone's whacked."

Carson looked at Chen's profile, at the flat nose, the broad cheekbone sprouting scraggly black hairs twisted into the strange goatee. He felt intense distaste. "It's all a big joke to you Harry, isn't it?"

Chen answered with unexpected sobriety. "No way. I been waitin' for this, waitin' a long time."

"What do you mean?"

Chen reached up to his topknot and fingered its ornament of garnet rosary beads. "Like I knew it, man. I mean, I didn't know exactly—just that someday I'd find my calling." His eyes were half-eclipsed by the epicanthic folds. "And I could just tell it would be big. Like I always knew I had this power, always knew I'd be performin' fucking *miracles,* man."

Carson's lips curled back, an instinctual response. He clenched his teeth and swallowed hard, and the distaste sank down into his gut. It lodged there, his anger and resentment wrapping around it, like it was the seed of some secret black pearl.

Elgin Smith was an irritable wisp of a man who Backwater introduced as the church's artistic director. "Everybody, if I could have your attention, please," Elgin shouted over his headset, voice rising with each word, echoing from hidden speakers.

The assembly gradually stilled.

"Now where is . . ." Elgin manipulated the small control pad hanging at his waist, eyes scanning the space before him, searching for the name on the projected display. "Where is Ezekiel?"

Someone gestured.

Elgin trotted down the altar steps and over to the Seraph. "Oh my," he said, when he saw Zeke's condition. "This simply won't do." He beckoned to an assistant, and their heads bent in whispered consultation. Then, "All right. If the angels will go with Robbie—" The Seraphim were led away through a door next to the altar steps.

Elgin walked over to Chen, planted his hands on his hips, and looked him up and down. His dry lips pursed. "Makeup, are we ready for the messiah?" he said into his microphone. *"Good."*

An hour later, Elgin reappeared on the altar, clapping his hands.

"Attention, could I have your attention please?" Scattered conversations gave way to silence. "If everyone could be seated, we're ready to begin."

Backwater, Alden, and Cherie slid into the pew in front of Carson. The administrative assistant blessed him with one of her redeeming smiles as the Reverend said to Alden, "Now, remember, the choir's bein' piped in from the rehearsal hall, but tomorrow, they'll be up in the stalls." He laughed. "Elgin was fit to be tied when we told him, but ah understand y'all don't want the cat out of the bag, specially with those rumors. Ah, now look at this . . ."

Carson followed Backwater's pointing finger. The altar steps were moving. They retracted smoothly and formed a curved wall of star-sprinkled blue.

As the lights dimmed, he realized that the oversize Seraphim had disappeared.

He took five breaths in expectant silence, then something flickered overhead: stars, winking from a midnight sky projected on the dome. Hushed organ chords vibrated in the dehumidified air. The stars streaked across the firmament, fading to nothingness. When the last one was gone, there was a pregnant pause, and then a bright pinpoint of light appeared at the apex. The chords came again, welling as the luminosity increased, until the dot was a radiating asterisk.

Soprano voices joined the organ in a high C major. Spectral waves of light pulsed from the star, rippling down the walls of the sanctuary, washing over the unfilled tiers of seats as the sopranos broke into verse. The hymn built to a crescendo, ending on the words "dawn of a new day." The lone star streaked across the dome, igniting the tip of the crucifix, and the giant cross lit like it was made of diamonds.

The bass voices intoned the second hymn as the brilliant crucifix extinguished to a pure moonlike glow. Panels slid back in the ceiling above it, and clouds of white smoke billowed from the opening. Then golden rays of light cut through the thinning clouds and lit the altar in a bright circle, sparking the stars in its carpet.

The hymn had swelled to symphonic accompaniment, full chorus. "Host of angels, servants to our glorious Lord," the voices sang, as the first Seraph descended along the artificial sun rays. Gabriel's robe caught in the faint updrafts, billowing around his dangling legs, as powerful wings brought him to a soft landing on the altar's carpeted floor.

Four more Seraphim followed at even intervals, forming an open semicircle as they landed. The hymn concluded with a final cresting note and laser beams bursting from the dark periphery of the altar, to converge before the cross in a giant holographic projection of a crucified Christ.

A new hymn began softly, as the projection vanished. Over the course of two verses, the Seraphim knelt, one at a time, until they were all kneeling, their faces raised expectantly to the overhead hatch from which large volumes of white smoke were now pouring. A tremendous orchestral fanfare sounded, then the chorus, at almost unbearable volume, shouted, "He is come, He is come."

The two oversize Seraphim descended through the opening, wings beating in a carefully coded approximation of flight. They faced each other, supporting a gilded throne in their outstretched arms. Behind and to one side of the throne, his hand resting on its high back, stood Zeke.

A bright nimbus surrounded the throne's occupant. He wore shimmering, iridescent robes and was crowned with a simple circlet of gold. His black hair and beard hung straight and smooth; his eyes hid behind round purple glasses.

The robotic Seraphim reached the floor and gently deposited the throne as the music ended. The messiah stood, raising his arms in benediction, and the kneeling Seraphim bowed their heads. Chen then lifted his face to the absent masses, smiled without showing his teeth, and in an echoing, soundless voice said, *I have returned.*

Riveted to his pew bench, hands crushing the edge of the cushioned seat, Carson answered within himself, with the only invocation that could endure his mind-numbing rage: *God help us.*

Riding back to the resort in the limo, Chen was quiet, a vacant smile plastered on his wide face. He hadn't bothered to rebraid his beard.

The rehearsal had not proceeded smoothly after the messiah's grand entrance. Chen tried to ad-lib the speech the Strategic Planning Office wrote for him, enjoining the world to accept him as their savior and support the mandate. "I am not gonna spout this bogus bullshit," he'd said, for everyone to hear. Alden had rushed to take him aside, and later announced he would deliver the speech himself. They'd wrapped it up quickly after that.

The service ended with Alden, the Reverend Backwater, the liaisons, and the dignitaries who would be present on Sunday filing up the steps to receive a personal blessing. Torrie had objected to Carson's participation, but Chen won out again, insisting that he had to have his brother on the altar.

Now Carson avoided looking at Chen, stared instead out the tinted window, watching the cars. He glimpsed night-hollowed faces, like phantoms blowing past, and he wondered what they would think if they knew who they were leaving behind.

His watch beeped. Surprised, he checked the one-line display. The icon for a calendar reminder was flashing. He pressed the SELECT button, curious as to what long-forgotten message he'd left for himself. The scrolling LCD read:

PUBLIC

ACCESS
CHANNEL
99 AT
MIDNITE.
ACK? M.

He caught his breath. It had to be Miriam. She'd rerouted the message through his scheduler; it was still set to automatically download to his watch. Trying to keep his expression bland, he pressed CONFIRM.

PASSWD:
M-----
ACK?

He pressed CONFIRM again. The display returned to status.

Back in his suite, Carson scanned the news to stop himself from pacing. The guard watched from a seat by the door, yawning periodically with boredom. The location of the service had been announced upon their return, and a crowd was already gathering on the church's lawn.

He donned the VR headset at two before the hour and keyed for PA99. It was a public access channel: Anyone could broadcast, at their own cost, but to receive you needed a password. He admired her ingenuity in using it to bypass the blocks they'd put on his console.

At midnight, he typed MIRIAM.

Visual and auditory static gave way to the inside of a familiar SunFleet starcruiser. Destiny's blue-haired Astra Naut sat at the com. The VR character wore flowing carmine robes. She also wore jeweled turquoise pince-nez.

"Identify yourself," the sultry voice requested.

He typed CARSON. The letters appeared in white alphanumerics at the bottom of his field of vision.

Astra said, "We are aware of your situation. We

can liberate you from ICARUS and the Herald Party. Are you interested?"

His stomach was filled with animated butterflies. He imagined their grinning, little bug faces. WHAT ABOUT ZEKE? AND WHAT'S THE PRICE?

"Instructions are being relayed to Ezekiel. The price is your help, during the rescue and after. You seem to be the only person the Seraph trusts."

Sweat prickled across his forehead. This was it, the Judas moment.

OKAY, he typed, pressing each key deliberately, as if he were activating some final code, committing himself to a future even more dangerous and uncertain than the present. WHAT DO I DO?

Seven

A parade of bare-chested men carrying a large wood cross blocked the road to the church. The messiah's motorcade slowed while police in orange riot vests herded the penitents out of the way. Seated beside Chen in the first limo, Carson watched the odd choreography of antagonism between the lines of protesters and pilgrims, both of whom had ensconced themselves on the church's front lawn. Signs bobbed above the crowd, lettered with slogans he'd seen before: Earth First, Heaven Can Wait, Angels Go Home.

It was nothing new, he thought, this dance of opposition. He was tired of it. Years before, a journalist had coined the phrase *neofeudalism* to disparagingly describe the global backwash of the Seraphic prophecies. The Herald Party, its opponents argued, was offering a medieval bribe: eternal happiness in exchange for the misery of the moment. Of course, the Party didn't say, "Don't worry about that new hole in the ozone," but those matters took on less importance when salvation was imminent. Besides, for thirty years prior, the threat of alien invasion had had the same diverting effect.

The motorcade turned into the drive, unobstructed thanks to sentry-lined barricades. As they parked at the church's back entrance, Carson saw that the crowd had overflowed onto the bank sloping up to the interstate. Beyond the guardrail, leather-clad bikers prowled the right-of-way, caged in by standstill traffic.

They went inside and took an elevator upstairs. Maartens led him through the boardroom, which was being used as a hospitality lounge for the Heralds, and into a small office overlooking the church's parking garage. "We'll wait here," the guard said.

Carson pulled out a chair from the desk and propped his feet on the windowsill. It was going to be a perfect spring day. The sun was climbing fast in a dome of pure blue, unadulterated except where air pollution smudged out the horizon's level edge. Two hundred sun-worshiping tourists would give themselves basal-cell carcinomas today if the stats were right.

He leaned back and shut his eyes. Harry was off being ministered to by Elgin's people, being transformed into a suitably regal savior. The thought didn't help his mood. He might be the betrayer, but he felt betrayed. Even in his disillusionment he had hoped that somehow it would all work out, that the messiah would return in his heavenly glory and that he, Carson, personal liaison to his Seraph Ezekiel, would be counted among the worthy, perhaps even among the *saintly*.

Saint Carson. He could have dealt with that. But this . . .

The betrayal wrapped itself around the black seed he'd swallowed yesterday, and the pearl grew by another secret layer.

An hour until the service. They'd be seating the congregation by now, those lucky three thousand who had paid dearly for the privilege of being the first to offer fealty to their savior. The butterflies from the night before fluttered in his stomach. He willed himself to relax. He needed to stay calm. Miriam's plan was simple, but it was a one-shot deal. He had to be ready when the moment came.

At ten minutes and counting, Maartens's phone beeped.

"On our way," the guard said. He gestured to Carson. The boardroom was already empty. They proceeded down the hall, past a door marked DRESSING ROOMS, to the elevator. He heard faint, murmuring voices. It seemed odd to him, the quiet.

The elevator arrived and a breathless Dr. Imogene Berthold, dressed in a severe navy suit, stepped out, pushing past them with a curt, "Pardon." She ran toward the dressing rooms, her hand reaching for the knob as the veneered door swung open and Chen, in his iridescent robes, dashed out. He slammed into Imogene, knocking his purple glasses askew, then stopped, dazed, as the physician took a wobbling step and caught herself with a hand against the paneled wall. Chen's gaze darted back and forth, then focused on Carson.

"Oh, man," he said, lunging toward him and tripping on the edge of his long robes.

Carson reacted, catching the messiah in his outstretched arms.

Chen peered up at him. "Carson . . . Carson, man," he whispered. "I seen it. I seen paradise."

They got Chen back into the dressing room and into a chair. Elgin's assistants talked over each other, trying to explain to Imogene what had happened

"We were working the hair, you know," said a short, chubby redhead.

"And he spazzed," interjected the other.

"I asked him was he all right, but he just had this glazed look," the redhead explained.

"That guy," the other assistant said, gesturing to one of Torrie's people, "made a call, said he was getting a doctor, and then Harry here just leaps up and charges out the door."

Imogene produced a little flashlight and, pushing back the heavy folds of the lid, shone it into Chen's right eye.

"Stop it," Chen said, batting at her hands.

She switched it off, asking, "Did you take something, Mr. Chen?"

Chen waved her away, found Carson in the small crowd. "I seen it, man. I seen the city of light. Beauty, I'm telling you. Paradise. Holy shit—"

Carson cut in, "Stop it, Harry." He shouldered past Maartens. "Space," he said to Imogene. Then to Chen, "You're wired, aren't you, Harry?" He grabbed Chen by the wrist and pushed up the iridescent sleeve. There were fresh burns in the zigzag.

Chen's focus had dissolved, but Carson saw him mouthing the words "I seen it," over and over. He wanted to smack him. Relax, Carson reminded himself. Imogene will straighten him out. The show will go on. It *has* to.

"All right, party's over," Maartens said, and led him from the dressing room.

The other liaisons, in identical charcoal uniforms, were already lined up in the hall by one of the sanctuary's side entrances. It was twelve o'clock. They filed to their seats in the front pews and were greeted by scattered cheers from the congregation. Maartens brought up the rear and slid into place next to Carson.

The crowd had been singing, but now they hushed expectantly. Nothing happened. A minute passed. The background noise of muted prayers increased. Someone shouted in tongues. Carson twisted around. A lot of the congregants were on their knees, praying. He looked up and saw reporters and cameramen ranked in the second balcony. Several of the seats were taken by large, reflective spheres. Global-vision cameras. They were even broadcasting in 3-D. The singing resumed.

He checked his watch: ten after. The choir stalls were still empty. The congregation sang louder. Ushers seated a few latecomers in the back.

Quarter after. Pulpit seats waited for Alden and Backwater. He shifted, glanced at the scrolling message on the pew-back screen: *Salvation, the Greatest Show on Earth.* The show will go on, Carson told himself. It *has* to.

And then, heralded by dimming lights, it did.

The reaction to Chen's telepathic pronouncement *I have returned* was palpable, a collective knee-jerk response of the congregation, followed by shrieks, cries of hallelujah, more shouting in tongues, people collapsing in the pews. Even the other liaisons dropped to their knees.

The ushers restored enough order for the service to continue. By the time Carson stood to follow the line of his colleagues up to the altar, his palms were slick with sweat and his nerves were frayed electrical cords throwing sparks across his retinas.

The wide, curved steps protracted. He was last; Maartens waited in his seat. Up on the altar, the Reverend Backwater was kneeling in front of Chen. High above the still-ecstatic congregation, the scrim-lined dome showed a fainter version of the pulsating star.

He mounted the stairs, pausing on each as the liaisons, in turn, genuflected to Chen. Zeke stood at his post, face drawn, eyes fixed. Synthesized symphony hummed over the speakers, embellished with wordless cries from the pews.

Three ahead of him now. Discreet glance upward,

the bright asterisk unimpaired. Zeke still staring with that gaze like dull metal.

Two. Chen smiling without showing his teeth. Choir singing in awed tones.

One. On the altar. Gold stars streaking across the carpet, carpet itself feeling like quicksand, each step heavier. Don't dare look at Zeke and—

Boom-boom-boom. The sanctuary plunged into darkness.

The last thin wire of his nerves snapped, throwing some internal circuit breaker, routing power to his legs. Zeke's reflexes were faster. Carson caught up with him behind the crucifix, grabbing him around the waist to support his injured side. The door was there, as Miriam had told him. They pushed through the narrow opening.

"That way," Zeke said, leaning into Carson.

He steered them to the right, down a long corridor. Shouts echoed on the other side of the wall. He could sense the determined tension in the slender body next to his, could almost feel the wincing pain of wrenched ligaments and fractured bone.

Their destination lay ahead: a glossy blue door with a flashing red EXIT sign above. He didn't see the package she'd promised.

"Wait," a voice rasped from behind.

Carson twisted his head and saw the Cuban running toward them, one hand reaching inside his suit jacket.

Zeke slowed.

"Come on," Carson said, desperate. "We can make it."

"No, the masks—"

He hauled on the Seraph. "Just a couple more steps—"

"Wait!" Strong fingers closed around Carson's free arm. A scream of fear and frustration welled inside him. Letting go of Zeke, he channeled it into one word of defiance.

"No!" he cried, as he drove his shoulder into Juan's chest. They careened backward and hit the linoleum floor with jarring force, legs tangled together.

"Carson, stop!"

He scrambled to get on top of the Cuban, yelling to Zeke, "Just go; get away!"

Juan was trying to reach into his jacket.

"No!" Carson yelled again, and slammed Juan's hand into the speckled floor.

"The masks," the Cuban gasped. "I have them."

Zeke was beside him, leaning against the wall. "Carson, listen: He's helping us."

His mind reeled in confusion.

Juan worked the other arm up to his jacket and pulled out two disposable respirators. "Take them," he said. "Hurry!"

Zeke already had one of the masks, was pulling it over his nose and mouth.

Carson hesitated, still confused, then grabbed the other, climbing off of the Cuban. He got it on as Juan pushed them out the exit into the wail of sirens and a blinding brown fog.

His eyes stung, but he got Zeke around the waist again, and they hobbled down the stairs to the asphalt. He couldn't see more than a few meters. "Where are they?" he said, his voice muffled by the respirator. They were still moving through the fog, and to one side he saw policemen bent over, coughing. Then he heard a roar, carrying above the sirens, and they hitched toward it, escaping the cloud of gas. Carson followed the direction of the sound and saw six motorcycles, their riders crouched low, charging down the bank from the highway. The crowd was already running, and they ran faster now, small herds scattering from the path of the sleek chromed cats.

The cycles gained pavement and squealed to a halt in front of them, the riders' faces concealed by their shiny helmets.

"Get on," one shouted through his built-in respirator.

Zeke grabbed the shoulder of the nearest biker for support and swung his leg over the seat, the corresponding good wing extending to clear the cycle. Carson mounted behind one of the others. His driver yelled, "Hold on."

Carson wrapped his arms around the man's chest, then the bike roared and they were off, swerving past the police and riding up onto the lawn. Carson gripped the machine with his knees as they swung a hard right and dropped off the bank, shooting across the highway ramp and bumping down the other side, through clouds of blue-flowered leadwort, onto another road. He couldn't tell if he was trembling, or if it was just the vibration of the ride.

As they streaked down the two-lane avenue, the four passengerless bikes veered off at side streets, but they kept going straight, following Zeke and his driver. The Seraph's silk robes billowed, catching the wind like sails. They were beyond the homes into a light-industrial zone, flying past old, stuccoed warehouses; newer, modular units with corrugated-metal siding; and lots hedged in chain link. Carson held fast to his driver, not daring to look back.

The bike squealed around a corner, then continued the turn into an alley between two concrete buildings the color of bleached cow bones. Dead ahead was a delivery truck. The back was open. Carson had a glimpse of someone crouched in the corner, maybe another person next to the gate, then Zeke's driver

ramped up the metal gangway and Carson's followed.
They skidded across the truck's floor, the back end of
the cycle sliding out, stopping centimeters clear of
collision.

The truck lurched forward and Carson heard a fading timpani as the gangway fell, hitting pavement.
Someone pulled down the door, and a rolling, metal
curtain dropped on the glare of the perfect spring day,
pitching them into momentary darkness.

A single yellow bulb flicked to life overhead. Carson
blinked, his eyes still burning from the gas, and realized his arms were locked around the biker's chest.
He ungripped one hand from the other, letting go,
and tried to stand, but his legs were shaking. He
plopped back onto the bike.

The air was humid and close. He felt sick. Remembering the mask, he pulled it off. His ears were ringing. He looked at Zeke. The Seraph had also removed
his mask and gave him a wan smile through the tight
lines of pain around his mouth. The truck took a
curve, forcing them to brace, and the queasiness
increased.

"Y'all okay?" a male voice asked. A young man
wearing a green visor and hot pink surfer shorts was
holding on to a handle by the door.

Carson nodded dumbly.

The kid pulled a bandanna out of his pocket and
went to Zeke. "Gotta cover your eyes," he said, and
blindfolded the Seraph.

The drivers dismounted and stripped off their jack-
ets. Underneath they wore matte vests of some thick,
dense material. Bulletproof. The truck took another
curve. It straightened, and they pulled off their helmets, revealing handsome, tanned faces. The two men
looked at each other, perfect white smiles cracking

their tense expressions. They embraced, then kissed, then embraced again.

This is it, Carson thought, the den of iniquity. But they'd risked their lives.

He tried to stand, making it off the bike this time, and staggered to one side, leaning against the warm metal of the truck's wall, trying to slow his heart. When he looked up, he saw that Zeke was still on the other bike, and someone was crouched in the shadows behind it. A batiked kaleidoscope of amber and green swirled through the silver spokes of the cycle wheel. Miriam.

There was nothing to sit on except the bikes. Zeke stayed where he was, but the rest of them settled onto the floor of the truck. The kid in the surfer shorts produced some cans of soda out of a coldpak. He had a flask of whiskey for Zeke. Carson gulped cola, jealous of the booze, but feeling less queasy despite the jouncing of the uncushioned ride. Occasionally he heard Miriam whispering in the corner. Perspiration trickled along his forehead, along his ribs. Zeke had stripped off his robe and wore only tapered ivory pants. Taking advantage of the blindfold, the men stared at him unabashedly.

He'd finished his drink when Miriam's face appeared above the cycle's chrome fender. She pushed away the mike of her headset and waved them over. They squeezed past the bikes, and Carson saw she had a laptop.

"Looks like everyone's out," she said.

The vid was keyed to some news channel. Carson peered at the small screen. The grounds of the Church of the Messiah seemed deserted. Barricades, signs, and clothing littered the lawn. Three helicopters hovered like giant dragonflies against the expanse of flawless blue sky. The broadcast cut to farther down the street, where the orange vests of the police bobbed among a surging crowd. The reporter stood in the foreground.

Miriam hit a switch and they had sound.

"—evacuation is complete," the reporter was saying. "Ezekiel and his liaison are not in the building. The other Seraphim and Harry Chen are being driven to safety. Meanwhile, police are attempting to move the crowd as far as possible from the church.

"The Gay Liberation Front is claiming responsibility for the attack. No one appears to have been injured in the earlier explosions, which were minor." Cut back to the church, looking again to Carson like a spaceship, afternoon sun setting fire to its mirrored surfaces.

Good, he thought. Now we just need to get far, far away.

The others were still intent on the screen. Zeke was slouched on the bike, blindfolded, making serious progress with the whiskey.

"The terrorist claims have been confirmed," the reporter's voice-over continued. "There are four sequenced charges bonded to structural supports. According to an Orlando Police spokesperson, the bombs are on an automatic countdown which was activated by coded transmission. No word yet on whether disarming—oh my God."

The spaceship was lifting off. A burst of fire circled the dome, licking outward, and disappeared. Carson drew one quick breath, a sharp intake of oxygen. The church seemed unaffected, and then the slabs of mirrored glass fell, sliding like mercury. An avalanche of reflected color hit the ground and shattered, glittering diamond shards splashing up in waves, sprays of quicksilver leaping off the grass, as the dome collapsed and sank from view behind the naked steel girders.

They were all silent for a moment, stunned. Then

the bikers applauded, the applause escalating to cheers and whoops of victory.

"Ezekiel, what did we ever do to you?" It was the shorter biker, the one with a scar along the ridge of his left cheek.

Zeke, still blindfolded, turned his face toward the sound.

"Why did you judge us?" the man added.

The Seraph told him, "We didn't."

"But your revelations say—"

"Yes," Zeke acknowledged. "We were asked the judgment of your god, and we answered."

The door rolled up on a drab, prefabricated building hung with a peeling sign that read FLAMINGO PLASTICS. They were in some sort of industrial park, deserted except for a row of identical trucks and a dilapidated Ford van.

While Miriam thanked the bikers, Carson helped Zeke across the steaming asphalt and onto a red sleeping bag in the back of the Ford. The only other place to sit was a tattered stadium chair decorated with a toothy green gator. Faded curtains sagging on plastic cord covered the windows.

The kid from the truck drove. Miriam rode shotgun for a while, then squeezed between the front seats and joined Carson in the back. Zeke was snoring softly, his bare torso sheltered by the good wing, the whiskey bottle clutched in one hand.

"Quite a sight," she said.

Looking at the Seraph, Carson felt an uneasy déjà vu.

"I think 'distraction' was somewhat of an understatement. People could've been killed." He tried to find her eyes beyond the mirrored lenses of the pince-nez, but saw only himself. His curly orange hair was flattened, and his cheeks looked hollow.

Her lips pursed as if she were considering something. Then she said, "It was a deal: We helped the GLF, and they helped us. The church was their target; they were already in, waiting for the right time. Our interests happened to coincide."

He remembered what Harry had told him about the church and the Klan. "So you got bikers and a diversion. What'd they get?"

"Explosives, gas grenades, and worldwide coverage."

"Oh. Earth-friendly explosives, no doubt. I didn't know environmentalists were so handy with bombs." He shifted, stretching his legs. His clothes were still damp with sweat.

She shrugged. "It pays to know others sympathetic to your cause, and to have favors that can be pulled in. The GLF was good cover. We had few options after Ezekiel's attempt to escape failed. It was fortunate his Easter appearance at the church got canceled, or they would have moved then." He found her casual tone unnerving.

"What about Juan? I tackled him when he showed up with the respirators. They weren't by the door like you said."

She frowned. "That was unfortunate. He's just a paid informant, and we took enough of a risk having him leave instructions for Ezekiel. Will the others expose him to ICARUS?"

"I don't know."

Zeke said, "What I have seen is hidden."

Miriam's brows crested above the pince-nez.

I'm not the only Judas, Carson thought. Torrie has a mole. He remembered the Cuban's warning after Zeke's disappearance. "Juan was on my case. Really had me fooled."

"Our suggestion," she said, to his surprise. "We didn't want you to lose your job before we had a chance to contact you."

He felt manipulated. Who was she, he wondered. He didn't even know the color of her eyes.

"Well, I lost it now." Hearing the words, he was suddenly heavier, as if their truth increased his personal gravity. "So what's next?"

"We're betting the Party will downplay this until after the vote. In the meantime, we're taking you someplace safe, where Ezekiel can rest."

She seemed to have everything under control. Even him. It was irritating. "Where?" he demanded, as if knowing would give him back his independence.

She just smiled.

Eight

The van turned onto a rutted road and the bouncing woke Zeke. Golden light of late afternoon poured through the windshield, encasing him in a faint aura. The Seraph stretched gingerly. He was still blindfolded.

"I think we're almost there," Carson said. "How are you doing?"

Zeke turned his face toward the sound. "It's broken in three places. I sprained my ankle. The rest are bruises."

"I'm sorry. The elevator locked. I should have remembered—"

"It wasn't your fault. I doubled back, thinking I could hide on the roof. They saw me." Zeke shrugged. Then he said, "Thank you for helping me to get away."

Carson swallowed a warm, salty lump of emotion, muttering, "You're welcome," as they slowed to a stop.

Ahead was a deteriorating fence of silvered wood, crowned with rusted barbed wire. A corroded metal arch spanned the gate, and hanging from it, curlicued letters wrought in black iron spelled out *STAR-GATE*. A sign was tacked to the fence, fluorescent yellow paint on rough cypress: PENISED PERSONS PROHIBITED.

Miriam climbed out and unlatched the gate. Beyond, wood cabins surrounded a ramshackle, three-story Victorian painted avocado and lilac. The steep slopes of its roof were shingled with black solar-conversion scales. They pulled into a sandy clearing next to the house.

Miriam opened the van's sliding door. "Let's get Ezekiel inside."

"What is this?" Carson asked, as he helped the Seraph to stand. The cabins looked abandoned, but a few potted plants graced the Victorian's porch.

"The perfect place to hide you: Men haven't been allowed on the grounds for over fifty years." She grabbed a blue nylon duffel from between the front seats. "It used to be a commune. We made the connection through one of the bikers. His therapist owns it." She looked at the Seraph, who waited patiently, leaning on Carson's arm. "When Ezekiel contacted us, he said he wasn't ready to accept our asylum. So we had to make other arrangements."

She slammed the door and waved to the driver. The van circled a clump of palmetto fans, turning around. Miriam added, "I know it's probably out of your comfort zone, but try to be nice."

Carson had taken a college course entitled "Spiritual Expansionism: A Comparative Survey." He was reminded of it now as they helped a lame and intoxicated angel across the sandy yard to the house.

The professor, a former Episcopalian minister turned shaman turned nihilist, came to class in his priestly collar and a grass skirt. His main premise for the "salad-bar spiritualism," as he liked to call it, of the last decades of the millennium, was that mankind, faced with the imminent triumph of reason, the disrobing of mystery, the discouraging finality of fact, *balked.*

Carson remembered one particular lecture in which his instructor ranted about the feminine rejection of what he called "phallicentric religious philosophy." It had focused on drum-beating white women, pagan lesbians, and a recent initiative to do away with separate bathrooms in public places.

The professor, he knew, resigned midyear amidst charges of unethical behavior. He had been caught playing witch doctor in his office with some young coeds. Carson always wondered what became of the pagan lesbians.

The crone who met them on the Victorian's wrap-around porch was seventyish, her slight frame swallowed by baggy denim overalls and a white T-shirt. She had gray hair pulled severely back into a long braid and was smoking a cigar.

"Why the blindfold?" she asked, as they guided Zeke up the steps, through a resinous, orange-scented cloud.

"So he can't see," Miriam explained. "The others get images from him. Are you Echo?"

"And you must be Miriam." They shook hands.

"This is Carson McCullough, Ezekiel's liaison."

Carson corrected, "Not anymore."

Echo didn't offer her hand. Instead she regarded him with faded brown eyes, the stub of the cigar working between dingy teeth.

"Thank you for having me here," he said, feeling his ears flush.

She grinned around the cigar. "Yeah, yeah. Come on in." She held open a screen door, real wood decorated with beaded spindles.

The front room was a library, shelves of books, not

a vid in sight. It smelled like smoke and patchouli incense. Cushions were arranged around a low, carved table inlaid with mother-of-pearl. There was also a collection of primitive statues.

"Goddesses," Echo said.

A large tiger cat was curled on one of the pillows. Her gold eyes focused on Carson and Zeke. She hissed, then slunk away.

"Don't mind Esmerelda. She's never met a man before." Echo grinned at them. "Or an angel. Come on back." She led them down a hall. "Bath's that green door, and you'll be staying in here." They entered a small room furnished with twin beds and a rocker. "And 'Zekiel, I don't care if you see me."

Miriam said, "There is a risk—"

"No," Zeke interrupted. "There is not." He removed the blindfold.

Miriam set her bag down on one of the beds, unzipped it, and pulled out a bottle of whiskey. "For you," she told the Seraph.

Echo hooted with laughter. "Now that's something the Heralds don't mention. They all have a habit, or just him?"

Carson snapped, "It's not a habit." Softening his tone, he explained, "It keeps Harry Chen out of his head."

"You read minds?" Echo asked, the grin gone.

"No," Zeke said. He was leaning against a scarred oak dresser. "But we can speak to each other, and, it seems, to you."

"Huh. ICARUS left *that* out of their 'comprehensive report.' " She puffed on the cigar.

Carson said, "I don't think they knew. Zeke didn't start using the ability until . . . well, recently."

Miriam was removing clothes from her duffel, making two piles. "We need to get you out of those glad rags," she said. "These are for Ezekiel."

Carson went to the paned window and pushed it open. "We near the beach?" he asked. Away from the cigar, he thought he smelled salt air.

"Yeah." Echo grinned. "Just follow the yellow brick road."

After dinner at an old chrome-and-red-Formica dinette in a corner of the kitchen, Miriam excused herself to make some calls. Zeke sat at the table, both legs stretched in front of him, wingtips brushing the black-and-white-checkered floor, one hand curved around a tumbler of whiskey. Echo puffed on a cigar while loading the dishwasher. Carson found the domesticity soothing.

When he was five, he'd sneaked a drag of his great-uncle Louie's stogie and nearly choked to death. His throat burned all night, causing him to lie awake wondering if he'd done himself some irreparable damage. Since then, he'd acquired a taste for pain, for the raw ache of whiskey. Eyeing Zeke's glass, he could feel the slow burn without actually drinking the booze, and it seemed somehow appropriate to him—like a deep wound he could always open, the origin of his profanities, his false utterances of faith.

He didn't quite understand what had happened, in the broader sense. Oh, the details of their escape were etched indelibly in his mind, but how had he gone, in the space of one week, from saint-candidate to this?

He glanced at the Seraph. Zeke was especially beautiful tonight, although strain and fatigue shadowed his eyes. There was something haunting about the narrow features, chiseled just enough to gender him male. He wondered if Echo, lifetime lesbian and high priestess of pagans, would make an exception for the Seraph?

Could any woman resist? Unexpected jealousy panged him. Maybe it was the company he'd been keeping.

And maybe it was the company in which he'd always belonged. The Seraphim had dictated a strict adherence to God's morality, a morality that did not tolerate homosexual acts—or deviant angels—but here they were.

Echo finished the dishes and disappeared, returning a moment later with an antique cane. The rod of polished mahogany was brass-tipped, its handle a winged female torso carved from the wood. Their hostess said simply, "You need it more than me," and leaned it against Zeke's chair.

The Seraph looked up at her. "That is very kind. So is your hospitality."

Echo sat, placing her hands on the table. They were age-stained and gnarled, with short, unpainted nails. "I'm not particularly altruistic," she said. "I would've given my eyeteeth for this opportunity. And there's something I'd like in return, though you're not obligated."

"What is it?"

"A prayer feather."

Carson said, "I thought you were a pagan, and that you didn't believe in them."

She smirked. " 'Course I do. I just don't buy all that patriarchal, point-the-finger bullshit. But I know—" She leaned forward, stabbing the lit end of the cigar at Zeke for emphasis. "That you are a cosmic messenger. And I won't split hairs over whether there's a god or goddess at the other end." She nodded at his wings. "Those are powerful. You can be sure I wouldn't use it lightly."

Carson was appalled. "That's why you let us come here, huh?"

She shook her head. "No. I let you come 'cause

I'd like to see that Party go down in flames. It's not contributing to the mental health of the planet." She grinned. "And 'cause I wanted a feather."

"Don't you think that's what everyone wants?" he demanded. "A feather, a hand, a miracle—wouldn't we all love that. Why do you think we banned reliquary?"

"Carson." The Seraph's tone arrested his tirade.

He looked away.

"You may have your feather," Zeke told her. "Perhaps it will carry prayers to your goddess, but I doubt it. These wings have not served me well."

"Thanks. I'll take my chances." Echo produced a long matchstick from the overall's kangaroo pocket. "Magic wand," she said, waving the styptic applicator. "We wouldn't want you to bleed to death."

Magic it must be, Carson thought, if it heals the wounds of angels.

The yellow brick road was just that, and it snaked between the cabins, through another gate in the fence, and across sand dunes, ending at a rickety flight of wood steps that descended to the beach. Carson carried the whiskey while Zeke tried out his new cane.

They settled into the shadow of the dunes and passed the bottle between them. A wing of pelicans floated above the sliding black surf, the birds distinctive even in silhouette. Stargate was on a secluded section of coast. Beyond the commune, the crescent of beach was unlit. "Little lesbian nook in the national parkland," was how Echo had put it.

Carson eyed the cane handle. "Maybe Echo's got a goddess for me, too," he told Zeke, breaking their silence. "I could use one." He laughed, embarrassed. The Party didn't require celibacy, but few opportunities existed which didn't compromise their standards of conduct, and he'd come to view his stint at the seminary as training for the last several years. Still, the plastic shrink-wrap of his self-denial was stretched to tearing. "So what happens now? What kind of deal did you make with Miriam?"

The Seraph turned from profile. "I didn't. She is hoping that given time I will." He handed Carson the bottle. "Torrie approached me yesterday, offering refuge with ICARUS. Michael says they have no intention of upholding the Special Visitor Resolution, that they are pretending to respect their law so they can discover our secret plan. That's why they wouldn't let me leave. Torrie may have thought I was ready to reveal our ulterior motives."

"You've been listening to Michael a lot," Carson said. He took a long draft from the bottle, enjoying the sear. He didn't like how much sense the devil made. "What does he have to say about the Infidels?"

Something rustled in the dune grass above them. They both looked up. Someone was at the top of the stairs.

Carson whispered, "Shit."

The person switched on a halogen torch, waving its beam across the sand and crushed shells, catching them in the spotlight. "There you are," Miriam called. She joined them, switched off the torch. "Better you had stayed inside."

Carson said, "We've been cooped up all week." A chill breeze brushed his face, riding in on the tide, but the slow boil of the whiskey warmed him.

"Have you thought about our offer, Ezekiel?"

Carson dug his feet into cold sand.

"I appreciate your aid," Zeke said. "But I left because I didn't want to be their puppet. I'm not going to become yours."

"We don't expect that." Miriam's tone was neutral.

"We weren't even certain, when we contacted Carson, why you had left. We have a tape of what happened on the beach in Daytona. You're entitled to an audience with the United Nations assembly under section 14.3 of the Special Visitor Resolution. Just to show that tape, to have you confirm that you were being held against your will, would do a lot of damage."

"And if I refuse?"

"You're free to go, if that's what you're asking. But I think you're going to need our help. I know Carson does."

Carson said, "What's that supposed to mean?" He strained to see her face. The glasses were gone, but he couldn't make out the color of her eyes.

"The GLF has denied kidnapping you two. The Party's hedging on Ezekiel's disappearance because of the vote, but Perez thinks that once they're past it, an international warrant will be issued for your arrest. Preemptive tactics. They know you might come forward to discredit them."

The whiskey was cooling fast. Cold crept up his legs from the sand. He pulled his knees to his chest.

Miriam turned back to Zeke. "Where are you going to go? You're stuck, at least until that wing heals. If we expose this, then maybe you'll have a real choice. Maybe the other Seraphim will, too."

"They're happy where they are," Zeke said, the bitterness returning to his tone. "And maybe they're right. Maybe we are angels. What then? You've still got Harry Chen to contend with."

"I'll take that chance. As for Chen, he's a wild card. We're not going to do anything about him yet. Enough people are indignant that he may do the Party more harm than good. I've arranged transportation, and I'd like to leave tomorrow. Would you reconsider our offer of asylum?"

"No. I am not going to Israel."

She made a little gasp. "I didn't tell you . . . Never mind. May I ask why?"

"Because it is at the center of the controversy that I am escaping."

"You'll be protected there; here we're on sovereign ground. Coming and going is difficult. The only place without those restrictions is Ocean City, and it's head-quarters to the Party."

The Seraph shrugged. "I have learned that 'protect' is a euphemism for 'confine.' I want to be free."

Miriam said, "Freedom comes only with confine-ment, of one sort or another. That is what I have learned, Ezekiel." She sounded weary. "But if you won't accept asylum, then we have to keep moving. Ocean City offers flexibility. Will you go there?"

"Ocean City, then," Zeke agreed.

"All right. And please think about the rest, both of you." She switched the torch back on, joining them in a circle of light. "We can help each other," she told them. Then the light cast upward and she stood.

Carson watched as she made her way to the steps, the beam flashing around her moving silhouette like a beacon. When she was gone, they sat in silence. He stared up at winking stars.

Finally, Zeke said, "I just wanted to get away."

Carson found the silver glint of the Seraph's eyes. "It's not that simple." His voice was quiet, but clear, in the moon-washed night. "It just never, never is."

Carson rolled toward the open window, where a square of checked cotton fluttered in the night breeze. Zeke was asleep in the other bed, his breathing rhyth-mic. Carson found it distracting. He hoped Miriam's accommodations in Ocean City were roomier.

The curtain lifted and he glimpsed one star, low on

the horizon. It reminded him of the burning asterisk . . . of the church . . . of Harry Chen.

Messiah. King of the Angels.

He tossed the covers aside and swung his feet to the floor. The wood planks were cool and slightly sticky. His pants were on the rocker, on top of the clothes Miriam had left for them. He pulled them on and padded out into the hall. The house was quiet, too quiet. He wasn't used to houses anymore. The peacefulness unsettled him; it was too much like the eye of a storm.

The other bedroom on the main floor was Echo's study. It wasn't locked. He pressed the door shut behind himself, switched on a ceiling globe of frosted glass. Where was Miriam sleeping, he wondered. Upstairs with their hostess?

In the center of the room was a heavy desk, fashioned from walnut, with ball-and-claw feet. The phone was there, an old black plastic handset looking oddly futuristic on the slab of oiled wood. He fished the card out of his wallet and keyed her number.

Tao's voice was fuzzed by sleep. " 'Allo?"

"Tao, it's me."

"Carson? You okay? News said you and 'Zekiel disappeared."

"Yes. No. Listen, Tao, I have to tell you what really happened today. Someone has to know, just in case—" He gave her the whole story this time, from his first meeting with Miriam up to that evening on the beach.

She said nothing except *"merde,"* repeating the expletive at each new twist.

He concluded, "I want you to be my witness. Tell Bloom." He took a deep breath, released it, feeling marginally better, and leaned back in Echo's desk chair.

"The offer still stands," she said. "I know the senator, and I know he'll want in. If you come forward, he can extend his privilege, protect you."

"I'm staying with Zeke. It's his call. Miriam wants him to testify at the UN, but he hasn't committed. I don't think it'll do much good for me to come forward without him. They'll just call me a liar. But I wanted you to know, because I don't trust her."

"You sure she's Infidel, Carson? This sounds out of their league."

He admitted, "I made an assumption; she didn't deny it." Remembering Miriam's surprise at Zeke's mention of Israel, he added, "Zeke might know. I'll ask him."

"If that bit about ICARUS not respecting the Resolution is true—and you know I believe t' worst—then 'Zekiel can't go to Geneva without some insurance. Tell that to this Miriam, that you have a link to Bloom. You don't have to say we already talked. The senator won't move without proof anyway. And speakin' of proof, what do you make of Harry's DNA?"

He sat up, elbows on the desk. "That was a whole other meeting, Tao. I don't think ICARUS has the first idea. Imogene was talking about gene-splicing, like the Seraphim might have done it. I'd say Harry's a fluke of nature, or a freak accident, except it wouldn't explain why the others think he's the messiah."

"Maybe it's part of their plot. If you believe the Earth Militia, this is a bloodless invasion. Michael reminds me of *Le Faucon,* our rebel leader back home, and you say 'Zekiel's loyalties are torn. Well, I could believe some aliens concocted Harry."

He allowed himself a smile.

"So you're goin' to O.C. tomorrow?"

"That's the plan. I'll call as soon as I can sneak off."

"Try to find a vid. I want to put you face-t'-face

with Bloom. And, Carson—be careful. You're at ground zero, ya know?"

He thought he'd been quiet as he climbed back into bed, but Zeke's hoarse voice sawed through the silence. "You were right."

He propped himself up on one elbow. "That'd be a first." It was too dark to make out the Seraph's features. He waited for a response, but Zeke said nothing more, and after a time, he heard the slow breath of sleep.

Zeke limped into the kitchen the next morning wearing jeans, a black *bandolero* hat with leather cording around the low crown, and a horseman's duster. The coat was made of oiled canvas, and its long, split tails hid the Seraph's wing tips. He held the cane in one hand and the bottle of whiskey in the other.

Carson had his back to the door and his face buried in the steam rising off a mug of black coffee, but he turned when Echo started laughing.

"Howdy doo, pahdner," she said, hitching her thumbs into the straps of her denim overalls.

Miriam looked at Zeke appraisingly over the jeweled rim of the pince-nez. She wore a mauve jumpsuit, cinched at the waist with a wide belt. "It's the best I could do. I think it'll work, at least from a distance."

"You look like a hunchback cowboy," Carson said, regarding the Seraph with amused skepticism. His own outfit was simpler: sneakers, jeans, a plain green T-shirt, and a hooded tan windbreaker. Echo would dispose of their uniforms, but for some reason he'd kept his silver-wing insignia, slipping it into his jacket pocket like a little nugget of denial.

Zeke spun a chair around and lowered himself onto it. He leaned the cane carefully against the table, then poured a shot of whiskey. The Seraph stared at the amber liquid before taking a small sip.

Echo set a muffin on a white plate in front of him. "Got a theory for you, 'Zekiel. Know how a beehive works?"

Zeke tilted his face up, regarding her from the shadow of the hat brim.

"There's a whole bunch of workers and back at the hive, one queen bee. Maybe you and the others are lost—"

Carson groaned. "So now God is a queen bee?" His head throbbed.

Echo sat down, laughing. "Just a theory."

"But it doesn't explain Harry Chen," Miriam pointed out.

Zeke took a bite of muffin.

Echo spoke, her tone more serious. "Chen is an interesting piece of work."

"Is that a professional opinion?" Carson asked, remembering that she was a psychologist.

"Sure. Christ complex." She grinned, then, "I don't know what to make of Chen. There's his DNA—awfully suspicious, though if you buy spontaneous mutation he might be the new, improved version of the species." She looked at the Seraph. "Care to comment?"

"No."

She smiled. "Didn't think so." Turning back to Carson, "But you mentioned he was using space. Lot of spacers out there think that drug makes 'em superhuman, and I know a few odd things about it, too."

"Like what?" he asked.

"Hmm." Echo rocked her chair back against the wall. "Let me tell you a story, children. It's called 'The Frog and the Fighter Pilot.'

"Once upon a time there was a green amphibian

called *Phyllomedusa bicolor.* The waxy tree frog lived in the South American rain forests—when there used to be South American rain forests. Anyway, our frog had the notable misfortune of coming to the attention of a team of·researchers working for the United States Air Force. Their task was to biochemically enhance the abilities of fighter pilots.

"You see, there were these eggs, and everyone was very worried about them, so of course the intelligent thing to do was to give lots and lots of money to the Defense Department so that if and when the Martians came, we would have all kinds of clever ways to blow them up." She gave Zeke a deferential nod, then continued.

"Our team of researchers found an old article about how a now-defunct tribe of rain forest Indians used to tweak the froggy's toes and get him so excited he secreted this potent peptide stew. Apparently the substance had all kinds of wonderful effects that made fighter pilots much more efficient at blowing up Martians: It increased strength and endurance, enhanced the senses, et cetera. There were some unpleasant physical side effects—namely, it made you piss all over yourself then pass out—but the researchers thought they could eventually synthesize an improved version. The other stuff about how the Indians used it to induce hunting visions was dismissed. After all, the researchers were men of science, and they knew better than to pay attention to superstitious nonsense.

"So the scientists conscripted several frogs, who had been enjoying the freedom of zoo life, into the service of their country. Project Medusa was initially successful. After coming to and cleaning up, our flyboys were better than ever.

"Then one of the lieutenants in the project reported a vivid hallucination, in which the new plane he was testing tailspun into the Pacific off the Baja Peninsula. This was duly noted by the researchers. Of course, when Search & Rescue fished the pilot out of the ocean after the crash, they considered it a coincidence.

"Unfortunately, other pilots started having coincidences. The coincidence outbreak was becoming very bad for flyboy morale, and the project was eventually sidelined because of it. The frogs were given honorable discharges and everyone lived happily ever after."

They were silent, each absorbing the story. Then Miriam asked, "How did you learn that?"

Echo said, "Latest batch of pre-Rising files Senator Bloom made them unseal. What's interesting is that chemically, space is a refined derivative of the frog secretions. I'd heard a rumor, years back, that it was developed by Dautrech Pharmacopoeia. Dautrech, you might recall, is part of ICARUS." She brought the front legs of the chair down. "So go figure."

Carson said, "Harry told me that he couldn't talk to the Seraphim until he used space. It was like the drug brought everything into focus, gave him access to the connection. Right before the service, he overdosed and freaked out. Thought he saw paradise."

"Well," Echo said, "either he's God, or there's another explanation." Her chair scraped across the floor as she stood. "Places to be, clients to see." This time she offered her hand to each of them, ending with Zeke. "There's no place like home," she told the Seraph. "I hope you find yours."

Nine

After breakfast, Zeke went to lie down, his ankle visibly swollen. Carson and Miriam watched the news on her laptop at the kitchen table.

Everyone had an opinion about Harry Chen. A mustached colonel of the Australian company of the Earth Militia stood in front of their outback observatory and training command, glaring at the camera. "It's what we've been sayin' all 'long, mate. It's a bloody invasion, 'cept it ain't, and if he's a messiah, then I'm a kangaroo."

The pope remained in seclusion, but a group declaring Chen the Antichrist had stormed the Vatican. The Italians didn't have an exclusive on that interpretation: There had been violent clashes in Buenos Aires and New York between those for and against the new messiah. The savior's identity was dividing the Herald ranks, and even people outside the Party, many of whom viewed the Seraphim as exotic celebrities, seemed nonplussed, except for the spacers. As one interviewee put it, "We aren't surprised at all. He's been king of our realm for years."

The latest statement released by Chairman Tepanov on behalf of the Planetary Security Council extended Special Visitor status to Harry Chen, and assured the global constituency that everything possible was being done to locate the missing Seraph. The network replayed a tape of Alden weaseling around the fact that the All-Seeing had apparently *not* seen where one of his own angels had gone. The messiah and the other Seraphim had departed Orlando earlier, and were now en route to Ocean City, where they would stop overnight before proceeding to Geneva for Wednesday's vote.

Miriam switched it off. "Time for your makeover." She showed him a package of platinum blond hair dye. "We're returning to the lion's den, and I don't want anyone recognizing you, so we'll nix the red hair. Don't shave, either. Grow a goatee."

Carson commented, "I'm not the one who'll be recognized."

She smiled behind the pince-nez. "True, but I don't think hair dye would make much of a difference in Ezekiel's case."

He followed her to the cramped bathroom and stooped his head over the pedestal sink. "How are we getting to Ocean City, anyway?" he asked, while she wet his hair.

"There's a private jet at an airstrip near St. Augustine."

"You fly?" He looked up at her, warm water dripping into his eyes. She was pulling on a pair of plastic gloves.

"No, two of my associates do. Sit over there on the toilet."

"Associates with private jets? Pretty high-class for an Infidel." Her expression was masked by the glasses. "Are they your connection to Israel?"

She shook the applicator bottle. "Close your eyes." He obeyed. Her fingers were strong against his scalp. The dye irritated his nasal passages. She asked casually, "How did Ezekiel know that?

"Probably the same way he knew how to contact you."

"I thought you relayed my offer."

"Nope."

"Then how—"

He squinted. "The devil. That's what Zeke says. His name's Michael, and he knew about your offer and how to reach you. He probably even knows who you really are. I was going to ask Zeke, but I haven't had a chance."

She stopped massaging. "The devil?"

"Haven't you seen *The Seraphic Revelations*?" He quoted, " 'The devil abides in darkness, ever whispering his lies to those who listen, ever seeking to thwart the will of God.' " He shrugged. "They said the messiah was coming, and now we've got Harry Chen. That should be enough to convince even an Infidel."

She continued working the dye into his hair. "I never told you I was an Infidel."

"And you never told me you weren't. But if you want Zeke to testify at the UN, he's going to need more than a bunch of militant environmentalists to keep ICARUS from snatching him back the minute he walks into that assembly. Michael told him they're just using the Party to keep tabs on the Seraphim."

"That's been addressed. Israel has offered an honor guard in addition to asylum." She finished, stepping back. "I wish you would convince him to accept it."

"I don't have as much influence as you seem to think. But I do have a connection, someone who could help with ICARUS. He'll probably want to know who you are."

She went to the sink and peeled off the gloves.

"I think you owe me one," he said, watching her in the mirror. "Especially after your little omission about the church. I'm just as stuck as Zeke, and I don't have a demon to let me in on your secrets."

She picked up the bar of soap. "We've been aware of your attitude problem, and Ezekiel's drinking, for several months, through Perez. I was sent to follow you, in case an opportunity like Daytona came along, an opportunity to defeat the mandate."

" 'We'? Who sent you?"

She rinsed and dried her hands, then turned, removing the pince-nez. Her eyes were hazel, just like his own. "Mossad," she said, her accent foreign. "Israeli Intelligence."

Of course. He should have realized from the start. She was watching him. He asked, "Do you know if what Michael said about ICARUS is true?"

She nodded. "That and more. My government wasn't willing to go along with the game when it meant giving up Jerusalem. ICARUS will try and push the mandate through the PSC, letting the Party take credit, especially now that they have their messiah. That's why we need Ezekiel. A public denouncement might be enough to make the Planetary Security Council reconsider."

"And what do you know about Chen?"

Miriam frowned. "Probably less than you. He's an enigma. This source Ezekiel has, this Michael, does he have any information?"

"Zeke said something about Michael's answers, but it's obviously a sore subject. All I know is that Michael is shielding him from Chen and the others." Talk of the devil tickled his spine like cold fingers. Carson shrugged them away.

She said, "Another enigma."

"Yeah." His scalp itched. He pointed at his hair. "Am I done?"

*   *   *

"Yes, I know who she is." Zeke sat on the edge of the bed, flexing his ankle experimentally.

"Why didn't you tell me?"

"It doesn't matter, Carson. I'm not going to Israel."

He tried to say it gently. "Zeke, Alden said your wing might not heal. We can't hide in Ocean City forever." He scratched his head. "I know you want to get away, but where are you going to go? You can't just become another drifter. You're a little too conspicuous."

The Seraph looked up. "Yes, I'm very aware of that. But if it does heal, there are still a few spots on this planet where strange creatures live free and undisturbed."

"You're not a strange creature, Zeke."

The Seraph's gaze issued the challenge. When Carson couldn't meet it, Zeke said, "You see, that's just it."

Frustrated, Carson went to the window, then turned, folding his arms. "What about the PSC? Miriam thinks if you go to them, it may stop ICARUS. And what about Harry? Has Michael told you his secrets, too? Maybe if you can explain him, it'll help get you what you want."

Zeke's expression became distant. "No," he said. "I doubt that very much."

"What is it, Zeke? What are you not telling me?"

The Seraph reached for his cane. "Lies, Carson. Or truths. As your species knows, both are relative." He stood up, the good pinion refolding itself. "When do we fly?"

Ocean City. It wasn't visible yet from the window of the small jet. Nothing outside except a uniform black void. Carson watched his handprint of moisture evaporate off the cold oval glass. He'd called O.C.

home for almost seven years, but he'd experienced the city in time lapse, rarely spending more than two consecutive weeks there, finding a new stage of haphazard expansion under way at each return.

Unlike the carefully planned, shore-linked ocean metropolises, O.C. was stateless. This appealed to the Heralds because they considered themselves residents of God's nation. It appealed to other Oceaners for different reasons. The advertisements of the Ocean City Cooperative billed it as True Opportunity, "Land of" being deliberately omitted. *Stranded,* the on-line, alternative weekly, preferred the double-entendred slogan Atlantis of the Alienated. Perhaps, in that sense, it was still his home.

Seven minutes after midnight, he made out the dim violet glow of Royal Atlantic Sea Farm field markers and the red warning beacon on the O.C.C. Utilities Plant, and then beyond, the glitter and wink of the city proper.

The jet banked, the skyline coming into view, dominated by the Herald Tower. Merbleu Bay was rough tonight; its waves fragmented the city's reflection into shards of light. Bounding the harbor, a horseshoe of artificial islands rose from the sea on giant pylons that reminded Carson of the Church of the Messiah. He remembered the waterfall of mirrored glass and shuddered.

They landed on Cooley Airstrip, taxiing to a charter bay, and took an electric courtesy car to the docks which, fortunately, were deserted. Miriam had the key to a four-seat skimmer with an Avis rental fleet sticker on the windshield. It was cold, the sea breeze biting through his jacket while he helped Zeke climb in.

She steered them north, toward the city. The white spike of the Herald Tower loomed as they followed their cone of light across the water. Centrus, the largest island, was a five-year-old joint venture between the Heralds and some private developers. The Party occupied the west corner of its two triangular decks. Topside, the Tower was headquarters and residence for the Seraphim, their liaisons, Torrie, and Alden. Directly underneath, on the lower level, was the port authority for the floating complex that adjoined the island.

Pilgrims Port offered moorage, but its main traffic was the frequent departures to the ocean site of the Rising. The pilgrims came year-round for the special baptism performed at the Sea Station, which the Heralds had purchased from ICARUS and converted into a visitors center. During Carson's last interlude in O.C., the port had been decorated with banners marking the upcoming tenth anniversary of the Seraphim's birth.

He and Zeke wouldn't be attending the festivities, that was for sure.

Miriam veered out of the commuter channel at Las Vegas, a pyramidal island that offered mostly rental lodgings and casinos. Immediately, Carson understood why she'd chosen it: Sea-level buildings formed the perimeter of the base. No need to sneak the Seraph up onto the island from some public marina.

They docked at a five-story structure whose neon proclaimed it The Pink Porpoise, letting by the week or month. Miriam raised the skimmer's bubble top, and Carson helped Zeke climb out onto a narrow walkway. A lone fluorescent tube lit the private berth walled by sheets of corrugated pale green fiberglass. A door in the back led to a gray stairwell with marred rubber flooring. At the landing, Miriam punched a key code, unlocking another door that led into the unit. Ceiling panels came to life, and he saw it was one rectangular space, partitioned by translucent screens framed in dull alloy tubing.

The section in which they stood held a kitchenette with hot pink countertops and a futon sofa covered in black canvas. Underfoot, the establishment's namesake dolphin repeated endlessly on stained carpet, providing the only other color break from the off-white walls and bent venetian blinds shading the seaward window. The back section was divided into two rooms by a short hall that ended with a painted-steel fire door, presumably the island-side entrance. He knew by Ocean City standards, the studio was spacious. It smelled of coffee.

Miriam dropped her duffel and touched a panel by the door. The air exchanger rattled to life.

"This is it," she said, then pointed to the smaller of the back rooms. "That's the bath." She went to the black fiberboard drawers that made up the sofa's base and pulled out a blanket and two pillows. "Here, give me a hand."

Zeke had to step into the kitchenette so they could open the futon.

"There's not much in the refrigerator, but help yourselves." She told the Seraph, "We left your liquor on the jet. I'll buy some more tomorrow. Can I get you anything else?"

Zeke leaned on the cane. "No. Thank you."

"Well, I think we can all use some sleep. Good night." She picked up her duffel and disappeared through the door opposite the bath.

Carson stared after her. When he turned back to the Seraph, Zeke gave him a tired smile. Carson cleared his throat.

"Okay then," he said. "Which side do you want?"

Carson woke to white feathers tickling his face. He rolled away from the Seraph and, standing up, went into the bath. When he came out, Miriam was in the kitchenette making coffee in a tiny hexagonal pot. She wore a jade silk robe, the smooth fabric snagging on her erect nipples. His smile widened into a yawn.

She whispered, "Strange bedfellow, no?" as he slid onto a stool at the bar.

Carson rubbed his eyes. Zeke had stripped down to boxers, but he'd slept in his clothes.

"Do you think he'll go to Geneva?" she asked.

"I don't know. But if he does, I want you to contact Senator Bloom. That's the connection I told you about."

"You know his aide, Chen's former lover." She nodded. "It might be worthwhile." She filled two demitasse with steaming black liquid.

Carson frowned at his coffee. He didn't like to think of how she'd waited, watching, cultivating him as her Judas. Looking up, he said, "I think Zeke knows something about Harry, something Michael told him. Did you ever use the VR version of *The Seraphic Revelations*?"

She nodded.

"In the beginning, when you're floating in the void, and the images come at you, hurtling out of the darkness—creation, crucifixion—it's like a recap of the old testaments. And then there's that blinding light, and when it dims, the egg has cracked open. Remember?"

"Yes. That's how they knew who they were. Supposedly."

"It's true. You can ask Zeke. Anyway, I've been thinking. When Harry's folks adopted him, he was slipping in and out of this catatonia. His mother would just sit there and hold him and tell him about Jesus. Tell him God loved him, and that he had to cast out the demons. Funny thing was, it worked. He got better. But whenever he was bad, she'd say he was letting

Satan in, and Harry, he'd start shaking, get that glazed look in his eyes."

"So?" She blew on her coffee.

"So Harry told me that when he was wandering Xiaoping during the revolution, the devil was there with him—with Harry Chen, the young messiah. But Harry's mother told him to cast the devil out."

"It works from a theological standpoint," she said.

"*If* you believe he's the messiah. And I don't. So if he's not the messiah, maybe Michael isn't the devil. But whoever he is, he's trying to get some sort of message out. Maybe the message explains Harry."

She put down her cup and sighed. "I'm not fond of Mr. Chen, but unfortunately, I have to restrict myself to sources I can interact with."

He looked down, away from her skepticism. "Yeah, I know. I'm just thinking." He tried the coffee. It was very bitter. Looking up, he said, "You asked me if truth matters. It does. Maybe Zeke knows the truth. But if he doesn't, or if he won't tell it, then someone else has to."

"Saint Carson," Zeke rasped from the futon.

Carson pivoted on the stool.

The Seraph pushed the covers aside. He wore white cotton boxers. Above the bandages, his chest was pale and hairless, the small nipples the color of eggplant. "Still crusading," he added.

Carson checked Miriam's reaction. She was staring. He asked, "Well, what are you gonna do, Zeke? Hide forever? It's a pretty small planet."

Zeke stretched, hands clasped above his head. "No. I'm going to Geneva."

"What?"

The Seraph rolled over, standing with his weight on the uninjured leg. He hobbled to them. "I've learned something these past few days." He brushed the fine gray hair away from his eyes with long fingers. "It's not going to work—the whiskey, this flight." He looked at Carson. "You asked me once if we Seraphim spoke in each other's minds. I thought it an odd question. After all, why? What would we say?" He shook his head. "Now I hide from sound and vision, seek refuge in the deafness of whiskey and the blindness of a god. But Harry Chen strengthens. Before, there was no need for words. In this artificial silence, words are all I have." He hobbled around Carson, heading toward the hall, then stopped and fixed Miriam with his magnetic gaze. "I wish to speak them at Geneva."

They both stared as he limped into the bath, shutting the door. Then they heard the rush of the shower.

"Well," Miriam said, exhaling, "I suppose it's time to call Bloom."

At age fifteen, Senator Josiah Bloom had been incarcerated for weapons possession and electronic theft. When he went into juvenile detention, he was a chocolate-skinned, African-American punk with a conical spike of jet hair, just three years short of the average life expectancy for his GRAEL—his gender, race, and economic level. By the time he was released, eighteen months later, he was an albino. Carson, along with most of GRAEL-advantaged America, knew his story well.

Bloom had been just another delinquent on the fast track to oblivion, which was what made him a good subject for exposure to B-312. And the Pentagon's alchemists had been right: B-312, their latest alien bioassassin, wasn't significantly harmful to human life. But there was one unforeseen side effect.

For Bloom, the side effect changed more than just his GRAEL projections. When he got out, he called the producers of *Deadwatch* and told them he thought the government had done something to him while he was in juv-d. It took five years, but they nailed the story. Bloom put himself through college with the royalties.

He ran for senator on a pledge to rip open the iron bowels of national security so the public could see the stinking shit inside. That had been nine years back, a time when ICARUS and its member governments were coming under heavy fire for their quarantine of the Seraphim, and their refusal, prior to the Rising, to release any prebirth images. They'd said such pictures might lead to premature conclusions—a position which, in retrospect, was not viewed sympathetically by the increasing number of people who considered the aliens to be heralds of God. Although he was not a professed believer, Bloom had exploited that situation, and his own story, to win by a respectable margin. He'd since proven himself a man of his word.

Carson was fairly certain the Pentagon now wished B-312 hadn't been quite so safe.

Miriam set up her laptop on the bar. When Zeke was finished in the bathroom, she got dressed while Carson explained Tao's offer to the Seraph. Then he made the call. Tao answered after the second signal. She wore a loose yellow dress and held a white towel. Her cropped mat of black curls was dripping, but her attention was fixed on his hair.

"What happened?" she asked. "You seen a ghost?"

"Disguise," he said, remembering the dye job. "But I called because Zeke has decided to go to the UN and wants Bloom's help."

Tao nodded. "All right. Let me link him in." She was replaced by her hold signal *du jour,* a recording of an African pygmy dueling with a snake in the reddish brown dust underneath an acacia tree. The pygmy leapt agilely away from the lunging serpent, vying for a position from which he could grab the snake and snap its neck. It was an anxious, deadly game, and Carson wished the randomizer had picked a different recording from Tao's video library of her homeland. Before either player could prevail, the screen image split, Tao appearing in one half and Josiah Bloom in the other. The senator's face was round and pale pink with a wide, fleshy nose and small, tight mouth. His hair was shaved into a white skullcap. Carson could just find the eyes behind the thick, tinted glasses.

"This meeting isn't happening, friend." Bloom's voice was deep and cold. His image vibrated against a standard blue security background. Carson guessed he was in a limousine. "What is it you need?"

He beckoned Miriam and the Seraph into vid range. Bloom said, "I see."

Carson let Miriam take it from there, explaining her mission, while Zeke confirmed what the senator had already been told by Tao. Bloom agreed to forward the Seraph's request for audience to the Planetary Security Council, and to meet Zeke in Geneva early the next morning. When the conference was done, he signed off, but Tao remained on the screen for Carson.

"Be careful," she said, leaning into the transmitter, her eyes wide with worry. "*Tout le monde* is looking for you, and all it takes is one wrong step—"

Carson came out of the bathroom after showering to find Zeke perched on a stool, holding lengths of bandage.

"Anyway, it was a long time ago," Miriam said, as she reached a strip around the Seraph's slender chest. "Long before you were born." She laughed. "Now *that* makes me feel old." Wrapping the bandage twice, she tucked in the ends.

Carson sat on the futon, wondering what she'd been saying. He guessed her to be in her early thirties.

"You're lucky," she continued. "Even if you don't believe you're an angel." Zeke handed her another strip. "Had you been different in any other way, the world would certainly have destroyed your kind." She tied off the bandage. "We treat each other as less than human; your only salvation was to be more." Her fingers hesitated, then stroked the injured pinion, smoothing the white feathers into place.

"Perhaps I am less." The Seraph pivoted on the stool to face her. "Man-beast," he said, and the free wing lifted. "A new trophy for the hunter's wall."

"Is that how you feel?" The question had an unexpected tenderness.

Carson interrupted, "Man-beast, you're being morbid."

A moment of uncomfortable silence.

"Well, I hope that's better." Miriam's tone was businesslike. "I have some things to take care of." She pulled on a khaki overcoat. "I'll be back in a few hours. Ezekiel, should I buy you some whiskey?"

"No. Thank you."

She glanced at Carson, who shrugged. "All right then." She left, and he heard the magnetic lock snap into place.

"I thought I was the priest," he told the Seraph.

Zeke tilted his head quizzically.

"Sounded like she was confessing."

"Do you remember Temley?"

The blood shunted from Carson's face. "Gilbert Temley, the U.S. president? Yeah." He hugged himself.

The Seraph watched him expectantly.

"It was a vicious election," he began, as if he were

a VR tutorial. "Temley's slogan was The Might of the Right. He said the country had been crippled by amoral social elements and now Judgment Day was at hand. Said decent, God-fearing people shouldn't live in fear." Zeke raised his eyebrows. Carson shrugged away the contradiction.

"Anyway, it *was* a fearful time. Not that long after you splashed down. Height of NOPE—Not On Planet Earth. The whole alien invasion craze. National debt was out of the solar system. Global defense had carte blanche. They threatened, said if Temley got in, there'd be hell to pay. They were right."

"Who?"

"Usual militant factions—at least they're militant now. It's not an era we Americans are proud of. It became another witch-hunt, the search for alien sympathizers. I guess we just couldn't accept that no one knew what was happening."

"Her mother was black," Zeke said. "She was killed in Brooklyn. Miriam doesn't remember. Her father was Jewish, and he decided to emigrate to Israel."

Carson's lips worked independent of his mind, forming the words. "Dad was coming home on transit. They threw firebombs into the train. It was two weeks before things calmed down enough for a funeral. I was eight." He shuddered. "After that, my mother found religion."

"And you?"

"I hated him for the longest time."

"Your father?"

"No." He regarded the Seraph gravely. "God."

The couple who arrived that night in a rented skimmer to pick up Zeke looked so much like European pilgrims that it took Carson a minute to realize they were the same pair that had piloted the jet.

"Just the rich tourists, eh?" Carson asked, as he and Miriam stood in her garage, watching the skimmer bounce away over the swells, streaming a blue-gray plume of exhaust. He felt helpless being left behind. Zeke clearly wanted *out*, and Carson sensed that he would avoid saying anything that pulled him farther *in*— and he feared the truth might fall in the latter category.

"Let's go back up," Miriam said.

It was awkward for him, when they were alone in her unit, and he realized Zeke's presence subdued his longing. At least when he was sober. He watched Miriam shrug out of her coat, noticing her narrow hips, the high curve of her ass. She turned to face him, and he pulled his gaze away. It found the flesh-toned bandage, coiled on the hot pink counter.

"You really care about him, don't you?" she asked.

"Eight years," he answered. "That's a long time."

She nodded her head. "It is. He's been with you most of his life."

The comment gave him pause. He'd thought of Zeke as older, maybe even eternal, but never as ten. "You don't believe in them, do you?"

She shook her head. "It's not about that. Religion is fantasy; hatred and suffering are real."

"Your mother." Hazel eyes stared at him. "Zeke told me. My father was killed. Transit firebombing."

She swallowed. "And so we're both crusaders."

"You don't like me, do you?" he asked.

"I've got a job to do, that's all." She yawned. "Anyway, I'll get you up early. Three-hour time difference, and we don't want to miss the big show."

Carson awoke later from a wet dream, embarrassed and unable to remember. He listened. Beyond the screen divider, Miriam made no sound. Feeling his way to the bathroom, he cleaned up, then climbed back onto the futon, glad now that Zeke was in Geneva.

The Seraphim didn't have wet dreams. The Seraphim didn't have sex. He couldn't ask Zeke, but he wondered, did they ever have desire? Their genitals, after all, were analogous to a human male's. But angels were sterile, according to ICARUS's comprehensive report, though Carson didn't want to guess by what indignity they'd ascertained it. Their gametes contained only a few notes from a vast genetic repertoire, and their celibacy was a foregone conclusion. Angels simply didn't screw. But more than once, during the endless public appearances, women had thrown themselves at Zeke's feet, begging, please, to bear the child of God.

He rolled onto his back, eyes open, watching the retinal fallout. What would Zeke do if he gained his freedom? He was ten; he could live to be a hundred. And what kind of existence would that be, stranded on an alien world with no hope of progeny? The Seraphim prophesied the opening of a gateway to paradise, an event, they said, that would mark the completion of their work and the salvation of man. Perhaps the Infidels were right, and Zeke wouldn't be staying much longer.

Carson drifted, his eyes closing—and saw it, the bright star, expanding, dilating in blackest space, opening to—

He was awake, upright, staring at the silver-blue shapes of the kitchenette, the hypnagogic image gone. Was this what Chen had seen?

Then he remembered the recording, broadcast years before, of the starburst phenomenon that accompanied the eggs' arrival. The rush of panic dissipated. He lay back down, pulling the covers up, and let out a sigh.

Tomorrow, Zeke would walk into that assembly, on the leading edge of a cyclone. But for now, Carson was at the storm's center, and the fact that the calm was fleeting made him treasure it all the more.

Ten

Morning. Carson sat on a stool, sipping thick, bitter coffee and waiting for the satellite feed. Miriam leaned forward beside him, fidgeting with the laptop's scanner. A pattern of rainbow chevrons filled the screen.

"Ezekiel got there okay," she said. She wore lavender sweats. A green bandanna tied her braids.

The image on the vid resolved itself.

"Ah, here it is."

He peered at the small screen. The United Nations amphitheater was filled with suits. The heads wearing the suits were decked with partials, into which they whispered a hundred different tongues. Legacy of Babel, Carson thought. The voice-over prattled above the background chorus of mutual incomprehension, speaking of the day's proceedings, the startling news that one of the Seraphim had requested an audience, the imminent arrival of Harry Chen.

Then it got quiet, too quiet, and even the commentator shut up, so that the only sound aside from the faint static of the satellite feed was the steady *tap, tap, tap* of a cane on the polished marble floor of the assembly chamber.

Zeke limped down the central aisle wearing his horseman's duster. He propped the carved cane against the rosewood podium, then shrugged out of his coat and removed his black felt hat. His chest un-

derneath was bare except for the bandages holding
the injured wing in place. He hunched over the microphones, facing the twelve members of the Planetary
Security Council.

All the suits sat immobile. The camera zoomed
again on the face that a decade before had smiled in
benediction over a waiting world. It was not smiling
now.

"I'm here," Zeke said, his tone less graveled with
sobriety, "alone. And I speak not for the Herald
Party, but for myself. My brothers are not with me.
As you know, they believe we are angels." He looked
straight at the camera. "I do not."

Whispers rippled up the stepped sides of the theater. Multihued faces pivoted above the suits.

The Seraph continued, voice raised in a command-
ing tone refined through ten years of evangelism.
"You have all seen *The Revelations*. In our prebirth
confusion, we did not have words, not like I speak to
you now. Yet we saw the sad story of your world and
its fall from grace. Through that story, we came to
understand our purpose. And when we emerged, your
words came to us, gave sound to sight. We learned to
name this source of vision, and to call it God."

Zeke scanned the tiers. The suits were rapt. He continued. "We showed you our vision. And you humans,
who need so desperately to believe, you chose to believe us. But I have realized that like you, I also have
a choice." His eyes were slivers of cold steel. "I will
not serve your angry god."

He gave the words a moment to penetrate, before
extending a hand to the council. "You granted us our
autonomy. This assembly gave us the status of Special
Visitors. The Herald Party presented itself as our host;
your own ICARUS as our protector. But it is a strange
hospitality we have been offered. Recently, I tried to

leave." He grabbed the bandages crossing his chest. "This is the result. I am hiding now, from my pursuers, but the hunter is not to blame. He is just the agent of your own uncertainty and need."

The Seraph paused for a deep breath. "I am hounded by a voice. I do not know who this messiah, Harry Chen, is. I do not know why he speaks as a god. But these are mysteries I cannot illuminate. I ask you this—" The good wing came forward, sheltering him. Zeke's final words were less authoritative, more hushed. "Please," he said, his gaze cast down, "seek your own answers. Let me be."

The Seraph bowed his head as the shouts and cries of the suits swelled and fell, discord crashing on the thin, wan shoulders and white-feathered wings.

Carson heard a tinkling sound. Miriam still held the slender porcelain handle of her demitasse, and the cup was rattling against its saucer. She quieted it with her other hand.

On the screen, Rajid Nehru, the Indian ombudsman, had joined Zeke at the lectern. Beneath the black turban, his face was flushed. He waved his arms, trying to referee the assault.

"What about the tape from Daytona?" Carson asked.

"That's next," she said.

They liked the tape, and Zeke's supporting testimony, even less than his speech. He kept it terse, mentioning his attempt during the fire alarm, and then his escape from the Church of the Messiah, but leaving out Carson, Miriam, and the specifics of how and why. Under other circumstances, Carson might even have found the Seraph's ability to confound his questioners amusing.

Zeke leaned against the lectern in his blue jeans,

looking tired, alone, and very much the nonconformist. The Japanese delegate to the council had the floor.

"You testified before us two months past," he said, addressing Zeke, "that the messiah would soon come forth, and that it was imperative to the future of man he assume his rightful place in a new Jerusalem. Now what is your belief about this event?"

The Seraph shrugged. "That it is no longer my concern."

The delegate placed both fists on the table. "Oh? You have abandoned your duty and your honor, it seems. I must insist on an answer more specific."

"What do you want me to say?" Zeke asked. "That I have seen a vision of paradise? Then, yes, I have seen this. Will gates open to it? I don't know. I have seen many things. But I have no interest in telling you what to do. I came here hoping to be relieved of that duty."

Nehru cut in. "This line of questioning appears unproductive. Let us proceed." He gestured Zeke to a seat beside the council table, next to Bloom. "The assembly will now hear representatives of the Herald Party."

The double doors of the chamber swung inward and two guards entered, carrying a throne of carved wood. They marched to the podium and set the velvet-upholstered chair down to one side. A small procession entered after them: the other Seraphim in their formal uniforms, Chen, and then Torrie and Alden. The messiah's beard and hair were combed smooth, his purple glasses gone. He wore new white robes with voluminous sleeves that covered his hands.

They paced solemnly down the aisle. When Chen was seated, with his entourage grouped behind, Alden approached the ombudsman. "Our Lord, Harry Chen, has asked that I respond to the statements made by the Seraph Ezekiel."

The ombudsman nodded consent.

Alden went to the podium. His right cheek twitched as he slid a disk into the prompter. He introduced himself, then said, "It is with great sorrow that we inform this assembly of the truth. The Seraph Ezekiel's behavior has become increasingly erratic of late. His ICARUS protectors were, perhaps, overzealous in their attempt to keep him from harm when he was found, obviously disoriented, in Daytona Beach. As for his other injuries, Ezekiel harmed himself further when he leapt off the roof of the Herald Resort. He was treated at that time by his personal physician, Dr. Imogene Berthold. It is the regret of the Herald Party that we were remiss in our duty to aid him.

"The messiah bears malice to no one, not even one of his own Seraphim who has been led astray by forces which seek to keep mankind from its salvation. He thus requests that Ezekiel be remanded to his custody, so that he may save him, as he will ultimately save all those who accept him as their Lord." Alden turned to Nehru. "With your permission, his holiness will now address the assembly."

Permission granted, Alden returned to Chen's side. The messiah's lips didn't move, but in his mind Carson heard the words clearly, even as the suits twitched in their seats, and Miriam jerked on her stool.

I'm the real thing. So cut the bullshit, and let's get on with the vote.

Alden looked almost as pale as Bloom, the albino. The suits were in an uproar. Nehru blinked rapidly, then remembered he was in charge.

The black pearl of Carson's anger absorbed the fear, expanding.

Miriam was breathing fast. "That was him? That was Chen?"

Carson nodded.

She grabbed his wrist. Her palm was cold and damp. "How can he do that?"

The fear surged for the opening, lashing out at her. "What did you think? That we made it all up? It's not so simple now, is it?"

Her fingers sprang from his wrist, and she pulled away. "Okay, okay."

He looked back to the vid. Alden was bent over, whispering furiously to Chen, who was enjoying the commotion. He pushed the priest away and went to the microphones. Silence descended.

"I've seen paradise," he said. His hand emerged from a sleeve and stroked his beard. "It's definitely real. So you—" He pointed a finger at the council, then paused, looking around the theater, confused. "Well, whichever one of you are the Israelis, you gotta let me in. Okay." He turned to the lone Seraph. "Zeke, what *is* your problem?" He jerked his thumb over his shoulder at Torrie and Alden. "These guys are getting on my nerves, too. But you said it yourself, man: I'm God. You can't hide from me."

Zeke's face was carved from stone. Chen waited for an answer. Alden appeared beside him at the microphones, but Chen shouldered the priest out of the way. The older man hovered behind him.

Chen shot one more look at Zeke, then returned his attention to the assembly. "Quiet down," he shouted. The suits stilled.

"Blasphemer! Devil! Cast him out!"

Chen searched the ranks for the heckler. "Yeah? Is that it?" he asked, the epicanthic folds rising like a cobra's hood. "When I tell you to go to hell, asshole, it's gonna be for real."

The suits gasped in unison, time-delayed by the translation.

"Now listen up. Things are gonna be different from here on out. I've got a new show coming. Give you the vitals. Bottom line, I don't need no mandate." He puffed up. *"I'm the messiah."*

The hoods lowered, and his tone shifted, became conversational. "You guys are whacked, right? Of course you are. Look at you! I seen hologens more lifelike. And hey, so I wasn't what you were expecting . . ." He glanced down at his robe, scowled, stripped it off. Underneath, he wore white drawstring pants and a plain white T-shirt. "That's better," he said, almost to himself. "It's too late," he continued. "Couple of thousand years too late for that airy-fairy bullshit. Not my idea anyway." He glanced accusingly at Alden, who had retreated into the shadow of the throne. Torrie stood to one side, turning crimson. He looked like he was going to explode. Chen said, "Miracles? You'll get 'em. The works." He pointed at Zeke, who watched him warily. "Those angels ain't here for nothin'." Chen's gaze darted back and forth. He seemed to have run out of things to say. He shrugged. "That's it."

"Are you okay?" Miriam asked.

Carson was trying to convince himself he was asleep, that the whole thing, including the Seraphim, was a very elaborate nightmare. He opened his eyes. The assembly was still in session, hearing testimony from Alden and Torrie. Chen sat cross-legged on the throne, braiding his beard.

"No," he said. "Or maybe I am, and it's just the rest of the universe that's screwed up." He shook his head. "They're all lying, even Zeke."

"What did you expect? The Party wants to keep

their support intact, ICARUS has to cover themselves, and the PSC has to maintain credibility by going along with it all, even though they've probably been briefed by that security chief. Ezekiel obviously wants to wash his hands of the whole thing. I'm surprised he even agreed to testify." She glanced at the screen sidelong. "And then there's Mr. Chen."

"Yeah." He rubbed his stubble with one hand, wanting to shave it. "Maybe that's why Zeke said hiding wasn't going to work. I think Harry's getting stronger."

"I'd say so."

According to the commentator, Chen's unspoken words had reached everyone watching the broadcast.

She added, "Though I'm not sure that performance will broaden his popularity. It's up to the PSC now. The question is whether they'll still go along with ICARUS."

"What about Zeke?"

"We'll get him out of there. I just hope he'll change his mind and accept our asylum. I assume you'll come with him?"

"I don't know that I have a choice. Or that I ever did." Carson pointed at the tiny winged image on the screen. "He picked me, you know. I hadn't even applied, knew I wouldn't make the cut. But I was there, working in the membership office. Zeke came in one day, just to give the legions a glimpse. Shook my hand. Then he said, 'Yes. I remember you.' That was it. Next morning, Alden gave me the job. Dream come true." He pushed off the stool. "I'm going for a walk."

"You can't," she said. "Especially not now."

"I need a drink. This is Las Vegas. No one's going to notice one more loser."

"Until you spill your guts to the guy on the next stool."

He shook his head. "You don't have to worry; I'm a quiet drunk. I've had a lot of practice."

"No, Carson. I have to insist."

He decided not to argue. She'd had two cups of coffee; she'd need to use the bathroom. When she did, he grabbed his jacket and let himself out the unit's front door, into a dim corridor that smelled like sweat and potato chips. At the end was an elevator. He rode it up to island level.

The alley in front of The Pink Porpoise was deserted except for a sleeping indigent wrapped in a silver tarp, and a pile of refuse bags. He shoved his hands into the windbreaker's pockets and walked toward the interior, feeling invisible. A dented orange rickshaw, pulled by a squat Asian wearing blue goggles, clattered by. Las Vegas seemed relatively unaffected by the events in Geneva, except for the Judgment Day specials advertised on the casino marquees. He found an open bar between a bustling Nosh'n'Net and the cyan-tiled entrance of a Tube station. Inside, out of morning's cold glare, he ordered a double.

The bartender was tall and thin, with a black Cleopatra wig and low-cut white dress revealing a swatch of blond chest hair. He placed the whiskey on a pink plastic coaster, then went back to the tabloid he was reading. The headline announced, "Shocking new evidence: Déjà Vu was an android!" In the accompanying photo, intricate circuitry replaced half of the psychic's birdlike face.

Carson's throat was raw from the chill sea air. The whiskey hurt. He liked it.

A vid above the bar showed news. The London, New York, Tokyo, and Beijing markets had decided, wisely, to suspend trading after last week's crash. Unfortunately, there were no fail-safes for human behavior. In New Delhi, an entire congregation had set themselves on fire, and a few islands over, on Centrus, the Herald Tower was barricaded against a panicked mob.

He drained his glass.

"Get you another?" the transvestite asked, putting down the paper.

Carson savored the pain like a fine wine. "Yeah. Keep 'em coming."

"That was very stupid," Miriam said, when she let him in. "How did you pay?"

"Currency voucher. Told you I had practice." He wobbled over to a stool. The bandage was still on the counter, pushed to one side.

"It's dragging on. They're in closed session." She grabbed the pot and sloshed coffee into his cup. "Here, sober up."

"Don't want to," he managed. The pink porpoises on the carpet were multiplying. It made him dizzy. "Zeke . . ."

"Is coming back here. They held your senator for questioning, but we got Ezekiel out."

Voices roused him from sleep. He groaned, felt for the fissure bisecting his skull. There was none. Opening his eyes, he saw Miriam helping Zeke to the futon.

"Welcome back," she said, as Carson sat up, groaning.

The Seraph's limp was worse. He removed his hat and shrugged out of the duster. His face was colorless, the eyes sunken. Zeke looked at them. "He's stronger. It's never been that loud before."

Miriam nodded. "*We* heard him."

"Why didn't you tell them?" Carson demanded, the

fear surging again. "Haven't you figured out that you can't run away? It never works, trust me."

The Seraph's eyes receded further. "Did you not hear my words, Carson?"

"I heard them, Zeke. I heard them loud and clear." The sarcasm spurted like pus from a wound. "You don't like your job. It's got too many pressures: God bossing you around, the devil trying to head-hunt you, and all of us dissatisfied humans expecting miracles. So you're ready to just fly off into oblivion, let someone else deal with the metaphysical mess. Don't you think that's a little bit irresponsible? I mean, I seem to remember that you had some part in all this."

Zeke spoke very softly. "I don't have the answers, Carson."

He wanted to scream, but the headache stopped him. "You do, Zeke. You do, and you just won't tell us what they are!"

"Take it easy, Carson," Miriam said. She dropped down next to the Seraph, her hand on his shoulder, brown fingers spread against the ash skin. "It's over."

"What do you mean?"

"They just made the announcement. Said Jerusalem should be 'protectively occupied' because of its significance, and that Israel was in violation of the Special Visitor Resolution. They all but accused us of kidnapping him. Only good thing is there will be a separate vote on the use of force." She shook her head, looking pissed. "They got their mandate."

Zeke was curled on the futon, asleep. Miriam came out of the bedroom, and glancing at the Seraph, whispered, "He's even more set against asylum now, and we can't stay in Ocean City, especially not with you running around." She gave Carson a meaningful look. "I received word that the warrant is being issued tomorrow. They're not beating around the bush in your case. The charge is kidnapping."

His hangover was suddenly worse. "What about Zeke's testimony? And Chen?"

She shrugged. "They're covering all their bases, going along with the other Seraphim while they position themselves to deflect an invasion, and try and hunt down Ezekiel to find out what he knows."

The Seraph jerked awake.

"Are you okay?" Miriam asked.

Zeke propped himself up. "Chen," he said, closing his eyes and taking a deep breath. He looked at them. "He's much stronger, and I believe he's . . . embarrassed that he can't locate me."

Carson glanced at Miriam. "You said Michael was shielding you."

Zeke bowed his head, silver locks fringing his face. "Yes, so far."

"What do you mean 'so far'?" Carson demanded. "Are you saying Harry's going to find you? Find us?"

The Seraph answered, "It may be inevitable."

Carson squeezed around the side of the futon and stood over him. "Inevitable? Well, before it's inevitable, you have to tell them. You have to tell them about Michael and about Harry. Don't you see that? You can't hide from this, and the longer you let it go on, the worse it's getting. People set themselves on fire today, Zeke, because of you! Doesn't that mean anything?"

The Seraph lifted his face. "And so you want more words, Carson? You believe they will quell the fire, like holy water? I wish I had such words. But I have seen the effect of your god's words, and now you want me to utter those of your devil. They will not extinguish the fire, Carson. They will fuel it. This I know."

Carson stepped back, into the wall. He extended his

hands, palms up. "Would you just tell me what they are, Zeke? Would you just do that?"

Miriam was beside him. She stood there, looking from one to the other.

"I don't care if they're lies. I just want to know!"

The Seraph didn't respond.

Carson grabbed for Zeke's shoulder, to shake the answer out of him, but Miriam's hand locked around his wrist. He let himself be led to the door.

"I can't believe I'm saying this," she said, "but go for a walk. Calm down. He's not going to tell you anything until he's ready." She went into her bedroom, returning with a pair of dark glasses and some cash. "Here. Be anonymous and get him some whiskey." When he started to protest, she added, "You two are drinking buddies. It might help."

It didn't. Zeke accepted the booze, but wasn't any more talkative after three shots. Finally, he just rolled over and shut his eyes.

I taught him well, Carson thought. Too well.

Miriam looked at the Seraph, who appeared to be sleeping. "Try again in the morning," she told Carson. "He's had a long day."

"So we just wait? What if Chen sees us?"

"I asked about that while you were out. He said this Michael will give him advance warning." She raised her eyebrows. "I don't think I want to rely on it. We'll just have to be persuasive." She said good night.

Now, as Carson listened to the Seraph breathing beside him, he thought of Alden, wondering if the priest really believed the statement he'd delivered, that Zeke had been led astray. Carson had never doubted the Herald leader's sincerity. Could he be right?

Although the Party's membership was much smaller, a majority of adult humans did accept the Seraphic prophecies as indicative of real future events. To Carson, that meant that most people were probably confused by what had transpired in the last week, and those who weren't, like the Earth Militia leader he'd seen interviewed, were certain the trap was about to be sprung. Carson wasn't convinced that an invasion fleet lay in wait, but surely *something* lurked beyond the limits of man's personal and technological perception, something named Michael.

Unlike the messiah, the Seraphim had never identified the devil as a human being, and since he didn't tread the Earth, he'd been far less interesting. Now Carson almost wished the fallen one would materialize in a puff of black smoke—he had a few questions for him. His answers might be lies, but lies usually contained a grain of truth, at least effective ones did, and from Zeke's equivocation, he suspected Michael's lies were very effective indeed.

His back was to the Seraph. He rolled over, being careful to stay toward the edge of the futon. He'd considered sleeping on the floor, but Miriam didn't have another blanket. His preference was to sleep with her.

Stop it, he told himself, as the longing stirred in his pants. You're in bed with an angel, for God's sake. He glanced at Zeke and saw the gloss of open eyes.

Carson whispered, "Are you awake?"

"Mmm." The eyes shut.

Carson woke to tapping sounds. Dawn suffused the apartment with weak ambient light that made the screen dividers look like parchment. Someone was knocking on the door.

He sat up, grimacing at his residual headache, unsure whether to answer. The futon beside him was an empty expanse of black. A curl of white down clung to the other pillow. He listened for sounds from the bathroom, but heard only the knocking, insistent, but subdued. Assuming it was Zeke, he hurried to the island-side door. The magnetic lock was still engaged. He fidgeted with it; finally, the door opened.

The old woman standing in the corridor was wrapped in a faux leopardskin coat, her rotund body perched on heeled red boots that laced up the front. Above the coat's black-furred collar, garish makeup set off huge green eyes. A pink turban covered her hair.

She shoved past him, into the apartment. He lost his grip on the door and it swung shut with a loud *click*.

"Woke you up, did I?" she asked, in a throaty voice. Before he could answer, she said, "Well, don't stand there gaping. There isn't much time. We'll talk on the way." She flicked magenta-clawed fingers. "Coat, shoes. Hurry, Carson!"

At the sound of his name, he froze.

Miriam's voice came from behind them. "You're not going anywhere."

He turned to see her in the silk robe, braids tousled, right arm bent casually against her waist, the strong fingers closed around the ridged plastic grip of a gleaming silver pistol.

"Tsk-tsk," the woman said. "Put that thing away before you hurt somebody."

Miriam demanded, "Where is he?"

Carson stammered, "Gone when I woke up. Just now. I heard knocking, thought he'd let himself out. It was her."

"I did wake the poor boy," the woman admitted. "As for your feathered friend, that's why I'm here. His whereabouts are known to me, so if you'll—"

"Who are you?" Miriam brought the gun forward, clasping it with both hands.

The woman looked pointedly at the weapon, penciled brows arching in disapproval. "Names are hardly important," she said, and slid magenta nails into her pocket, withdrawing a business card. "But allow me to introduce myself."

Miriam ordered, "Stay where you are." Then she told Carson, "Read it."

He took the card, peering. It was printed black-on-black, in fancy script. An address and then two lines:

> *Madame ViVi Vestala*
> *Psychic Extraordinaire*

He laughed, knowing it was probably hysteria.

"Turn around," Miriam ordered.

The woman sighed, but pivoted with mincing steps.

Miriam snatched the card. She glanced at it, then said, "What do you want?"

Vestala answered, "Only to take you to Ezekiel." She regarded them over her shoulder, batting false eyelashes. "But we really must be going."

Miriam's tone was very cold. "You happen to know where he is. And why is that, because you're psychic?"

Vestala smiled, showing worn teeth, smudged with coral lipstick. "No, dear," she said evenly. "Because I watch the news."

Eleven

The laptop was still on the bar. "Turn it on," Miriam said to Carson. Her gaze never left Vestala.

The psychic told him, "Try C-12. They have one of their talking heads down at the port."

He keyed for the channel. A reporter stood on a cantilevered deck that jutted over the ocean, wind whipping at his burgundy trench coat. Some distance behind him, Carson saw the granite base of the seamark crucifix belonging to the Heralds' port authority. A Seraph perched on the horizontal beam like a giant seagull, his back to the camera. He was naked. Carson's first thought was: Harry must be God after all. This is his sort of perversity.

"Zeke's on top of the cross." He heard the edge of panic in his own voice. Looking at Miriam, he repeated, "Zeke's on top of the cross at Pilgrims Port." This isn't happening, he told himself.

Vestala said, "And if you want him back, you'll put that nasty toy away and get dressed."

"We're not going anywhere. Now who are you, and how did you know where to find us?"

Vestala sighed, exasperated. "You have my card, dear. Michael told me where you were. He's the seventh Seraphim and he's dead, but I'll explain all that later."

Miriam's sharp glance met his.

Vestala continued, "Oh yes, he's quite real. You can ask your pet bird. That is, if we get to him in time." With one arching magenta nail, she pointed at the vid.

The cross rose from the guard wall surrounding the deck. Ocean City Rescue & Response had cordoned off a semicircular area around its base, but they were hanging back, for fear Zeke would leap—and plummet twenty meters into the Atlantic.

"We have to help him," Carson said. He didn't know whether to believe the psychic, but if Zeke died, it wouldn't much matter.

"The boy is right," Vestala chimed in.

He waited for some tacit sign of agreement from Miriam, and when he got none, said, "I'm going, with or without you." His shoes were on the floor next to the futon. He went to put them on.

Her tone was flat. "There's nothing we can do."

Vestala said, "*Au contraire*. The necessary arrangements have already been made, assuming R&R doesn't find a giant butterfly net. But we must get back to Shipside to meet him."

Carson looked up at Miriam from where he knelt, tying his shoes. "You can stay here, play your spy games. I have to try." He straightened, grabbing his jacket.

"Don't." She raised the gun.

"Go ahead. Put me out of my misery." It cost him all his courage, but he strode past her, to the door. As he pulled it open and stepped into the corridor, he heard Miriam say, "Wait." He kept walking, toward the elevator, imagined bullets ripping through the air around him. No shot came, just Vestala's footsteps right behind.

"Carson, do slow down."

Whatever she had to say, he didn't want to hear it

now. He sped up, opting for the stairs. Taking them in twos, he realized he had no way of getting from Las Vegas to Centrus. Then he remembered the bar he'd found. It was next to a depot for the Tube, the submarine subway that connected all the major islands. Gaining the alley, he broke into a jog.

She caught up with him inside the crowded compartment of the train. They rode in tense silence, Vestala on the plastic bench opposite, her eyes green and owlishly large. Puckers of fat pinched her small nose, the coral-stained lips.

Triton station. Their compartment half-emptied. The port was next. He shut his eyes as they accelerated again, and tried unsuccessfully to dredge up some recollection of Zeke's departure.

Her whisper intruded into his private darkness, carrying the scent of tobacco and clove. "I just risked my sweet derriere on Ezekiel's behalf, so be a polite boy and listen." He opened his eyes. She sat beside him now, stockinged legs crossed at the ankle above the red boots. "Michael needs your help. He's not really the devil; he's just gotten a bad rap."

"How would you know?"

"I *am* psychic," she said, her tone dripping condescension. "I can hear him." She added, "He would have preferred to deal with one of his own kind, but the rest won't listen. And obviously poor Ezekiel has been rather traumatized by the truth. So he needs us."

There was something distinctly unsettling about her, something too costumed, that suggested disguise. He said, "I don't know how you came up with that name, but I don't believe you. And even if I did, I'm not in the habit of cutting deals with the devil."

"Well, you should." Impatience hardened her words. "You haven't got much choice, since I doubt you can get him down from there on your own."

"And you can?"

"Michael will take care of it. But we need to get back to my place to meet him." The train was decelerating. "I'm not enjoying this, Carson. And there isn't time to explain everything. You're just going to have to trust me."

The train shuddered to a stop. He was up, pushing toward the door. Vestala was talking about a miracle, but he'd spent too much time with the Seraphim to expect one of those.

As he crossed the platform, she struggled to keep pace, puffing, "Wrong way. We can transfer here. The red line goes to Shipside." Her face was a gaudy mask, sheened by sweat.

He hadn't risked being shot by Miriam, only to fall into another trap. "You obviously know where to find me," he said. "If Zeke ends up at your place, just bring him back." He jammed himself onto the perpetulift, knowing that with her bulk, she'd have to wait for the next car. The continuous-motion elevator whisked him upward, then slowed, moving sideways in front of the unloading quay.

He exited the station on Centrus's lower level, across from the port authority. Anniversary banners for the Rising, emblazoned in silver with a winged form and the number ten, snapped at the tops of flagpoles surrounding the tiered, triangular building. He ran through cold morning mist to the deck on the southwest side. A large crowd had already gathered near the giant steel crucifix. Sunlight blazed across its surface. He saw with grim relief that Zeke was still atop his perch.

Carson skirted around the onlookers to the guard wall rimming the deck. The wind was brutal, razoring his face. He hunched into his jacket and squeezed toward the cordoned area. If he got close enough to yell to Zeke, he'd most likely be recognized, arrested. But desperation drove him on. I have to try, he thought. I can't just—

Something fell, wrenching screams from the assembled crowd.

A whiskey bottle.

On top of the cross, Zeke hoisted himself to a standing position. The spectators surged inward, screaming. Carson grabbed the concrete wall, fighting for ground, neck craned back, one word caught in his throat as Zeke straightened, hands free. The Seraph wavered, swaying with each gust of wind. The crowd froze in jarring stillness.

Silence, then

whistling rush of air.

No—

Zeke dived like a tern, wings clasped to his body, arms rigid, legs spread slightly, forming a V.

After the horror, there was a moment of anticipatory euphoria, when Carson felt certain the descent would slow, then reverse itself, life going into rewind, as God realized a terrible mistake had been made.

But Zeke's god was Harry Chen, and the Seraph kept receding toward the green-blue darkness where the rescue boats waited, little white toys on the vast, unwelcoming sea.

He was bruised by the time he worked his way out of the crowd. His ears ached from the sharp wind. Zeke hadn't resurfaced. The boats were making incremental circles from the point of impact.

"He's not dead." Vestala appeared from the shadow of the building's entrance as he passed. He kept walking, ignoring her. "Did you hear me, Carson?"

"It's over. Leave me alone." He blinked back hot tears.

"Oh, stop being so morose. He's not dead, but I can't wait here any longer. I know you want proof, and if you'll just come with me—"

He stopped. "Proof?" he said, his voice rising. "Proof? Okay, lady, give me proof: one Seraph, alive and kicking. You deliver that, and I'll do whatever Michael wants."

She rolled her eyes. "I'm telling you, Carson—"

He cut her off. "No, *I'm* telling *you*. It's over. Now leave me alone." He walked on, blinking faster.

She called after him, "Shipside Slips, K-9. I won't be responsible for what happens if you don't change your mind!"

He wandered Centrus's lower level for a bleary half hour in search of a private phone booth, eventually finding one next to a pair of vacant tennis courts. Carson stared at the receiver, deciding whether to place the call. Bloom would help him. He trusted Tao on that. He could surrender through the senator, cut his deal, be done with it. Let someone else save the world. It wasn't his job, not anymore. Not without Zeke.

Tao picked up on the first ring. She'd already seen the news. "Why'd he do it, Carson?" she asked.

"Hell, I don't know," he told her, choking back a sob. "I woke up this morning, and he was gone." He fought for self-control. "I think it was too much yesterday. But, Tao, I kept telling him that he was trapped, that he had nowhere to go. I never thought he would . . ."

"Easy, man. Breathe deep."

An elevated tram hissed around a corner five stories overhead.

He wiped his face on a jacket sleeve. "It's not just Zeke. Things are getting weirder by the minute." He told her about Vestala.

"We're living in Harry's world now," she said. There was no humor in her voice. "What do you think she meant, that Michael was the seventh Seraphim?"

"I don't know what any of it meant, Tao, or that it means anything. Zeke said the devil was one of them, the fallen one. But this woman was a kook. He's gone. I saw him hit the water. I was close, so close—"

"I know." Then she said quietly, "They haven't found a body. Wouldn't you expect 'Zekiel to float?"

"Tao, *I was there.*"

"I know that, Carson, but I also know that things are happenin' which we don't understand. I've been watching the vid, and the Party hasn't released any statements since he jumped. Mighty strange, don't you think?" She gave him a chance to respond. When he didn't, she added, "Could it be that 'Zekiel's alive and the others—or even Harry—have some sense of it?"

He wiped his face again, ignoring the possibility. "Haven't you heard about the warrant, Tao? I called to surrender. I want Bloom to arrange it, try and make sure some of the truth gets told."

"Carson, right now both the Party and ICARUS need a scapegoat bad, and you're number one on the list. This woman has information, and she seemed to want to help. You need help, and unfortunately, not the kind Bloom can deliver. It's your life, but if it was me—"

"What? Go back to Miriam? The Israelis don't need me now. I'm a liability."

"My guess, Miriam's long gone. But you said the psychic gave you an address?"

He didn't want to think about Vestala. He didn't want to think at all. "Get Bloom."

She sighed. "Carson, realize the situation has changed. You're a fugitive, and he has to follow the rules, somewhat. Are you sure?"

He wasn't sure about anything. It took conscious effort not to attack her for asking. "No," he said.

"Then think about it," she told him gently. "I'll be here."

Carson stared glumly at the reflective letters spelling SUD, as the Tube wheezed into the station. His search for an open bar and anonymity had led him here, to the laissez-faire colony of recommissioned semi-submersible drilling rigs anchored at Merbleu Bay's south end. Enclosed gangways connected the tiny pseudo-islands. He crossed three before veering into an entrance labeled simply The Tavern. Two old Soviets wearing their lambskin shapkas were ensconced in a ripped red vinyl booth, a game of checkers and small glass vials of vodka on the table between them. Carson slid onto a stool and ordered his whiskey.

The bartender was a burly man with a gold tooth that looked as if he kept it polished. A flannel shirt was rolled back from his tattooed forearms.

"What terrible day," he said, after he'd served Carson. He hunkered down, elbows on the varnished wood of the counter. "You see this news, yah? The angel?" He made a diving motion with one hand, and a whistling sound, like a falling bomb.

"Yeah. I saw." Carson drained half his glass.

The bartender watched him, nodding sympathetically. He set the drink down.

"That Party," the man went on, shaking his big head. "Why they not let the angel go?"

Carson shrugged, wishing some other customer would come to distract the man. The bartender took it as an invitation.

"They not find the body." He waggled a stubby finger for emphasis. "Now that Party say they know the angel is not dead. Pah! That is crock of shit." He nodded knowingly.

Carson paused his drink in midair. "The Party's saying he isn't dead?"

The bartender nodded. "That is what they say. That Alden. That man is a fool. Worse!"

Trying to keep his tone casual, he asked, "Do they know where he is?"

"No! But they say this, because they are embarrassed, what they have done. They should throw them off the cross when they get back, all of them!"

Carson still had his glass half-raised. The man noticed. He straightened, frowning. "But what do I know?" He gestured helplessness, then disappeared through a swinging door at the end of the bar.

Carson managed to set the drink down. Alden might be a fool, but as Tao had pointed out, he had access to five Seraphim and Harry Chen, all of them linked to Zeke. What if the Party was telling the truth? What if Vestala had been right? He shut his eyes and clenched his teeth, thinking: No, I will not do this.

The bartender returned with a box of Carpathia lager tucked under one arm.

"Do you know where Shipside Slips is?"

"On the old island, by the docks. Not a nice place, that. Why you go there?" He clicked open a utility knife and severed the box top in four swift cuts.

Carson tossed back the rest of his whiskey, leaving the question unanswered. Then he fished Miriam's change out of his jeans pocket, paid for the drink, and left.

Shipside was the oldest island, and it completely lacked Centrus's meticulously planned order and grace. Most of the deck was given over to warehouses supporting the industrial docks on the east side. The

Tube lifts were fixed to the northwest corner, an obvious and somewhat unstable afterthought. No elevated trams here, no Vegas rickshaws. Leaving the station, he headed east, making his way across the small island on foot, until he found a break in the perimeter buildings where a strip of dune grass anchored by two benches passed for a park. ATLANTIS WILL SINK AGAIN was sprayed in fluorescent lime paint on the guard wall. Through chain link, he saw piers jutting into the open sea, a conglomeration of cranes, stacked orange cargo cubes, and rusting storage silos. The outlook had little to redeem it except the water. The sea was choppy; sunlight danced across the tufted blue waves.

He spied the marina in the shadow of a white processing plant that looked like a giant beer still decorated with Christmas-tree lights. A hundred or so geriatric schooners, trawlers, and pleasure craft were ranked along a series of narrow walkways. Overhead, an arrangement of power cables dropped a feed down to each slip. Hooked up that way, the motley fleet appeared to be on life support. He couldn't tell which one was K-9, but he doubted Zeke was aboard it. His optimism seemed foolish now. O.C. Rescue & Response had kept other vessels out of the area beneath the cross; certainly none of these boats would have made it near.

Wind lifted off the docks, bringing with it the smell of diesel. His hands were getting numb. He shoved them into his pockets and found cold metal. When he pulled the thing out, silver glinted at him like a winking eye.

His Herald pin. He should cast it into the sea. It was more than a badge of rank: It had also been his passkey to the electronically secured heights of the Tower. They said it registered with the sensors in Party HQ, letting the security system track movement of individuals throughout the building. For a paranoid instant, he imagined they had ways of tracking the pin *outside* the building. He shot a glance behind him, almost expecting to see Maartens and Juan. Or had they ferreted out the mole?

Then it occurred to him: He could call Juan.

No, he told himself. This is insanity. If Vestala really had Zeke, she would have come and gotten him by now. After all, she'd known where Miriam's apartment was. Zeke was gone; they'd find his body eventually.

But he was already heading toward a MerMart he'd seen near the Tube.

His hand shook as he keyed Juan's number.

The voice rasped, "Perez."

"If they catch me, they catch you," Carson said. "You know who this is?"

Pause, then curtly, "Yes."

"Two questions. First: Are the others saying Zeke's alive? Yes or no."

"Yes."

"Do they know where he is?"

"No."

He hung up, feeling the tension like tethers between his shoulder blades and spine. If there was even a chance—

The marina's location had seemed obvious from his vantage at the park, but it was another matter getting there. He aimed for the odd angles of the processing plant, eventually finding it and a sign that directed him to a rusted, expansion-grating catwalk from which twenty or so plaswood ladders descended, leading to the various walkways of the slips. Each was labeled with an orange letter. Making his way through the alphabet, he heard blaring music in the distance and the drone of machinery from the plant. A drunken prostitute wearing metallic blue underwear was slumped against the rungs of B; at F, two men loitering on the catwalk argued in Spanish. He tried to limit his breaths of the fetid air as he hesitated at the top of K, nervous sweat condensing under his arms. I should have called Tao first, he thought. There was a houseboat with peeling green paint in number eight. He didn't see anything beyond it except ocean and a dangling power feed.

He climbed down the ladder anyway. Waves splashed against salt-crusted hulls as he approached the ninth slip, sneakers silent on the rubber grid of the walkway, dread and disappointment closing around him like jaws. Then he saw the low deck, camouflaged to blend in to the water, except for a name printed in black: BAUHAUS.

A scale model of a Seapod personal survival craft hung from the ceiling of Harry Chen's living room. The real thing was docked in Shipside Slips, K-9.

Carson stared at the small, half-submerged submarine. Its four starboard portholes were covered. Above them, a shin-height railing surrounded the sloping deck and central hatch. I don't believe I'm doing this, he thought as he leaned out, grabbed the railing, and climbed aboard. Knock once, no one answers, and I get the hell out of here.

Squatting, he rapped on the hatch. Very faintly, he heard something bang.

He waited, then cursing himself, rapped again.

Faintly, *bang-bang-bang.* Then three slower *bangs,* followed by three fast ones.

His heartbeat accelerated. He looked around. The two men were still on the catwalk, but they weren't watching him. The prostitute had disappeared.

He rapped a third time and got the SOS in response. He tried the handle. It turned, and he lifted the weighty hatch. Peering down, he saw a short ladder and, at its base, a man in dirt-streaked coveralls, bound and gagged, lying on his side. *Bang.* He kicked the bottom rung with the heel of a black work boot.

Carson let go and the scuttle fell. It was his heart banging now. He twisted around, expecting some sort of ambush. The walkway was empty.

When he opened the hatch again, the man's brows drew together in concern. "Arrrh. Arrrh." Growling sounds escaped past the gag.

Carson knelt, sticking his head down for a better look. The man was in a closet-sized antechamber with another scuttle set in the epoxy-coated steel floor. An opening in the aft bulkhead led to a cluttered cabin. It was very dim, but he didn't see anyone else. The man kept growling. Reluctantly, Carson descended into the sub. It smelled of tobacco and clove. Stepping off the ladder, he saw a panel of switches and pressed the top one, flicking on a caged bulb. Then he squatted by the man. Duct tape bound his wrists and ankles. He said nothing when Carson removed the gag, which looked like half a dish towel.

"Are you all right?" he asked.

The man sighed, squinting at him from underneath thick dark brows. His hair was chestnut brown, frizzy, but shaved around the back and sides so that it stuck up in an unruly shock. Acne scarred his cheeks. He couldn't have been much past twenty-five.

Carson lifted him into a sitting position. As soon as he was upright, the man scooted toward the cabin. Straightening, Carson saw ViVi Vestala seated on an upholstered bench that ran the length of the starboard hull. She was bound and gagged, but her green eyes regarded him with owl-like intensity. The man reached the psychic and snuggled against her thigh.

Carson pressed the second switch, lighting a fringed

lavender shade suspended from the cabin ceiling. It was a compact and functional living area, furnished with the bench, a dining booth, and opposite, built-in storage, all of marbleized scarlet Formica. The hull surfaces were drab epoxy, a blankness covered by an eclectic assortment of decorative touches, like the Victorian shade and a gleaming rapier hanging above the vid screen.

He approached Vestala and untied the other half of the dish towel.

She said peevishly, "It certainly took you long enough." The coat was gone; she wore smocked gold velvet. "You'll find scissors in a drawer by the sink. The galley's through there." She nodded at a low doorway between the booth and the storage cabinets.

"What happened?" he asked. "Are they coming back?" This fear was different; it made the hair on the nape of his neck prickle.

"Not for some time," she said. "But my calves are cramping."

He went to the tiny galley and got the scissors. More scarlet Formica. Returning to the clutter of the living area, he noticed underfoot a woven tapestry depicting stylized Japanese men and women in a variety of sexual poses.

"Who did this?" he asked, as he cut at the duct tape.

"Your little spystress. Apparently, she found me more interesting than you did. She was waiting by the time I got back here—I told you we needed to hurry—and she is quite proficient, as you can see. Poodle had gone to fetch—"

"Poodle?" Her wrists were free. He came around to kneel at her feet, next to the man.

"He's very good at fetch. And he'd gone to get a birdy, hadn't you, Poodle?" The man smiled up at her.

Carson looked from one to the other, revolted. Then it clicked. "A birdy? Are you talking about Zeke?"

"Carson. If that much isn't clear to you by now, then—"

He cut her off, demanding, "Where is he?"

"Miriam has taken him to Israel. I got the impression it would have been rather difficult trying to sneak a dead Seraph and two prisoners out of Ocean City, so she left us like this, intending to send someone later, I suppose." She wiggled her red boots, prompting him. "Do get on with it, Carson."

He finished with the tape at her ankles and started on Poodle's wrists. He wasn't sure whether to believe the psychic. "How can he be alive? I saw him fall. He didn't resurface so—"

"Is this *really* necessary, Carson? You think he's alive; that's why you're here. Even your precious Party admits it. As for how, this is a submarine, which has certain advantages. Poodle dived out the air lock and retrieved him."

He snipped the tape from Poodle's ankles, then stood up and went to the antechamber. After a check of the walkway, he sealed the hatch.

"You needn't worry," Vestala told him. "We'll have plenty of warning. Michael's watching out for me."

"Well, he's not doing a very good job."

She stroked Poodle's hair. "That's because of Ezekiel. Michael was able to intervene in some fashion when he jumped. Really quite miraculous, but it kept him preoccupied, so he wasn't able to warn me about your Mossad agent. Then, when Ezekiel came to, there was quite a flap. It was all any of us could do to keep him from flying off—" His skeptical expression stopped her.

"Zeke can't fly," he said.

"He can now. I told you it was miraculous." She sighed. "I can see this is going to be *very* difficult. Poodle, be a good dog and fetch my pouch. The yellow one."

The man obligingly got up. He ambled through one of the doors set into the antechamber bulkheads.

Carson asked, "What is he, your pet?"

"Poodle leads an alternative existence." She dismissed further questions with a wave of her magenta claws. "Let's start at the beginning, and you can swallow this one bite at a time. Originally, there were seven eggs—"

"Six. There are six Seraphim."

"Yes, but there were *seven* eggs." Poodle returned with a tasseled, yellow silk pouch. She took it, then shooed him away.

"What happened to the seventh?"

"They dissected it. Don't you remember the rumors?" She extracted a small packet of rolling papers and a lacquered vermilion tin of potpourri, proceeding to expertly construct a cigarette.

Carson's legs felt weak. He sat on the bench next to her. Of course there had been rumors of a dissection. ICARUS had always denied it, and whether or not they were telling the truth had been an ongoing debate—until the Rising. Then it was assumed, at least by believers, that if any such desecration had occurred, the Seraphim would know.

Vestala went on, "With his unformed body dead, Michael was released into the Realm." She held up her index talon. "*Don't* ask me to put that in religious terms. I won't, I won't, I won't." She fished a mother-of-pearl holder from the pouch, tapped her cigarette into it, and handed him a gold lighter.

He humored her by clicking a centimeter of flame that she drew in with a pursing of her lips. "The

Realm? As in the spacers? Are you saying that's where they're from?"

She shook her head. "It's not a place, and no, I don't think so. Now consider this: You want to communicate, but you have no body, and the only physical beings that hear you are the others of your kind, maybe one or two gifteds such as myself, and a very strange child named Harry Chen."

At the name, he leaned forward intently, hands clasped between his knees. "What do you know about Harry?"

"Ah," she said, giving him a smug little smile. "You'd like to know his evil secret, wouldn't you? Of course, you're already aware of his odd DNA."

She knew too much. He was tingling with anticipation and nerves. "All right, Vestala, let's say I believe you. So are you going to jerk my chain all day, or are you going to tell me what's going on?"

She tilted her head back and sent a jet of smoke toward the cabin's ceiling. Then her gaze leveled, eyes like green moons peering out of the colorized face.

She said, "It's very simple, Carson. The messiah has come, and now it's your job to stop him."

Twelve

He was going straight to hell. He was positive. That conviction brought with it a certain calm. "Tell me the rest," Carson managed.

Vestala balanced the holder on the bench next to her right thigh. Ashes drifted to the lewd rug. "My understanding is that after the dissection a couple of geneticists from old Red China pilfered DNA samples, taking them to a lab in Xiaoping, where they performed some experiments the rest of the UN team would *not* have approved of. Only one embryo took. They used some poor wretch from a state institution as their incubator, and *voilà*, Mr. Chen was born."

"Harry was *genetically engineered*?" He imagined Chen's fury at the idea, the rat tail quivering as he sputtered with rage, the purple glasses coming askew. It was a gratifying picture. "Then what is he?"

Vestala shrugged. "That depends on who you ask. He obviously thinks he's God. Michael considers him an abomination. Of course, he considers Michael to be the devil. Very reciprocal, don't you think?" She smiled.

"And Michael told you all this?" He popped up, unable to sit still. Vestala watched as he paced to the galley and back. "How did he know?"

"He couldn't do much except watch and wait. The others were incommunicado until shortly before they rose. He tried to reach Chen, and apparently got his attention for a while, but then Chen's new family encouraged him to cast the devil out."

He stopped pacing, arrested by her choice of words. "You mean that literally, don't you?"

She nodded.

"Then why do the others think Harry is God?"

"Well, dear, this is where it gets rather complicated for the likes of you and me." She plucked the dead cigarette from its holder. "According to Michael, their shared awareness is of more than just sensory information. Chen is a sort of weak link in the chain, and because he was around first, when they *became* they didn't discriminate between his beliefs and their own. Keep in mind that we're talking about creatures that don't learn, they *know*. And they rose *knowing* what Chen knew."

He returned to the bench. He'd hungered for the truth. He'd wanted to hear that Chen was a ghastly mistake. Now the truth was giving him indigestion. "You're saying they're not angels."

"I told you not to ask me to put this in religious terms." She waggled a magenta claw at him. "I won't do it." She returned the holder to the silk pouch, pulling it shut with a quick jerk on the tasseled drawstring. "It's rather ironic, don't you think? We've created our god and our devil, too."

Carson wasn't amused. "You said it was my job to stop Harry?"

"Ah, yes. Well, Michael's in a bind, as you can imagine. He's been trying to get the others to listen for ten years, hoping to enlighten them before Mr. Chen—and the Seraphim—became aware of their unusual abilities. Ezekiel was the only one who would, and obviously he hasn't been very successful in resolving his identity crisis. You made an offer, I believe.

Michael kept his end. He resurrected Ezekiel." She smirked. "And now you get to straighten out Mr. Chen."

Carson said, "I can't straighten out Harry; he's permanently bent. Besides, I can't even hear Michael. Why don't you do it?"

"Let's just say my past is rather sordid, and credibility might be an issue."

It was her first statement that he immediately accepted as true. "I thought you watched the news," he commented. "Mine isn't much better."

She arched a penciled brow. A smile tugged at the corner of her mouth. "Oh yes it is. Besides, I've made my own deal with Michael. I'll be his interpreter, that's it. You're already involved, and you have a special relationship with Mr. Chen."

He rubbed his forehead. "I don't know." He stood up, adding, "I don't know that I even believe you." He went to the doorway. Speaking slowly, he laid it out for himself. "You want me to go convince the messiah that he's a mistake, that the angels are misguided, and that the devil—who I'm not even sure exists—was murdered." He turned back to her. She looked at him expectantly. "Assuming I even could do it, why should I?"

"Because I'm offering you a chance to save the world, Carson. Or would you rather live in the age of our Lord, Harry Chen?"

"No." He remembered Chen's performance at the vote. They'd passed the mandate anyway. "Why don't you just tell ICARUS? They want an explanation more than anything, and they already know about the dissection."

"Don't be so naive." She adjusted her pink turban with magenta pincers. "ICARUS may not be religious, but they do believe that starburst was the gateway to the heavens, and they've been waiting forty years for a key. They think it's Chen. That's why they were behind closed doors yesterday, convincing the Planetary Security Council to play their game a little longer." She waved a dismissive hand. "Your precious party has been an expedient means of baby-sitting the aliens, because our fearless leaders are far too paranoid to give a bunch of deluded extraterrestrials free rein. I doubt very much they'll be sympathetic to Michael's cause."

"But what is the truth?" he demanded. "What are they, and why are they here?"

"I don't know what they are. And I don't know that it's a question they can answer," she said, crossing her legs, "or that we could understand the answer if they did." She shrugged. "For that matter, what are we? As for why, I hadn't asked."

He stared at her, disbelieving. "You don't know, and you haven't asked? Then why are you doing this?"

Her patience had expired. "Oh come, it's not like you've known anything for certain all these years that you've run around in your Party uniform. 'They're angels.' What does that mean?" She frowned. "Perhaps they will even continue the charade, just so long as *they* know that's what it is. Michael assures me that he's attempting to save us from our own folly that created Chen. Personally, I trust him, but I can't offer you any guarantees. It always comes down to this, Carson: What do you believe?"

He sat, hunching forward, and buried his face in his hands. "I don't know."

"Then what don't you believe?"

He answered automatically. "That Harry Chen is God."

"Well, good," Vestala said, her tone softening. "That's enough."

Carson walked to the end of the catwalk, sweating, but not because of the sun, which burned in a depthless blue sky. After demanding some sort of proof and getting a number Vestala claimed would reach Miriam, he'd needed to leave the Seapod, give himself distance from the psychic and her story. After so many shock waves, he was almost beyond reaction. Most of him—that personal tableau of assumptions, expectations, hopes, and dreams—lay in ruins. He wasn't sure what part was left intact.

Sitting cross-legged on the rusted grating, he cradled Vestala's phone in one hand, smelling diesel and rotted fish on the wind. Cranes glided over the docks like praying mantises. The scene amazed him, that reality could shift so drastically and yet remain the same. The business of living went on, despite aliens, despite angels. He shook his head, keying the phone.

He didn't understand the word Miriam used to answer, but he recognized her voice.

"It's Carson."

"How did you get this number?"

"ViVi Vestala told me, after I untied her. Is Zeke with you?"

She was quiet. Then, "Are you on the submarine?"

"I'm at the slips. Miriam, I need to know. She said Zeke was alive, that his wing was healed, and that he left with you. I want to talk to him."

"Carson, listen: Some of my associates are on the way there. They won't hurt you. Go with them. They can meet you at—"

"*I want to talk to Zeke.*"

Her tone was extremely patient. "He's not available, Carson. But if you'll go with my friends—"

"What the?" His first thought was: Earthquake. He'd been in Tokyo when a 5.3 hit. Then he heard Miriam gasp, and realized, simultaneously, that she felt it, and that it wasn't the Earth, but *him*.

It rolled in like thunder, across the wrecked landscape of his inner self. And like thunder, it attended a flash of illumination: *Chen*.

It would be described later as a psychic storm, the guttural, wordless outburst of an angry god.

As it faded, Carson knew that last part of himself was no longer intact. A pearly black seed, it flowered now, petals of fear and rage opening, overlapping, like scales.

His armor.

Returning the phone to his ear, he heard, in the background, an unearthly howl. His voice shook. "Miriam? Miriam are you there?"

"Call back," she said, and hung up.

When Carson reboarded *Bauhaus,* Poodle was lying in fetal position underneath the dining table. A collection of carnival masks hung on the bulkhead above it. Carson stared at a fanciful owl with gold feathers. It reminded him of Vestala.

"Well, that was rather *rude* of Mr. Chen," the psychic said, entering from the galley. She held a glass of water and a fresh cigarette. All color that wasn't painted on had faded from her face.

The armor gave him a sense of invulnerability. With something like detachment, he asked, "What happened?"

"The inevitable," she said, sliding into the booth. "Mr. Chen just saw the light."

Carson sat opposite, careful to avoid kicking Poodle. "What does that mean?"

The smoldering tip of the cigarette quivered as she

raised its holder to her lips. "Well, at the moment, he's in a state of shock, but in the long term, it means trouble. At least from where we sit, *here.* Michael cannot control him from *there.* So you'd best get on with it."

Annoyed, Carson said, "I haven't agreed to anything, and Miriam wouldn't let me speak to Zeke, so as far as I'm concerned, there's no proof that—"

She interrupted him, "You're after a guarantee again, Carson, and I've already told you I can't provide that."

He stood. "Well, you may have a T-1 phone line to the afterlife, but I don't, so for us *mere mortals* proof will have to suffice."

Under the table, Poodle growled.

He snapped, "Oh, shut up."

Vestala wore the expression of a patient parent indulging her child's temper tantrum. He glared at her, thinking that she looked like an old man in drag.

"I'm sure you know Senator Bloom's involved; he and the Israelis can handle this. Bloom can take it public, force ICARUS into admitting the dissection. When the others see the proof, they'll realize Michael wasn't lying, and then they'll listen. That will work."

"Certainly," Vestala agreed. "As long as the Seraphim share your proof obsession, and Harry Chen hasn't done any irreparable damage, and the PSC doesn't become so rattled that they revoke the Seraphim's autonomy, and the frenzied masses calm down when the biggest scandal in the history of the species—"

"Stop it!" Carson felt deflated, like he was caving in under the armor. He sat. "I don't even know that Michael exists. I've just got your word and Zeke's." He ran a hand through his hair.

Vestala bent over. "Poodle, dear, my other pouch."

The man crawled out from under the table and, with a resentful glance at Carson, ambled into the antechamber.

Carson said, "As for Bloom and the Israelis, how do you know I haven't already told them? I did reach Miriam and—"

She rose, going into the galley, and returned with a yellow plastic headset and transceiver. It was a cheap, flimsy rig, probably meant for joggers who didn't want to break stride when they had a call. She dropped the set onto the table and looked at him unapologetically. "A small precaution."

He accused, "You were listening in."

"Yes. Had you and Miriam been more cooperative earlier, we could have all sat down with Ezekiel and had this little chat. But since he's in denial and on his way to Israel, it's up to you."

Poodle returned with another silk bag, sage green this time, then disappeared.

Vestala extracted a small perfume bottle blown of iridescent glass and pushed back her sleeve. He saw the loose, puckered skin of her forearm was mottled with scabs.

"You're burning space."

She gave the flacon a close-lipped smile. "Well, dear, I've had many years to experiment with chemical aids, and I must say this is the best."

He cringed as she took the lit end of her cigarette and made a new burn. With two magenta pincers she removed the applicator rod and rolled black powder across the open sore. Color flushed her face. Her pupils narrowed to dark pinpoints, and she regarded him with unnerving intensity. "I should have used some this morning, but I didn't expect to have to give chase."

Curious, he told her, "Harry's burning. It's why he noticed his . . . capabilities."

"Hmm. I wouldn't doubt it. From what Michael has said, Chen buried that awareness as a child. And this expands it."

"So is that why you can hear Michael?"

She dropped the flacon into its pouch. "Not a simple question. You remember Mr. Chen's unidentified genetic objects? Well, I have a few of those myself."

"But why did Michael wait all this time? He could have just told all you psychics what's been going on and—"

She placed a hand against her chest, feigning insult. "All us psychics. *Really.* Didn't you read my card? I am not 'all us psychics'; I am ViVi Vestala, Psychic *Extraordinaire.*"

He wasn't impressed. "So you're special, eh?" he asked, remembering Déjà Vu. The androgyne had erased the effects of aging with cosmetic surgery, maintaining a counterfeit youth until his death at sea, but Vestala obviously needed the makeup and clothes to hide years of self-neglect. She looked old enough.

"If you're so extraordinary, how come you didn't know the eggs were here, like Déjà Vu?"

She frowned and said sourly, "Déjà Vu may have had talent, but he was vulgar and irresponsible. Better he'd kept his big mouth shut. I imagine he would have been far too self-interested to do the right thing if the opportunity presented itself. As for why Michael waited, I told you: He was intent on reaching the other Seraphim. But that is neither here nor there. You're well aware of the issue at hand. Now, if you'll excuse me, I need to use the loo." She minced out of the cabin.

Carson pressed his face into his palms, breathing deep. The air was saturated with smoke. He felt nauseous. There was nothing to stop him from leaving, though, and Vestala couldn't edit his conversations if he did. But would Bloom or the Israelis believe him, would they risk so much on the rantings of a medium? Zeke hadn't mentioned Michael at the UN assembly . . .

Michael, spirit of an angel. Wasn't that somehow redundant?

The devil wanted him to straighten out Chen, and no doubt he had some fantastic plan, like the one he'd used to rescue Zeke. The seventh Seraph probably did exist, Carson reasoned, because on their own, Madame ViVi and her Poodle didn't seem capable of much other than eccentricity.

He opened his eyes, peering between spread fingers, and saw Vestala's pouches. On impulse, he grabbed the green one. Under his thumb, the sage fabric slid over iridescent glass.

Space. It acted like a biochemical amplifier . . .

He reminded himself: You're not psychic.

And neither are all the spacers who say they visit the Realm, he argued. If Michael was watching, if Michael was real, if he, Carson, could hear him—

He fished Vestala's lighter out of the smoking pouch and seared his inner wrist with its orange flame, grimacing at the pain and the smell. Charred skin flaked away under his nail. Tapping powder from the bottle, he dusted the raw flesh, then rubbed it in with a fingertip.

He felt suddenly feverish. A burning pulse spread from his chest, outward. Shutting his eyes to wait for the voice, he heard only his heart pounding. A big hand reached over to squeeze his shoulder. "Have a good day at school, okay?"

"Sure, Dad," his child-self answered. He smiled up at the freckled face.

And then something crashed through the windshield of the car. Hungry flames licked upward from their feet, and he was screaming, but his father still smiled, that big hand holding him down as the fire swallowed them whole.

"Carson! Carson, can you hear me? Open your eyes."

Vestala, her hand on his shoulder. The blood seared his veins.

Her voice played on pipes, each tone distinct. "You've been a very bad boy. Let's get you over to that bench to lie down."

"I don't hear him. Where is he? I want to hear him." But he leaned on her, his arm bearing down into the fleshy shoulders.

Lying on his back, he started to shake. "Try to be still," she told him. But he couldn't stop shaking.

Hot urine seeped through his jeans.

Then nothing.

The shakes were gone when Carson woke, his jeans, too, and he found himself covered with a plaid wool stadium blanket. No light shone through the porthole shades, and only the galley was lit, but his vision was sharp and bright. He looked around, marveling at the vividness of the colored masks, the discreteness of the rapier's blade against the dull epoxy. Standing, he tucked the blanket in like a sarong. The wool was rough against his bare skin. It was very quiet. He pushed up one of the shades and gasped. Beyond the sub was a black void, dotted above with stars.

They were at sea.

"Vestala!" he called. "Where are you?" No response. A couple of strides took him into the antechamber, where he was met with three doors. "Vestala, answer me!" He tried the nearest, got a glimpse of a toilet, and slammed it shut. His hand was on the knob of the second when the last door opened.

Vestala emerged, wrapped in an embroidered gold kimono. The pink turban was on crooked; tufts of grayish hair stuck out around her left ear. Most of her makeup was gone, and she smelled like lotion.

"Calm down, Carson." As she pulled the door closed, he glimpsed a cramped bedroom, Poodle sprawled naked on a quilted, black-satin coverlet.

"Where are we?" He felt panicked, but his body didn't notice. His heartbeat was regular and slow.

"A few leagues east of Ocean City, dear. I thought it best that we not be there to greet Miriam's colleagues." She frowned. "I must say you surprised me. But your choice of this afternoon to begin experimenting with drugs was not particularly astute. Mr. Chen's recuperated, and he's already annoying his keepers."

"I didn't hear Michael."

"Ah. Proof again. Tsk-tsk. You could have saved us both some trouble. Your pants, by the way, are hanging up in the loo."

He looked down at the blanket.

"Oh don't be embarrassed. I rather enjoyed it." She smiled, then added, "Now that you're awake, we need to discuss the messiah-napping."

He shook his head. "I'm not going to do what you say just because I'm stuck out here."

She rolled her eyes. "This is becoming tedious, Carson. If it's prophetic vision you want, Mr. Chen's new episode should be on in a few minutes. I suggest you watch it. It may just make up your mind for you." She retired.

His jeans were stiff and damp. Carson put them on, then settled onto the bench with the control pad on the floor next to him. The VR headset was old, padded cups to cover both ears and bulky goggles. He adjusted the clumsy thing as best he could.

He'd programmed for *Freak Follies*. At eight o'clock the console tuned itself in.

The show's lead-in exploded around him, accompanied by the dissonant theme music.

Faithful minions, welcome to the Freak Follies, and the first-ever 4-D simulcast!

It was less shocking, somehow, hearing Chen's soundless voice when he was in virtual. Carson tensed, but kept the headset on, thinking: Only Harry would come up with something like this.

Then once again he stared up at a crucified Chen illuminated by moonbeams. But now slowly, deliberately, the messiah wrenched himself free. He dropped to the ground, crouching. Iron nails pierced his hands and feet. He yanked them out, first from each palm with his teeth, then from either foot. Blood splattered toward Carson.

Chen looked at him through purple glasses and smiled. Then he straightened, pulling himself up tall. And taller. Taller still. As he grew, the desert landscape shrank until the curvature of the world was obvious. Carson stood on a miniature Earth, replete with cloud swirls and continents. One of Chen's feet was planted firmly on the Middle East; the other was ankle-deep in the Atlantic Ocean. Chen eyed the moon, floating like a dust mote in front of his nose. Opening his mouth, he swallowed it whole.

His entire body lit, as if it were a bulb.

Now Chen stooped over and squinted one eye at the cross. His giant thumb and forefinger flicked it off the planet. It hurtled away into the depths of space and disappeared.

The crucifix left a hole in the world. A hissing sound came, the escape of air. Carson looked down. The globe on which he stood rippled, shrinking, then shot away after the cross, a deflating Earth-balloon.

He fell—into the giant hand of Harry Chen.

Chen raised him to eye level. The face was too close, a yellowish moonscape sprouting black hairs like obelisks.

Holy shit, said Chen, his voice reverberating in Carson's ears and his mind. *It's the end of the world as you know it.*

Flaring suns and whirling nebulae, streaking comets and funnel-shaped black holes, all interspersed without regard for relative size, appeared around them. Chen's distant other hand formed a fist. He smashed it into the cosmos and they cracked, a web of hairline fractures spreading. The whole of creation shattered and fell. Beyond it was blinding light.

In his real body, Carson shuddered.

The whir of an approaching motor. A dark speck appeared in the brightness. The speck grew larger, took on form. Red, his wings a blur, flew by with a jaunty wink and buzzed up toward Chen's ear.

What's that you say? Chen asked. Then, *Stop it! Get the fuck away from me!*

But Carson's ears heard Chen say something else, something he couldn't understand. Endless ranks of people were marching in from the brightness, everywhere he looked. They advanced heedless of gravity, toward a center point: him.

ICARUS bastards! You can't do this!

Confused images of the ranks closing, and flashes of Torrie's face, jaw set but eyes scared, a hand descending with a needle, claustrophobia as they marched toward him from above, below, all sides, marched into him, pain of collision, his face smashed, and the needle plunging into his arm—

I'm God! I'm fucking GOD! Nooo—

Echoing screams. The images gone. Taste of blood, smell of smoke and old wool.

He lay on the floor where he'd fallen, facedown, the VR headset he'd pulled off still clutched in one hand. The control pad was under his left shoulder.

He rolled onto his back. Something dripped from his nose, trickling along both cheeks.

Footsteps. Embroidered gold silk swirled beside him. He looked up into Vestala's green eyes.

"Satisfied?" she asked. "Or do you need more?"

"I didn't just hear him: I saw. At least, I think I saw," he told Vestala, as she wiped blood from his cheeks. "It was bizarre, because I was still in virtual. But Torrie was there. Someone with a needle, too."

"Yes, I know. Mr. Chen is getting stronger. Michael says they drugged him, which may be convenient." She rinsed out the washcloth in the galley sink and folded it over a chunk of ice. Without makeup, her face was tired, androgynized by age. "Keep this on your nose. I'll get dressed."

He still felt claustrophobic. Need some fresh air, he thought, putting down the ice.

In the antechamber, he climbed the ladder and opened the hatch, standing on the top rungs with his torso above deck. A cold, wet wind lifted off the ocean, soothing his bruised face. Despite everything, an apocalypse didn't seem possible. The universe felt solid. Stars still winked from the night sky. *Some aren't really there.* It was his own irritating inner voice. *But they look real. Don't rely on what you can see.*

"Fuck you," he said aloud. Harry was a man. Maybe a man with creative DNA, but a man nonetheless. Flesh and bone.

So was Jesus. Miriam's voice, remembered.

"Fuck you, too." He was scared.

He sat down on the rim of the hatch. Teeth clenched, he fought the thought for as long as he could.

Maybe it was the space. Maybe it was an irrational sense of responsibility. He'd never be sure. But there it was: *He had been called.* By the devil, he told himself. That doesn't count.

But Carson knew it did.

Thirteen

The Seapod's antique engine sputtered to life as Carson sealed the hatch. Vestala stood in the antechamber, wearing a felt cloche and a pantsuit of black-and-white-checked wool. Her lipstick and hat were cherry red.

"Where are we going?" he demanded, stepping off the ladder.

"Back to Ocean City, of course." She raised a clawed hand, silencing him. "Don't bother protesting, Carson. It's there in your eyes, the resignation."

He scowled. "Tell me something, Vestala: Why are you doing this?"

She pointed at the rapier with a magenta talon. "Because I don't have the right fashion accessories for *hara-kiri.*" The sword's double-edged silver blade extended from an ornate hilt with a scrolling gold handguard. "But it's a long story, too long, and time is of the essence."

"All right." He scratched at the burn on his wrist. "Let's say I'm willing to try and convince Harry. He's locked up in Party HQ. So how does Michael plan to get him out?"

"He doesn't. He doesn't plan to do anything. You're the one who's going to do it, and you're the one who's going to figure out how."

He shook his head, incredulous. "Hello? *Hello?* I'm

not a spy. I'm not even good at the VR adventure games, and you're talking about kidnapping Harry from people who are."

Vestala sighed. "Oh come, Carson. You're not alone in this. You've got me and Michael and that man on the inside. What is his name?"

"Juan? Juan Perez? He's Miriam's man on the inside. She bought him out."

"Good, then he's for sale."

"Not in my price range, assuming I could even risk using credit, which I can't."

She flicked his argument away. "Money isn't an issue. I've plenty of it and nothing better to buy than a messiah." She told him a number. "That's your budget. I suggest you call this Perez and make him an offer he can't refuse. The two of you should be able to find a way to smuggle Mr. Chen out."

He stared at her.

"Well, what are you waiting for?"

"Who *are* you?"

She smiled sweetly. "Your fairy godmother, dear." The smile vanished. "Now call Perez; Michael says he's alone."

"Juan, it's me. Can you talk?"

The Cuban was quiet for so long, he thought he'd lost the connection.

"Juan, you there?"

"Yes. Go ahead."

"I've got a job for you," Carson told him.

Silence, then, "And if I'm not interested?"

He tried to imitate Juan's menacing tone. "Then Torrie gets a phone call."

The Cuban didn't sound intimidated. "You are hardly in a position to make threats."

He gave up the pretense. "Let's help each other,

Juan. I'll tell you what I need, and you can name your price."

"What about our female friend? Does she know of this?"

Miriam. He hoped money would buy some sort of discretion. "No. But I assume you can handle the conflict of interest?"

"I see." Pause. "What is it you need?"

"Harry Chen."

Juan laughed hoarsely.

"I mean it. I have to get him out of the Tower. ASAP. Name your price."

It was a fraction of the budget, and still enough to retire on. "Assuming you have an acceptable plan," the Cuban added.

The price doubled when Carson admitted he didn't.

Pilgrims Port. The *Bauhaus* bubbled to the surface between two charter yachts, their polished white hulls dwarfing the low-slung Seapod. It was a tight fit. Through one of the portholes, Carson saw dark water churning against the boats, reminding him of the spreading bull's-eye from Zeke's nosedive, barely a day before.

Planning Chen's rescue had taken most of the night.

"No time like the present," Vestala whispered, the words crackling in the earphones of the plastic headset. Its transceiver was clipped to the waist of his jeans.

He answered, "Yeah, I hear you." The microphone was against his cheek, concealed, he hoped, by the hood of a waterproof navy shell belonging to Poodle. It smelled of stale beer and sweat. Underneath, he wore the man-dog's coveralls over his own clothes.

She flipped the phone shut. "How do you feel?"

"Good. Too good." The space hadn't worn off. His

surroundings had a hyper-realness akin to virtual. The entire scene—Vestala, the *Bauhaus,* the marina outside—felt artificial, like it could be switched off. So did his confidence. He looked into her unblinking green eyes and repeated, "No time like the present."

Cold, dank air greeted him when he climbed through the hatch. The *Bauhaus* was nosed in at one end of a series of docks fronting the public terminal. He closed the camouflaged scuttle, then leapt over the Seapod's deck rail onto the platform, landing with a wooden *thump* that sounded loud in the predawn quiet. Bright puddles spilled from ranked lampposts, and he avoided them as he walked quickly toward the entrance.

Inside the terminal building, anniversary flags for the Rising hung from a framework of white girders, alternating with banners that read HE IS COME.

Not for long, Carson thought, attributing his cockiness to the drug. He'd told Vestala he was no good at VR games, but now he imagined himself to be playing one. This terminal was the first level and predictably simple: a vast hall of gift shops, ticket windows, and passenger lounges, empty other than for a few vendors preparing for the anniversary rush. All he had to do was sneak through a door labeled AUTHORIZED PERSONNEL ONLY, and take a service lift up to his next challenge, the port authority on Centrus's bottom deck.

His hand slid under the shell and felt the metal of his Herald insignia. He'd provided Juan with Torrie's passwords, courtesy of Michael. The Cuban had used them to log on as the security chief and reactivate Carson's pin, giving it unlimited access and changing the owner ID. If it worked as Juan had promised, the Party's electronic logs would note only that a John

Doe had passed through. If it didn't, then the system would register an intruder alert and—

He didn't want to think about it. Dampness under the layers of clothing. He whispered, "Vestala, you there?"

Her voice crackled, "Yes. Michael says proceed."

Holding his breath, Carson approached the door. The red proximity indicator flashed, then winked off. He heard the lock click open, and exhaled. Ahead was the lift that would take him to Level 2.

Inside the cubicle, he whispered, "Vestala, how's it look?" Slight jar as he was whisked up twenty meters to the second floor of the port authority.

Crackle. "It's clear. I said I'd tell you if Michael sees a problem."

The pilgrims were audible once he exited the restricted area for a catwalk to the port offices. Looking down on the concourse, he saw them camped in small groups, with blankets, pillows, prayer books, and bags of food. Some slept, most were singing. Several guards in hunter green port-security uniforms were gathered at the doors to the crucifix deck. Vestala had warned him about the all-night vigil for Zeke.

Leaving the catwalk, he crossed a broad lobby, deserted except for a janitor vacuuming around the reception kiosk. The man's back was turned. Striding purposefully, Carson veered down the first hall. His pin clicked him through a plain white door. Beyond was a small carpeted vestibule and his ride to Level 3. "I'm in the private elevator," he whispered.

"Good. Michael informs me the doctor is dozing off. If you hurry, you may catch her napping."

He reached for the control panel, his finger stopping a millimeter short. "What will you do if I'm caught?" he asked. Anxiety was edging out the confidence.

"Beyond getting my sweet derriere out of here? I've

told you, Carson: I'll figure something out. But I'd really prefer not to have to."

He clenched his teeth and punched the button.

The elevator was a private link between the port authority and the Herald Tower on Centrus's top deck. Seconds later, it deposited him one floor below the residential section. He stepped out into a darkened hall lined with executive offices. Sensors picked up his motion and the overhead fluorescents switched on. It was a good sign. They'd scanned his pin and it had registered as authorized personnel.

"Vestala?"

"Onward and upward."

He followed the hall around a bend to the stairwell, feeling something like relief, not because of his celestial lookout—he wasn't fully convinced that Michael existed—but because he knew this building, knew the scent of its musty, processed air, the give of the shaved carpet underfoot, the crossed-wing insignia on the nameplates affixed to each of the paneled doors. He still felt as if he belonged here, and that sense of belonging assuaged his fear.

The stairwell was cooler and brightly lit. Up one flight, then he clicked through another security door. It led to more stairs, but now he was in the residential section. They were keeping Harry in Zeke's suite, three floors up. He climbed the steps with ease, feeling the enameled handrail sliding underneath his sweaty palm.

At the top, he listened. Quiet on the other side of the stair door. "This is it," he told Vestala.

"All clear," she answered.

He cracked it just enough to squeeze through. The door was set in one wall of a corridor; the other was half height, topped by archways open to the birdcage, Carson's secret term for the four-story, domed atrium created by cutting away the center of the residential floors. It was intended as a personal flight arena for the Seraphim, but with its vaulted ceiling and elaborate architecture, it reminded him of an antique finch house. The carpet here was thick gray pile. Wing-shaped sconces of pearl glass dotted the outer wall.

"Still snoozing," Vestala's voice hissed in his ear, as he stole past the recessed door of his own small apartment and came to Zeke's. The silver handle was a polished lever set in a raised medallion. He entered a combination on the keypad, then pressed down with slow, even pressure. The door gave, swinging open on silent hinges, across the floor of vanilla marble. Carson listened, hearing only the rush of the air vents.

He crept along the ivory plaster wall and came to the bedroom door. It was ajar. A nightstand lamp partially lit the room beyond. Over the back of a velvet armchair pulled up next to the bed, he recognized Imogene's silver-blond bob. Her medical case sat on the floor. There was a prone form under the woven coverlet; he couldn't see Chen's face.

Sweat trickled down his sides. Reaching inside the shell, he withdrew a plastic respirator from the breast pocket of the coveralls. A small canister of anesthesia was attached to the mask that Vestala had found in the Seapod's original emergency kit. He positioned his thumb over the release button, then inched toward Imogene's chair.

With each step, his heartbeat accelerated. Chen's face was visible now, mouth slack, eyes shut. He snored intermittently. Imogene's head nodded and Carson froze, certain she would wake. He was within arm's length of the chair. Two more steps and he was there, over her. Remembering to breathe, he took one long inhale, then depressing the button, he clamped the mask over her mouth and nose, grabbing her across the chest with his other arm.

For an instant he thought she would just slide from sleep to unconsciousness, then she reacted with a muffled scream, body jerking forward, hands locking around his wrists, trying to pry herself free. He held on, pushing all his weight down to keep her in the chair. She was in good shape, but no match for him and his space-boosted strength. A count of twenty and she went limp. He waited another minute before removing the mask, to make sure she was really out. When he let go, she slumped forward, head resting on the edge of the bed.

He stared down at her, stunned. It wasn't a game anymore.

Vestala's voice crackled over the headphones. "Stop admiring your handiwork, Carson. It's time to play doctor."

He tossed the respirator aside. Vials, steriwipes in little foil packets, and a ripped plastic bag of syringes littered the nightstand. He fumbled with the tubes of medicine, whispering their labels to Vestala until she recognized the antagonist for the sedative they'd given Chen. Hands shaking, he drew it into a needle.

Pushing back the coverlet, he saw they'd tied Chen's wrists to the side rails with webbing straps. He still wore his white drawstring pants, and a silver pin was fixed to the waist. Carson stuck the needle in Chen's left arm, doing his best to hit a ropy blue vein. Blood spurted from the puncture when he pulled the needle out. He dropped it on the nightstand and unlashed the straps. Chen groaned as Carson got an arm under his shoulders, sitting him up.

"Harry," he whispered.

Chen's eyes opened, rolled, closed.

"Come on, Harry." He shook him. "Wake up."

Chen's lids fluttered, and he groaned again. Then the folds rose and his dark eyes focused on Carson.

"Harry, don't transmit. You hear me, Harry? *Don't transmit.* Okay? Don't send any telepathic stuff. Harry, do you hear me?"

Chen's voice was hoarse. "Carson . . . that you, man?" He coughed. "Where you been, man?"

"Harry, did you hear me? *Don't transmit.*" Carson willed himself to stay calm. Chen looked at him, blinking. "I untied you, okay? I'm gonna get you out of here. Just don't say—send—anything."

Chen squinted and raised his hands to his forehead. "Oh . . . I feel like shit, man." He noticed the blood on his elbow. "Wha'?" His face scrunched into a scowl. "Those assholes—"

"They drugged you. I know. But I'm gonna get you out. So let's get up, okay?"

Chen's face darkened with anger. "That prick," he sputtered. "That prick, he drugged me! They can't do that—"

"Harry, *listen to me.* We don't have a lot of time." He pulled Chen's legs to the edge of the bed, then stripped off the shell and the coveralls underneath. "Come on, Harry, put it on," he said, dressing him like a child. Chen was still scowling and muttering, "That prick." Carson zipped him into the coveralls and pushed the shell down over his head. Their hoods could wait until the elevator.

"This stinks," Chen said. "And I'm pissed at you for taking off—"

"I know, Harry, I know." Carson tried to ignore his racing heart. He got Chen around the waist, hoisting him to his feet. "That's it, Harry. Can you stand?" He let go. Chen wavered, but stayed upright.

Vestala said, "Just get him out of there."

He took Chen by the elbow, leading him around the bed.

When Chen saw Imogene, he stopped. "That bitch," he said, his voice rising. He stared at the syringes on the nightstand. "That fucking bitch."

Carson put himself in front of Chen. "Harry, look at me."

Chen met his gaze.

"We gotta get out of here, okay? And you can't transmit, do you understand?"

Chen peered at him. "Yeah . . . you came back for me. I get it, Carson."

"Okay." Carson sighed, relieved, then saw Chen's bare feet. "Shoes." A pair of sandals was on the floor at the foot of the bed. He kicked them over to Chen. "Here, put these on."

Chen stepped into the sandals. "Where have you been, man?" he asked. "Hey, you're growin' a goatee. Looks good on you, but the hair—"

"Right, Harry. Let's go."

Chen let himself be steered to the door of the suite. "That prick is gonna pay," he said, as Carson peeked out into the empty corridor. "He doesn't know who he's fucking with. I'm gonna—"

Carson turned around, shushing him. "Harry, later. We gotta be quiet now."

Chen pressed his lips together in exaggerated co-operation. *I'm gonna make that asshole pay. I'm gonna—*

Carson grabbed him by the shoulders, shaking him. "Harry, stop it," he hissed. "You can't do that, do you hear me?"

"Hey, let go," Chen said, his tone irritable. Carson released him, and Chen made a show of brushing off his sleeve. "Where we goin' anyway?"

"Down to the port, and then someplace safe, okay? But we have to go *now*." He took Chen by the wrist, pulling him out into the corridor.

"I knew you'd come around, man," Chen said, stumbling at his side as Carson half dragged him toward the stairwell. "It's your nature. We'll stick together, here on out. Fuck this party."

They reached the door and it clicked open. When Carson went, Chen pulled back. He turned to see the messiah smiling at him.

"What, Harry? Why are you smiling like that?"

Chen said, "Hold on a sec."

"Why?"

Before Chen could answer, Vestala explained for him. "He's calling the other Seraphim. Go. *Now*."

Somehow Carson forced him into the stairwell, but Chen caught hold of the rail with both hands. "Stop shoving me, Carson. We got to wait for them."

Carson tried to wrench Chen's hands free of the enameled tubing, but he held tight. "Harry, if you don't let go, I'm leaving without you. We can't wait for them." He took two stairs to prove his threat, hovering his foot over a third.

Chen's gaze darted to the door and back. Indecision registered on his face. "They need to be with me, man, and—"

He pleaded, "Harry, there isn't time. *Please.* We'll get them later." He took another step, fighting the instinct to flee.

"Aw, man. I can't do that. I can't just leave them. They're mine, man, and I got to have—"

Inspiration struck. "Tell them to use the windows," Carson said. "They can meet us at the port." Chen had let go of the rail. Carson leapt up the three steps, and taking advantage of Chen's hesitation, towed him down the stairs. "Just tell them that, Harry. The windows in their rooms open. They can climb out and fly to the docks, okay?"

"Good idea, man." Chen picked up the pace. They rounded the first landing. "Shit, I wish I had wings." He was panting. "Feel kind of dizzy still," he said, as Carson led him down the next flight.

Vestala corrected, "Bad idea. They just set off an alarm. You've got to hurry."

Carson snapped, "I am." Chen whined, dragging behind him, going slower and slower as they descended, his pull like a giant rubber band, and Carson feared that just short of the *Bauhaus* it would recoil, slamming him headlong into ICARUS's grasp.

They made the hall of executive offices, Chen stumbling now, his whines interspersed with groggy moans. Carson forged toward the elevator. Hit the button. The doors slid open, and they were in. Chen collapsed against the carpeted wall; Carson punched for the port. A slight sensation of weightlessness as the elevator began its forty-meter drop, then a jolt.

They weren't moving. The control pad readout said they were between decks. Carson pressed frantically for emergency override. The elevator didn't respond.

Almost gently, Vestala told him, "Too late."

Carson's stomach plunged all the way to the sea.

"Quite the shit, isn't he?" Vestala whispered. "With Seraphim flying the coop, security decided to check the messiah's location. They're assembling a welcoming committee right now."

Chen moaned again, then slid to the floor, oblivious to their predicament.

"Vestala, you promised if this happened—"

"Yes, dear, and despite my rather numerous shortcomings, I am a man of my word, so to speak. Rest assured—"

He snapped, "Would you shut up and do something?"

"I can't do anything *right this minute*, Carson."

Tears caught in his lashes. He blinked at them, focusing on Chen. The messiah sat with his back against the blue-flecked carpeting that covered the elevator wall, head lolling forward, legs splayed, like a rag doll. The rage cleared Carson's mind. He dropped down on his knees by Chen. "Harry, look at me!" No response. He smacked Chen across the face, hard, taking pleasure in it. Chen's eyes popped open at the stinging impact. "Tell the Seraphim to go to the old Seapod moored at the end of the public docks."

Chen squinted. Drool glistened along his chin.

Carson shook him. "You want them to drug you again, Harry?"

Chen's voice was very weak. "No."

"Then, do it!" The elevator hummed. They were going up. "Do it!" he yelled in Chen's face. "Tell them to go with the woman on that pod. It's moored between two white yachts. Tell them, Harry!" Chen nodded, his eyes closing. Carson wasn't sure if he was sending the telepathic command or passing out. "Is he doing it, Vestala?" he demanded, breathless. The elevator slowed. "Vestala, are you hearing this? Take the Seraphim!"

Static answered. Chen slumped over, as the doors slid open.

Carson looked up, into Torrie's jaundiced scowl. He wore striped pajama bottoms and a red velour bathrobe. A black automatic protruded from his left hand. Behind him stood three men in charcoal Herald-security uniforms, silver-wing patches on their shoulders.

"Welcome back, McCullough," Torrie said, and slammed the gun into Carson's right temple.

He saw a flaring grid of light. Then, as consciousness snuffed itself, Carson thought he heard Vestala whisper, "They're coming."

Fourteen

The pain in his forehead was relentless. It pulsed through Carson's dream of climbing Escher-esque stairs that led both up and down, his goal an ever-distant minaret where he knew, somehow, that Zeke roosted. At last, steps led him to the Seraph's aerie. He burrowed his way through gold straw and surfaced inside the giant nest. Miriam was there, reclining in her jade robe. Zeke crouched over her like a vulture. Seeing Carson, the Seraph rose, wings whipping up a maelstrom of hay, and flew off through an arch.

Sharp, ammoniac smell, and he opened his eyes. The light drove twin daggers into his brain. His lids snapped shut. He heard himself groan.

Warm fingertips pried his right lids apart. A blinding, pencil-thin beam and a blurred image he gradually recognized as Imogene. Cold metal bit into his wrists. He was sitting up, hands cuffed behind the back of a chair. Memory came, white-hot like the pain.

Unhurried, she checked his left eye. Then, "Mild concussion. Some aspirin, perhaps."

A chill breeze ruffled his hair. He shivered.

"Perhaps." It was Torrie, nearby. "Thank you, Doctor."

He heard Imogene snap her black case. A door opened, shut. Silence. He counted time to the throbs in his right temple.

"Open your eyes, McCullough. Enjoy your last view that isn't the inside of a prison cell."

Carson cracked his left lid. Torrie stood before a square of pale blue-gray. A window. Dawn was approaching. The security chief lowered a pane of glass and the breeze stopped. He'd changed into brown slacks and a plaid shirt. The pistol hung under his right arm in a glove-leather sling.

"I admit I underestimated you, McCullough. My mistake." Cracking his knuckles, he came to lean over Carson, and added, "Now you're gonna tell me where the 'Phim are."

Carson croaked, "Don't know," thinking: They must have gotten away. It was a small wellspring of hope.

Torrie snapped, "What was that?"

Tilting his head back, Carson looked up at the security chief's stubbled chin, and repeated, "I don't know." He squinted both eyes. They were in the living area of one of the Seraphim suites, the careful work of a team of designers who had debated long and passionately about the appropriate decor for angels, until Alden lost patience and ordered them to do their quarters in white.

Torrie regarded him for a moment, then he grabbed a low-backed chair, custom-designed to accommodate wings, and positioned it on the textured rug, opposite. "I got time," he said, lowering himself onto the chair. "We'll just sit here until you remember." He glanced at his watch, adding almost casually, "There's an ICARUS transport coming to take you to Geneva for arraignment. Six counts of kidnapping Special Visitors." He shook his head. "The jerks that grabbed Uriel should be out in a century or two. Of course, that was only *one* count." He folded his thick, hairy arms across his chest, smiling close-lipped. "When your memory comes back, just say so."

"How about some aspirin?" The throbbing had spread across the right side of his skull. He added, "I didn't kidnap anyone, and you know it."

Torrie raised his eyebrows. "I know that you dragged Zeke out of that church."

He saw the lure, despite the fog of pain. "Bullshit. Zeke wanted to get away; we all knew that. And if your goons hadn't hog-tied him the first time he tried to leave, maybe none of this would have happened."

"What has happened, Carson?" The question was disarmingly polite.

Carson shrugged his stiffening shoulders. "You're the ones saying Zeke's still alive. You tell me."

Torrie stood abruptly. Carson's windbreaker, headset, transceiver, and pin were laid out on a low table of sand-blasted glass. The security chief picked up the insignia, tossing it into the air, and caught it, his stumpy fingers closing over the silver wings. "So who's been helping you?"

Carson ignored the question.

"You realize that we'll find out who it is, and when we do, he'll sell you out to save himself. Or is it a she?" Torrie replaced the pin. "Unless . . ." He returned to his seat, letting the invitation hang there.

Carson ignored him again, sliding his gaze to the window, where the sky was blushing. He wondered how long he'd been unconscious. And if it had been long enough for Vestala to come up with a plan.

The security chief's phone beeped. When he answered, a shadow of something—annoyance maybe— masked his face, then he said, "Send him in."

The door clicked. A few footsteps as the newcomer crossed the marble foyer, then only the whisper of his clothes. He entered Carson's field of vision from the right. Alden looked ready for the cameras in his pressed navy suit of fine worsted wool. He stopped when he saw Carson's temple, and in an abrupt tone, asked, "What caused that?"

Torrie said, "Don't worry about it. We got him. That's what's important."

Alden's pale round face swiveled toward the security chief, then back to Carson. "At least remove the manacles."

Carson glanced at Torrie. The shadow was back.

"He's dangerous, Alden. I have a responsibility."

"Yes. And I'm quite certain you can fulfill it without Carson being handcuffed. Please remove them." When the security chief made no effort to comply, Alden said, "If you don't do it, I'll find someone who will."

Torrie stood, tension showing around his mouth, but he unlocked the cuffs. Carson brought his arms to his sides, shaking them, and giving Alden a small, appreciative smile which the priest didn't return. Instead, he took the low-backed chair, crossing his legs and clasping his hands around his knee.

The priest said, "I'd very much like to know where you've been, Carson." His eyes were small, bright sapphires set in the faded face.

Torrie stood off to one side, fiddling with the cuffs. He pocketed the steel bracelets and lowered himself onto the arm of a couch slipcovered in white linen. "Mr. McCullough hasn't been very talkative."

Carson glanced at the security chief, then down to the rug.

The priest caught the hint. "I'd like to speak to Carson alone," he said.

"Can't let you do that, Alden. Least not with him unrestrained."

The priest turned to look at the younger man. "I

appreciate that he is your prisoner, but he is also Ezekiel's liaison, and there are issues at hand which exceed even ICARUS's jurisdiction."

"Be reasonable, Alden. You know the charges against McCullough."

Pause. Then the priest countered, "Charges which I will publicly dispute unless you cooperate, Torrington. Now which is it going to be?"

The security chief's left hand squeezed into a fist. He stood up stiffly, gaze riveted on the priest's face. For a moment, Carson wondered if he would swing.

Alden met his glare, unintimidated. "And we'll have our chat in my apartment. Come with me, Carson."

Each step sent an aftershock of pain through Carson's temple, but Alden was already opening the door. The priest waved the guards aside, and proceeded, unhurried, down the corridor. Carson followed, averting his gaze from the open arches that circled the empty birdcage. He heard Torrie bark an order, but no one interfered with them.

Alden manually latched the door to his suite, then faced him, dark blue eyes unreadable. They stood in a square foyer, under a welcoming copper lamp.

"I didn't kidnap them," Carson said, feeling obligated to speak. "The Seraphim left on their own. Even Zeke."

"And what of Mr. Chen?"

"They drugged him and—"

"Sedated."

"*Drugged,* Alden. He was strapped to a bed. Did you know that?" No answer. He continued, "I was rescuing Harry. He's a prisoner, him and the Seraphim. The others left because Harry told them to."

"We are not keeping anyone prisoner. And certainly not our Lord and his host of angels." The words lacked the priest's usual conviction.

Carson said, "You aren't. But ICARUS—" A sudden sinking feeling accompanied by a question stopped him. Had the whole confrontation been for his benefit, to get him to talk? He eyed the priest suspiciously. "I suppose Torrie's listening in?"

The answer was quick and firm. "No. That is why I brought you here: This apartment is not bugged. I've taken my own precautions to ensure that." When Carson said nothing, the priest added, "I am not pleased with Torrington's handling of this affair."

Carson weighed his options and decided to go for it. "I've found out some things since last weekend. ICARUS is using you and the Party to keep tabs on the Seraphim. The Special Visitor status is a sham."

"That may be, Carson. But God sees all. They too shall be judged—"

He blurted it. "By whom, Alden? Harry Chen isn't God."

He expected anger, but there was none. Instead, the priest's gaze searched his face, as if he might find something written there. At last, Alden gestured to the living area, saying, "Then come. Sit. And tell me what you've found."

Carson sank into a leather club chair, its comfort slightly diminishing the throbs in his skull. The priest listened with bowed head as he repeated Vestala's explanation. Occasionally, Alden raised his gaze to study him with that same searching look. He's unsure, Carson guessed. A week with Harry would shake even a saint's faith.

When he finished, Alden asked, "But how can you be certain, Carson, that this is not the devil leading you astray?"

It wasn't a question he wanted to answer, but he did, with surprising ease. "Well, if Michael is the devil, then Harry Chen is God. I prefer the alternative."

"That the Seraphim are not angels? That our salvation is yet to come?" His tone was defeated.

Carson empathized with the priest's pain. He told him gently, "I don't know, Alden. I couldn't get a straight answer on that. But if it helps, think of this as a test of faith. If you really believe in God, then you have to believe that somehow the Seraphim are part of his grand design."

"Is that what you believe, Carson?"

The question caught him off guard. He'd been trying to make the explanation palatable for the priest. But thinking about it, he said, "Yeah. I guess that's one reason I went with Zeke."

Alden nodded. His hands trembled against the blue wool trousers. "I think we have lost sight of that grand design, Carson. We have been impudent, and now we must pay the price." His face creased in a sad smile as he got to his feet. "Come. Let us speak with Mr. Chen."

The uniformed guards outside Zeke's door wouldn't let them pass.

Alden didn't argue. "Torrington," he said, into his phone, "Carson and I need to speak with Harry Chen." Pause, then, "My previous statement applies."

A minute later, the door opened. Torrie stood there, anger burning his sallow skin. Alden brushed past, and Carson followed. Entering the living area in daylight, he saw his one gift to Zeke, an acrylic-encased moon rock, resting on a maple console. Once, humankind would have considered it a little piece of heaven. Zeke had appreciated the irony. And maybe that was his problem, Carson thought, that he *could* see the irony.

Well, now he would give the Seraph a better gift.

Maartens was posted at the bedroom door, his bleached blue eyes targeting them as they approached.

Carson wished he felt Alden's apparent calm. Could

it be this easy, he wondered. March in, have a talk with Harry, explain the problem. What then, a press conference? "Sorry, folks, our mistake. God isn't back after all."

The bed linens were pure white, the wrought-iron four-poster centered in an expanse of oyster carpeting over pickled wood. Chen lay there, looking pretty much the same as when Carson had sneaked in earlier that morning. Imogene now sat on the far side, facing the door. At the window to her right, Juan Perez turned from a view of striated clouds and saw them, his face registering recognition, nothing more.

"He is sleeping," Imogene said. Her medical case rested on the nightstand next to her. The litter of syringes and vials was gone. So was the respirator.

At the bedside, Alden studied Chen's placid face. Then he pushed away the coverlet, untied Chen's left wrist, and folded the messiah's limp hand around his own. "Harry," he said, stooping over. "Harry, do you hear me?"

Chen's eyelids fluttered.

Alden perched on the edge of the mattress. "Harry, I need you to wake up now."

Chen muttered something.

"Carson . . ." The priest tilted his head toward Imogene.

Carson went around the bed and unlashed Chen's right hand. He had to squeeze in front of the physician and her cold, disapproving stare. "Harry," he said, "wake up." He almost pitied Chen, king of the Angels, soon to be dethroned.

Chen blinked. Once. Twice. Then his eyes stayed open. Groggily, "Wha'?"

"It's all right, my son," Alden said, patting the messiah's hand.

Chen twisted free. "Carson? Shit, what are you . . ."

He propped himself up on his elbows, brow furrowing. His gaze darted around the room. The confusion narrowed into recollection, then anger. "You? I remember—"

Struggling to his feet, he towered over them in his white pants and bare chest, hair wild and arms waving. *You're going to hell, all of you,* he shouted with his mouth and his mind. *Think you can lock me up? Don't you know who I am?*

Carson had his hands over his ears, a futile gesture. He could feel Chen's rage, like he had yesterday on the dock. It entered at his bruised temple and vibrated his thoughts into nothingness. Fighting for language, he yelled, "Just listen, Harry! Just for a minute!"

Chen continued his tirade, interrupting himself with ineloquent strings of profanity. He kicked at Torrie who was trying to get to him around the priest. Maartens hovered in the door, as if Chen's fury repelled him. Imogene fumbled with a syringe. Alden was begging him to stop.

Chen did. Seemingly without cause, his rage gave way to mirth. Smug chuckles erupted into raucous laughter. He looked down at them, his eyes slitted under the epicanthic folds.

Carson's relief at the assault's sudden termination was replaced almost immediately by fear. He was in the *Freak Follies,* peering up at Chen from that same awful perspective as when the virtual messiah had dwarfed a shrinking balloon-Earth. Tearing his gaze away, Carson saw Alden's blanched face, Torrie's appalled stare.

And then the room darkened. Something crashed, followed by a razoring noise and a blast of cold air.

Oh my God, Carson thought. It's too late. He heard an ominous sound carrying in on the ice wind, like the beating of giant wings.

Torrie and Alden's heads turned in unison, horror and realization dawning on their faces.

All the bats of hell, Carson thought. And in slow motion, he pivoted, following their sight . . .

To the smashed, opened window, where Gabriel crouched, naked except for boxer shorts, white hair flying about his face, eyes like bullets, wings still pounding, and grasped in his right hand, the long, gleaming blade of Vestala's rapier.

The Seraph was in the room and to the bed before Imogene screamed, his brothers coming through the portal after him. Carson tripped over the doctor and fell into their path. They seemed a single creature to him now, all snow-wings and diamond-hard eyes. Seraphim of the ancient prophets' acid dreams.

He scrambled on all fours away from *it*, toward the wall.

Hypocritical assholes! Drug me now!

Fingers closed around Carson's arm. "Go!" the Cuban ordered, pulling him to his feet. Juan pressed something small and sharp into his hand. A silver pin.

Chen's face bobbed above the thing of wings and eyes. The door was open. Carson inched toward it. Near, and he saw Gabriel holding Maartens and Torrie at bay with poised sword. Uriel, dark as a shadow, plucked a gun from inside the guard's jacket.

"Now be reasonable, Chen," the security chief said, backing toward the corner already occupied by Alden.

On your knees. Chen danced over the pristine sheets. *Beg my forgiveness.*

Torrie's left hand whipped his pistol from its sling. Carson froze.

Torrie brought the gun up, gaze riveted on the Seraph's blade. "I don't want to do this, Chen. Tell Gabe to put it down."

Chen shrieked, *How dare you?*

Alden was behind Torrie and Maartens. He scooted along the wall, trying to get around them. "Please, stop this! *You must listen!*"

Torrie's left thumb twitched, releasing the safety.

Gabriel commanded, "You will not harm him." He closed his other hand around the gilded hilt and took a meaningful step forward. Sinuous muscle bulged under the pale skin.

"Stop this!" Alden cried, dodging between them.

Pop. The priest convulsed, then straightened, crimson staining the torn back of his navy jacket. Alden collapsed as Gabriel's blade swung and connected: *crunch.* Torrie's pistol skidded across the oak floor. The security chief reeled backward, his empty left hand dangling from his wrist like a child's mitten, blood spurting over a jag of white bone.

Carson had seen enough. He ran blind from the room, navigating by memory. It didn't include the two uniformed guards. One got him from behind in a vicious embrace. He pitched forward, bent double, hoisting the man off his feet. Carson took three staggering steps that way, and then heaved to one side with all his strength. They flipped, the guard's head hitting the floor with a sickening *crack.* His arms went limp. Up, Carson lunged for the suite's entrance.

"Call for medics!" It was the Cuban. A bullet splintered the wood as Carson flung the door open. "Do it! I'm after him."

Carson dashed into the corridor, on legs that felt like they would snap off at the hip. The pin bit into his palm. Stairs, he thought, and his legs were already taking him there. Shouts as the door clicked open for him. *Pop.* Another bullet missed. He didn't look to see who was shooting. Down the steps, two at a time. He heard footsteps pound overhead. On the landing, he glanced up and saw the Cuban's sharp face.

Three flights to go. Sweat drenched his thin green T-shirt. The pain in his temple was red, misting his vision. He made the executive floor, remembering his earlier capture as Juan's pin released the lock. And then he saw it: The Cuban had followed as a decoy. Without his pin, the security system would log him as the intruder, not Carson.

The elevator doors took an eternity to open, but the descent to the port was longer. It wasn't until he exited the vestibule and saw, at the end of the hall, a cluster of officials around the lobby's reception kiosk, that he realized sneaking out was going to be a big problem. It was morning, the offices and restricted areas were occupied, and he had no hood. Not even a pair of sunglasses. He opted for the anonymity of the public spaces. Walking fast, one hand raised to shield his bruised temple and face, he followed the lobby wall to the escalators.

Chen's psychic barrage had ceased—he couldn't remember when—but that didn't matter to the panicked crowd on the concourse. They ignored the masculine voice coming over the PA with its assurances that there was no danger. A chorus of terrified wails and shouts echoed off the high ceiling. They moved in sudden eddies, streaming for the doors, or just circling. "It's the end, the end!" one woman screamed from atop a ticket counter. A pair of uniformed guards were trying to revive an old man who'd collapsed amid the mess of luggage, clothing, and trampled food. As Carson sidestepped the frightened pilgrims and tourists, it occurred to him they had no way of knowing Chen's outburst wasn't directed at them.

The lift to the terminal ejected a full load of hysterical passengers. He rode down alone, smelling the lingering scent of their fear. When the doors opened, the surging mob nearly crushed him. Tenth anniversary weekend, and the pilgrims had come in record numbers for the Rising-site baptism boats. He fought his way out of the lift and into the relative calm beyond. Those who had stayed were singing and praying. He threaded his way toward the exit.

All but one pair of dockside doors were locked, and that was flanked by port security. An officer raised his bullhorn, announcing, "Folks, everything is under control. We are continuing our scheduled runs. This is the last call for the 7:50 departure. The 8:15 will now begin boarding. Those with tickets, please proceed to dock C."

A large group locked arms, and still singing, moved en masse toward the exit. The hymn was "Our Lord Awaits Us." Carson knew it by heart. Mouthing the words, he sidled up to them.

The pilgrims funneled out the door. Carson was eight or ten bodies back when he saw one of the guards listening intently to something coming over his receiver. The man shouted to his partner and got a nod of acknowledgment. They both moved closer to the pilgrims, their eyes scanning the crowd.

"One at a time, folks, one at a time."

Carson bowed his head and wormed toward the center. He was almost out.

The guard shouted over the hymn's chorus, "You in the green T-shirt!"

Carson didn't look up. The threshold was steps away, the crowd too tight for him to turn back.

The guard ordered, "Hold it, folks. Hold on a second."

He sensed the crush of bodies parting to his right.

"You in the green T-shirt—stop!"

Carson shoved forward and out the door. The berth where Vestala had dropped him was down an empty, exposed stretch of walkway. He broke free of the singing pilgrims and ran toward the baptism boats instead.

The 7:50 was sounding its horn as he charged down dock C. The 8:15 was moored on the other side, and the first passengers were already boarding. Carson ran past. A dockhand in crisp whites saw him and shouted, "Sorry, fella, she's outa here."

He caught up with the 7:50 as it cleared the landing. The gangway was gated with a net of orange straps. Pure impulse, he leapt. For an instant he was over the churning water, then his foot caught in the gate, and he flew forward, palms tearing on the deck's sandpaper surface, legs twisted painfully into the net. Looking back, he saw someone in the hunter green uniform of port security run up the dock and shoulder his way onto the other boat.

As Carson unhooked the net, freeing his legs, a murmur rose, swelling to shouts and cries of hallelujah. Limping into the cabin, he saw passengers crowding wide windows that showed clouds pulled like wool over a deepening blue sky. And something else. He squinted at the strange sight.

To the west, over the indigo waves, a small flock of Seraphim held close formation. They flew low, weighted by their burden.

The boat tipped alarmingly as the captain's amplified voice entreated, "Folks, please move away from port." But the pilgrims paid no heed.

Beside him, an incredulous whisper: "They're carrying someone."

He stared at the synchronized wings, the limp form dangling below them by its arms and legs.

Prey of angels.

Harry Chen.

Fifteen

He watched as the Seraphim dipped toward the ocean and disappeared from view. The baptism boat was still lopsided, the pilgrims still loud in their expressions of shock and awe. "Oh my God, where did they go?" someone asked, horrified. "Do you think they *drowned*?"

Carson took a seat, painfully aware now of his twisted ankle. The Seapod's low deck wouldn't be visible at this distance, he reasoned, but they had to be on board. It was a thirty-minute ride to the Sea Station Visitors Center. Party security might be waiting for him, but short of jumping ship, there wasn't much he could do. At least it wasn't his job anymore; Vestala could explain things to Harry.

Shaking from cold, exertion, and nerves, Carson hugged himself, closing his eyes, and saw Alden fall, a crimson hole in his back. His lids popped open, hot saline pooling in the corners. Dead, he thought. Alden's dead. Maybe Torrie, too. Maybe even Harry.

From a speaker, the captain's voice told them, "Folks, I've just been in contact with Herald Party headquarters. In an hour or so, they'll be making an announcement. No word yet what it's about, though I think *we've* all got an idea."

The pilgrims began to sing.

Carson. Chen's soundless voice. Apparently God wasn't dead yet.

I see you, man. Hang tight. We're gonna meet you there. Pause, then, *Guess I showed them, huh? I mean it's my decision, right? Life and death and all that. Like I'm God, right? Shit, man, I wish you could answer me.*

Carson buried his face in his hands, thinking: And when I do, Harry, what then?

Twenty minutes later, Chen said, *Almost there, man. I gotta tell you something: I hear them. They're all calling out to me. I hear their prayers! Can't fucking believe it. Weirdest thing, too. Used to wonder about that when we were kids. I used to wonder how God could hear everyone at once. 'Course no one said nothin' 'bout him actually listening. Ha.*

Or about him talking back, Carson added to himself, trying to make light of Chen's latest revelation. The visitors center was ahead. With its Plexiglas dome, it looked like a flying saucer that had landed on the ocean, except for the Rising anniversary flags snapping at the tops of their poles. The boat slowed, aiming for one of the covered docking bays. Passengers were already lining up at the gangway to disembark. "A miracle awaits us," someone shouted, eliciting a ragged cheer in response.

A young woman—a freckled brunette in a pale blue uniform—waited on the landing as they coasted into the bay. The captain's disembodied voice announced, "Welcome to the Sea Station, folks. Sarah will be your acolyte today. It's been our pleasure to bring you here, and we'll be back to pick you up in two hours. Until then, God bless."

Carson shuffled off the boat after the others, into dank air that smelled of exhaust.

"Welcome, pilgrims," Sarah said into her headset's

microphone. "It's a great day to be saved!" The group cheered. Carson felt trapped.

She would be taking them to the changing rooms, she explained, where they could don their baptismal robes, and then to the chapel for prayer. After that, they would descend to the old air lock, now a font in which their sins would be cleansed by the holy water from which God's own angels had risen. She added, "If anyone has not come for baptism, then you may take the escalator to the main deck."

The main deck reminded him of the port terminal: souvenir stands, waiting lounges, and snack counters, plus a walk-in display on the eggs and their inhabitants. More banners, too. It was crowded and loud. The True Believers' latest hit rang over the PA. He scanned for guards and, finding none nearby, took another escalator up to the dome. Doors there exited to a catwalk that circled the Plexi bubble. From this vantage, with the sea breeze numbing his face and evaporating the nervous sweat under his arms, he studied the surrounding water. Another baptism boat approached from the direction of Ocean City. He saw a Japanese fishing fleet to the west, heading toward one of the outlying processing plants. No sign of the *Bauhaus*. Carson leaned both elbows on the railing, taking the weight off his bad ankle. Perhaps Vestala had thought better of it. If they didn't come for him, he'd have to risk the ride back to port.

I am coming.

The intrusion was almost welcome. Good, Harry, he thought, straightening up. Now where do I meet you?

I am coming to answer your prayers.

Harry, just . . . The pilgrims near him weren't chattering. He turned, saw their wide, awe-stricken eyes. A child screamed.

Chen wasn't speaking just to him.

ICARUS tried to stop me. They failed, man, 'cause I've got a host of angels on my side. Ha. Let them try to stop me now. Y'all know what I'm saying, don't you? I heard your prayers, and I'm on the way. Is that God or what?

They'd fallen to their knees, some of them. One lady wept; another fainted. The catwalk was suddenly flooded with people, pressing to the rail.

Carson held his ground, waiting.

They burst from the Atlantic, twenty meters or so to the northwest. White feathers glistened in morning sun as the five Seraphim hovered above the ocean. Each held a rope that disappeared beneath the waves. And then their wings pulsed faster and the ropes pulled taut.

Chen rose puppetlike from the sea, two lines around each wrist and one binding his chest. When he was vertical, with arms stretched overhead and legs just clear of the surface, the Seraphim flew toward the station, the messiah hanging below them, feet pedaling the water, kicking up spray that flashed rainbows before falling to white froth. The angels' wet pewter skin had a molten, computer-generated quality in the sunlight, and as Carson watched them advance with their bizarre marionette, he felt, once again, like he was in the *Freak Follies*.

The pilgrims piled up against the rail, screaming. Chen neared the edge of the station, and the Seraphim climbed higher into the sky, the sound of their powerful wings sickeningly familiar. Carson fought nausea and the crush as the messiah ascended to the level of the catwalk. He dangled there, dripping wet, purple glasses fogged, as a hundred pairs of arms reached for their god. Then the pilgrims had him and they pulled Chen aboard. He disappeared into the crowd.

The Seraphim dropped their ropes and alighted on

the railing, one landing centimeters away. The throng nearby turned and, like one body, slammed into him as they went for the angel. Gasping, Carson was thrown at the Seraph's feet. He looked up into Gabriel's hard face. No sword, just soaked boxers and bare skin.

No blood, either, Carson realized.

The waters had washed the angel clean.

He was still pinned against the railing when the drone of a helijet reached him through the pilgrims' deafening screams. Squinting, he saw that it was blue with a silver-wing insignia. Herald Party markings. The aircraft passed overhead, then circled toward the landing pad on the station's far side.

Chen's voice thundered in his mind. *The ICARUS bastards are here. They've come for me, just like when the Romans came for Christ. Y'all gonna put up with it this time?*

It was as if someone had turned down the volume on the crowd.

I'm not going with those bastards. They're liars. Liars! Y'all hear me? You gonna let them crucify another god?

Chen must have said the magic word. The crowd roared, the noise gradually resolving into a mantra: No.

Then let's go show 'em.

Chanting their defiance, the pilgrims poured back into the observation dome, carrying Chen and the Seraphim aloft, like heroes returning from war. When he had room to move, Carson found his legs were shaking and he could barely stand. Limping along the rail, he went inside.

Chen commanded, *Put us down here.* The messiah climbed onto a tier of monitors that displayed actual footage of the Rising. *Some of you guard outside. The rest go below.* Chen waved his arms, gesturing the telepathic commands. The Seraphim closed ranks around him as the crowd obediently dispersed.

World, you are the witness. This is your god, Harry Chen, coming to you live from the Sea Station. Chen paced the monitors in bare feet, lips forming his words. *The ICARUS bastards are at the gate. They drugged me. They tied me up. That's the establishment for you, man. Typical.*

But it's too late. I'm free. I'm here with my angels, and they can't stop me. It's Judgment Day, man, in a major sort of way.

Carson rested against a panel of Plexi, waiting for the pilgrims to clear the dome. Chen's speech was stoking his headache. Looking out, he saw the helijet lower itself onto the center of the square landing pad. The first wave of pilgrims raced across the tarmac and surrounded the aircraft. A group on the catwalk, going to watch, blocked his view.

The observation deck had emptied. He crossed to stand before the messiah and his honor guard of angels. The five Seraphim regarded Carson with clinical detachment. They were almost naked in their wet white boxers. Chen was bare-chested as well, and equally exposed in cotton drawstring pants.

He stopped pacing and peered down at Carson. "Hey, man," he said. "I almost forgot you were here."

"Well, I didn't forget you," Carson said, his voice cracking. "And Harry—we *really* need to talk."

Chen said, "It can wait." His eyes lost their focus.

"No, it can't." He took one step forward, and Gabriel's hand caught his shoulder, stopping him. The Seraph's touch sent a chill down his spine. "Harry, please. It's the whole reason Vestala and I came for you. I risked my life, you know?"

Chen saw him again. "Man, that lady is weird. Didn't like the vibes I got off her *at all*. And she was a real pain in the ass about giving me the rope. Wanted to keep us cooped up on that stinking sub. No fucking way."

Carson backed to a row of plastic chairs and sat, drawing in a deep breath. "Harry, I have to tell you this before ICARUS gets up here, so please, just—"

Chen sneered, "They ain't coming up here. Look around, man. I've got an army on my side now. Not to mention these guys." He pointed at Gabriel, saying half to himself, "Fuckers should've known better."

Blood coursed to Carson's face. The anger encased him, like an exoskeleton of loathing and rage. His armor still held. Raising his voice, he asked, "What about Zeke?"

Chen's eyes narrowed behind the glasses. "What about him?"

"He's not with you. Don't you want to know why?" He played his ace. "I know where he is, Harry. Do you?"

Chen's jaw worked.

"Let's talk, Harry. Just give me a few minutes."

Chen said coldly, "I don't need you, Carson," but his eyes held their focus.

Carson glanced at the Seraphim. "All of you should hear this," he said. It made him nervous to address them directly.

They looked askance at Chen, but the messiah didn't notice.

Carson plunged in. "ICARUS lied to the world. There was a seventh egg. They dissected it right after it splashed down."

The Seraphim betrayed little emotion, if any. Only Raphael's gentle face showed outright interest.

He went on. "They killed one of them, Harry. And

then some geneticists from old Red China took the DNA in secret. They gene-spliced a human embryo. And a baby—well, a baby was born, Harry. You."

Chen was smiling. Carson stared at him, confused.

"Sure," Chen said, still smiling. He looked pleased. "Told you it was immaculate conception, didn't I?"

Carson clenched his teeth for self-control. "Harry, I'm telling you that you're not God! Don't you get it? You were an experiment, an illegal genetic experiment that got lost during the revolution." He pointed at the Seraphim. "The only reason they think you're God is because you were born first."

Chen shook his head. "No, man. That doesn't matter."

"Yes, it does!" He was yelling. "You shouldn't ever have been born. I mean, someone like you, your DNA. They fucked with nature, Harry, and here you are. But you're not God!"

Carson, don't piss me off.

"Stop that shit!" He appealed to the Seraphim. "Don't you see it? He's a mistake!" His voice choked off. This day had been too much.

Gabriel spoke. "How would you know what is intended and what is not, Carson? The methods of the Almighty that return his son to walk amongst you? Do you know the mind of God, Carson?"

He saw again the sword recoiling, laced with blood. "None of us do," he screamed, managing to stand. "Except maybe Michael. Know who he is, Harry? The seventh Seraphim. He's not the devil; he's the seventh Seraphim! Why don't you ask him about intent, huh Gabriel?"

Michael? The rat tail twitched. *I don't have to listen to this shit.*

The Seraphim advanced and strong hands grasped

his arms, dragging him forward. He blinked up at Chen's face, which was twisted with scorn.

You're a failure, know that, Carson? A failure! And you're jealous, man. It's written all over your pathetic face.

"Maybe I am, Harry, so you go on, start a few wars. Maybe you'll even manage to end the world. But if I'm right, then *you'll* be the one rotting in hell!" He screamed the last words as the Seraphim hauled him out the catwalk doors, past the shocked pilgrims, who backed away along the curve of the dome.

They surrounded him, and more strong hands grasped his ankles, lifting him up. Again he heard the terrible beating of wings, but this time from the center of the thing, where crosswinds buffeted his bruised face. His limbs wrenched at their sockets. Airborne. Through the blur of feathers, he saw golden sun rays and flashes of azure sky. Their hold burned his skin. Searing pain lanced his shoulders.

There's no one to hear your prayers, Carson, no one but me!

And then the hands released him. He fell, away from the light and the angels, cloud-strewn heavens rushing by.

The sea hit him, a hundred lashes. He sank into the frigid darkness, salt water filling his mouth, consciousness sliding like a droplet on a pane of glass.

One thought left: *Up.*

He broke the surface, choking, blind. Coughing and gagging, he spit out most of the seawater and regained some sight. His eyes stung, but he made out the station. Hard to judge distance over the tossing waves; he thought he could swim it. If he didn't freeze up first. Already he was losing sensation below his waist. He sensed as much as felt the dogged treading motion of his legs. Reaching with his arms, he chopped at the water, taking in more mouthfuls. Each cough seared his throat. The pants and T-shirt dragged him down, but he didn't have the motor control to strip them off. He heard the drone of another helijet. His water-logged ears couldn't peg the direction, and it was too hard to see.

Reach, chop, cough, kick. His teeth chattered uncontrollably. The horn blared twice before the sound registered and he turned his head. The tall hull of a baptism boat cut the waves, clipping toward him. He saw someone in white uniform leaning over the bow, orange flotation donut in his hands. The deck was packed with people.

He stopped swimming and watched his rescuers approach. As the vessel slowed, its engines growling into reverse, it occurred to Carson that rescue meant capture.

The deckhand heaved the donut. It sailed over the waves toward him.

And then he was under again, pulled back like a babe into the womb. There was the vaguest awareness that something had him around the legs. His eyes opened to stinging blue. A shadow, below. He told his body to kick free, unsure whether it obeyed.

Down, still going down. Silent liquid scream. Bead of water sliding into blackness.

Gone.

Sixteen

He had no body.

Floating, he thought: I'm dead, but I'm not in hell. This isn't so bad.

Warmth. Someone was there. Michael? No, not Michael. Miriam. She was crying. He tasted her tears. Her wet mouth closed over his, leechlike.

But he didn't have a mouth—

Carson convulsed forward, seawater bubbling up through his pickled lips. His body was back with a vengeance.

Whoever it was, pulled away.

A voice, familiar, but the words made no sense. Taste of vomit.

And then floating.

Carson, wake up.

No, Harry, not again. Leave me alone. He burrowed back into his dream.

"Carson, I must insist. Open your eyes."

The deep, throaty voice wasn't inside his head. There wasn't room for it. His skull was filled with hot sand. The rest of his body had been crushed in a compactor. He was two-dimensional, a figure of pressed lead between warm sheets.

"Open your eyes, Carson."

He still had those. The lids pulled apart like chewing

gum. His head was turned to one side and he was looking at a creased white trouser leg. Raising his gaze, he saw it belonged to a stocky old man in a navy blazer with shining brass buttons and a pocket square of red silk. He wore a white captain's hat decorated with gold braid. Striking green eyes watched Carson intently from under the visor.

"Good boy. Here." The man lifted a glass of water with a carefully manicured hand and held it to his lips. He smelled smoke and cloves, but the water tasted of salt. Or maybe his mouth did. Carson was suddenly aware of his empty stomach. "Nearly lost you in the drink, old chap, but all's well that ends. Well . . ."

Carson peered up at him, then croaked, "You look familiar."

The man pursed his lips, colorless eyebrows disappearing under the hat's brim. Firelight danced across his pale face. Carson realized it was coming from a fake torch mounted on the wall. The wall itself was trompe l'oeil, painted with orchids and overgrown tropical plants whose canopy of leaves covered the low ceiling. At the head of the bed, which took up most of the small room, mosquito netting cascaded to the floor. He noticed a subtle rocking motion.

Painfully turning his face back to the man, Carson demanded, "Who are you? And where am I?"

"Aboard the *Sea Safari*."

He didn't remember a yacht. "I drowned . . ."

"Almost drowned. My sea dog rescued you."

Sea dog? Carson stared into the green eyes. Something familiar, the smell, the voice— "Vestala?" It was the same face, without the gaudy mask. "You *are* Vestala."

"Was, dear boy. And no longer."

It hurt, but he propped himself up on an elbow.

"What happened back there? And what happened to you?"

"My loyal sea dog rescued you, Carson. Dived out the air lock and snatched you—"

"Nearly killed me, is more like it. But this isn't the *Bauhaus.*"

"Well, I'm glad to see your powers of observation are keen as ever. We've had a change of venue since you were expelled from paradise. I am now a man of leisure, and this is my private craft. At least for the month. That was the minimum rental. Anyway, you've been out a good twelve hours, dear boy, and much has happen—what is it, Carson?"

He sat up, clutching the black satin sheet to his hips. Everything hurt. "*Who* the hell are you? *What* the hell are you? Some kind of eccentric billionaire with nothing better to do than get me killed? What about all that psychic mumbo jumbo? That just part of the act? In the trash now with good old ViVi?" Glaring at her through the wavering haze of pain, he said, "I want the truth. All of it."

"Well, I suppose you do deserve an answer." Vestala stood up and removed the captain's hat. Underneath, her hair was reddish gray and tufted, like feathers. Her green eyes glowed in the false firelight, and Carson was reminded more than ever of an owl. Fat coarsened the once-delicate features, but still—

"Allow me to introduce myself." Vestala executed a courtly bow in the cramped space of the cabin.

He knew that birdlike face and archaic gesture. "I've seen you before. You're—"

"*Précisément,*" the androgyne said. "I am Déjà Vu."

Carson gawked. Of course he knew that face; it had ghosted the tabloids ever since the psychic's presumed drowning a few days before the Rising.

Vu replaced his cap and pulled the yellow silk pouch

from a pocket of his immaculate trousers. Sitting down, he proceeded to roll a cigarette on the bamboo nightstand. "Oh do shut your mouth, Carson, or something nasty might fly in." The nimble fingers smoothed white tissue into a perfect cylinder. "I suppose you want to know why," Vu said, without looking at him.

"That would be a good start." He leaned back against the pillows, pulling the covers up.

Vu twisted the cigarette into its holder. The lighter clicked, and the psychic took a long drag, then exhaled over one shoulder. "It's a bitch coming out after all these years." He crossed his legs. "It's as much a curse as a gift, you know. The third eye." He tapped his forehead for emphasis. "Half the world doesn't believe you. Sometimes you don't believe yourself."

"I'd say you were well compensated."

"I made an obscene amount of money," Vu acknowledged. "Desperate times, they were. Are." He blew out another cloud of smoke. "Fear makes for easy prey. And I'm good. Probably the best ever, at least of those who've come forward. But even then, it's still touch-and-go. You see, there's no real control. The voices, visions—whatever—are just *there*. And when they're not, they're not. I have always found that rather . . . disconcerting." He paused for a long inhale. The green eyes focused somewhere across the room. "I felt used, Carson." Exhale. "Yes, I think I did." The gaze met his. "Much as you have, I'd imagine. A puppet. And one wonders what sort of god is pulling the strings."

"Where does Michael come in?"

Vu went on as if he hadn't spoken. "You see, I knew. I knew as soon as the eggs arrived. And I knew about the dissection."

Carson stared.

"My own private preview of the Rising, if you will. I knew what they were and what ICARUS had done, but I said nothing." He shrugged and raised the cigarette to his lips.

Carson caught Vu's wrist.

"Let go, Carson. I bruise easily."

He didn't. Liquid nitrogen filled his veins. Frozen, crystallized, the realization struck him like a tuning fork, setting up a harmonic resonance of shattering grief and rage. "My father died." He heard the vibrations in his own voice. "My father died because of that hysteria and *you knew*." His arm was shaking. The cigarette dropped into Vu's lap.

The psychic snatched it with his free hand, but not before it burned a brown hole in his trousers. "Let go of my wrist, Carson." Vu tried unsuccessfully to pry his fingers loose.

His breath came short and fast. "I hated him for letting it happen. But it wasn't God." He yanked Vu down and almost gasped the words: *"It was you."*

The psychic's jaw quivered. Fire shadows tongued the pale face. "I can't close that wound, Carson. I can't bring you back to life."

"You're not even sorry!"

"Sorry enough that I'm here now. I don't have to be." Still bent forward, the psychic added, "I never wanted to save the world. When the opportunity was tossed into my lap, I tossed it back. But fate is a harsh mistress, not easily denied. If there is a God, I'll answer to him or her, not to you."

Carson's grip relaxed, leaving white finger marks. "Get out."

As Vu left, a column of ash broke from the cigarette and fell like gray snow.

Later, Poodle brought him food and his clothing. The man-dog wore a new jogging suit of shiny green synthetics.

Carson eyed the clothes piled at the foot of the bed. Vu's past didn't change the present. There was still Chen, conspicuous by his silence, and the rest of it. He had too many questions that needed answers.

He was stiff and bruised, but nothing felt broken. He dressed and then found Vu above, in the yacht's living room. The psychic was at one end of a pink raw-silk couch, feet resting on a small elephant carved from teak. He held a goblet of red wine.

Carson went to the window, curtained with drapes of silk hanging from a long ceremonial spear. He pushed the fabric aside. The O.C. skyline glittered in the distance. A crescent moon hung low over the Herald Tower.

Without turning around, he asked, "What happened to the *Bauhaus*?"

"Nothing," Vu answered. "But it was getting too risky. Miriam, Mr. Chen, the Seraphim—they'd all been aboard and seen poor ViVi. And ICARUS is bound to think of a submarine. I thought it best that we abandon ship for a bit."

"You shouldn't have given Gabriel the sword."

"I didn't. He took it."

Carson turned around, forcing himself to look at Vu.

The psychic must have read the accusation in his face. He put the goblet down. "Yes, I know what he did with it."

"That's another death on your head."

Vu's tone was resigned. "Maybe so. You sent them to me. They wanted to rescue Chen, and I timed it so you'd have a chance at escape. Quick thinking on Mr. Perez's part, giving you the pin. The Seraphim brought Chen back, but he wouldn't listen to reason. He's much stronger. I was concerned he'd sense Michael's presence. As it was, he heard the pilgrims, and egomania got the better of him.''

Carson shoved his hands into his pockets. "I told him about the dissection and the experiment. He thinks it just proves he's God. Called it immaculate conception. But when I brought up Michael—"

Vu flicked his fingers. It was Vestala's gesture without the magenta claws. "He had you baptized. I know. And it's a good thing Poodle is so proficient."

Irritated, he told him, "The point is, Harry didn't listen to me. And he definitely isn't going to listen to Michael. I tried to straighten him out, and he's more bent than ever." Carson's ankle hurt. He left the window and took a low curving chair with a tasseled, zebra-striped cushion. "So what's going on? Is he still at the visitors center?"

"Yes. Quite the standoff. They've shipped in a squad of ICARUS commandos from Powell Space Base. The local authorities weren't about to take on God, unaided. Of course, it's difficult to launch a surprise raid against someone who's omniscient. Mr. Chen has had a field day with it. He's been rambling on, lambasting the ICARUS bastards and proclaiming himself King." Vu wrinkled his nose in distaste.

"He's awfully quiet now."

"Makes one nervous after a spell, doesn't it? Amazing how quickly we adjust. Reality can be rather insistent that way." The androgyne sighed. "It's unfortunate you weren't more persuasive. He's problem enough as a living god, but if he dies with that delusion intact . . . Well, for all our sakes, I hope ICARUS doesn't shoot him."

"Why?" Carson snapped, letting the irritation mushroom.

"Because, like Michael, he's more than his body.

Killing him won't release his hold over the other Seraphim, it will just make him *really* pissed off.''

Carson tried to comprehend.

"You'll just give yourself a headache," Vu said, watching him. "If we could understand, we wouldn't be what we are. As it is, our vision is far too coarse to see that kind of truth." The psychic took a sip of wine, then added, "Except for Harry Chen and his magic purple glasses."

"So how do we stop him?"

Vu shrugged. "I must admit, it's looking rather grim. At the moment, Michael is occupied elsewhere. But I would guess—"

Carson's mushroom cloud of irritation was dispersing. Anger radiated underneath. He interrupted, "No, let me guess: You don't have a plan. Michael doesn't have a plan. I'm the one who's supposed to—"

Vu regarded him, head tilted to one side like an inquisitive bird.

"Forget it," he said. "Where's the vid?"

"Who are you going to call, Carson?"

"ICARUS. NewsNet. Senator Bloom. Anyone who'll listen."

"Not advisable. I've explained to—"

He cut Vu off. "I don't give a damn what you think is advisable!" The anger was volatile, a core of radioactive fury. "I don't think Michael's the one who wants this under wraps; I think it's you. I see now why we played it this way. Your way." Mimicking the androgyne, he said, "Hide in the shadows. Don't get involved. Know, but don't tell. Leave it to someone else to save the world." He stood. "Well, I'm someone else. You tossed me the ball; now we play by my rules. Either tell me where the phone is, or drop me off in O.C. and I'll find a booth!"

Vu's fingertips were pressed together, his head

bowed, as if he were praying. When the psychic looked up, Carson saw something new in the green eyes: fear.

Vu said softly, "I'm afraid the ball is out of your court, too."

"What's that supposed to mean?" Carson demanded, as his skin prickled. The hair on his arms was sticking straight out.

Vu bowed his head again.

"Answer me, damn it!"

The psychic only shuddered.

He doesn't have the answers, Carson.

The soundless voice came somehow from behind him. He turned to look without thinking about it. A life-size holograph of Harry Chen floated in front of the window. In his confused, first reaction, Carson glanced at the varnished floor, expecting a projection base. Chen twirled in slow motion, his bare feet dangling several centimeters above the wood planks, his arms extended horizontal. It was a pose perversely reminiscent of crucifixion.

Projection, Carson realized, but not a hologen. He stared. "Harry . . . oh my God."

Chen smiled. *Rad, huh?* He drifted across the room toward Carson, the image's resolution blurring, resolving, and blurring again. It was less luminous, more lifelike than a holograph, but still transparent. *I'm going to give you another chance, man.* Chen's lips moved, forming the words. *Come on back. You can still be my disciple.*

Carson glanced at Vu.

That old freak doesn't have the answers. Told you he did, hey Carson? Told you I was some kind of mistake. I ain't no mistake. I'm a cosmic inevitability, man. If I'm a mistake, then so's the whole fucking universe!

Trying to keep his voice steady, he said, "Okay, Harry. Then tell me what Michael is."

Michael? Michael ain't piss. He tried to hide Zeke from me, but I see it all now. He tapped his glasses. *Eyes of God.*

"Do you see your birth, Harry? Do you see Michael's death?"

Chen's expression soured. *You're gonna piss me off again, man. They dissected him. So what? You heard Gabe; it don't change what I am. And what he is. He's the devil, the fallen one. He's just a liar. No integrity. What are they if they're not angels, huh? Why are they here?*

"Then why not tell the world?"

'Cause it don't matter.

Vu asked, "Doesn't it, Mr. Chen? Or is it that you don't want anyone to find out?"

Carson stood between Chen and the psychic. The projection swept *through* him, inducing a nerve-splitting sensation, like the squeak of foam.

Shut up. You tried to turn my brother against me. You're gonna be the first one I send to hell.

Vu looked up at the floating messiah. His face was drained of all color, as ViVi's had been after Chen's first outburst. The green eyes were wide and glazed with fear, but his tone was distant, even calm. "That's not it, is it, Mr. Chen? You're not here because of Carson. You're here because we know, and you don't want anyone else to find out. We know you're not some cosmic inevitability: You're a product. You were engineered. And if we made one, we can make a hundred. Or a thousand. We can mass-produce our gods. That doesn't make you very unique, does it?"

Chen's face twisted with rage. The image lunged for Vu, ghost hands reaching for his throat. And passing through. Chen pulled back.

"You'll have to come in person if you wish to strangle me, Mr. Chen. You'll have to do it with your bare hands, like a man."

A wordless scream echoed through Carson's mind. And then something snapped. He felt it as a shock of static electricity. Chen reached for Vu's throat again, but now the projection looked different. Its outline was defined, the light brightest at the edges. The ghost hands extended, straining against their shimmering perimeter.

Vu climbed onto the back of the couch, in a futile effort at escape. "Stop this madness."

Carson watched, realizing with a peculiar horror that there was nothing he could do because Chen wasn't actually there. But the projection still reached for the psychic, straining against its own boundary, as if Chen's astral self was encased in an embryonic membrane of light that isolated him from the physical world.

Vu whispered, "Michael." The name was a plea.

Chen's hands found the rolled fat of the psychic's throat. Fingers indented the pale flesh. Vu gasped. His mouth froze open.

Then Chen shrieked again, and his clutching hands passed through. The projection was suddenly dimmer, the membrane gone. One more mind-quaking howl of rage, and it disappeared.

Vu slid down onto the pink seat of the couch, rasping for breath.

Carson swallowed. The muscles in his back burned with tension. He went to the old androgyne. "Are you okay?"

"Not particularly."

"Serves you right." He hadn't meant to say it.

The psychic gave him a cold look.

"My way," he said. "Whatever Harry is, he's not listening to reason. Tell me where the vid is. Now."

Vu stood up shakily. "Very well, Carson." He pointed to a cabinet painted with a veldt scene, antelope grazing tall, windblown grass.

Carson opened it, seeing the square void of the non-reflective screen. Chen fighting to free himself from the light . . . The image was vivid in his mind's eye, and just before the projection vanished, he'd seen something familiar—

A winged shadow. Or had it been his imagination? He called to the psychic, "What stopped him?"

From the stairs, Vu answered, "Not what. *Who.*"

Carson pulled up a routing form and listed recipients: Senator Josiah Bloom, ICARUS, the Planetary Security Council, NewsNet. His first message would be brief, just the most relevant facts. ICARUS might trace it, but by the time they caught up with the *Sea Safari,* he'd have composed his second transmission, telling the truth about the last two weeks. And that truth, he hoped, would eventually set him free.

Poodle loped up the stairs and disappeared behind a bifold door.

The wood floor vibrated as the yacht's engine engaged. Glancing out the window, he saw they were heading due south, parallel to the city. The blue glow-lines of a farm gridded out the dark plane of the sea.

"Carson . . ." Vu's face appeared at the stair's iron railing.

He turned away from the vid. "Where are we going?"

Vu mounted the last few steps. He held a very small pistol in his right hand, not much more than a finger-width alloy tube. "To the airstrip."

Carson reached for the control pad.

"Don't," Vu said. " 'Twould break my heart, but I *will* shoot."

He allowed himself sarcasm. "Sorry, the shock value's long gone."

Vu waved his other hand. "Step away from there. Go sit down on the couch."

He complied.

Vu took the chair with the tasseled, zebra-skin cushion. The gun rested on his thigh, pointing in Carson's general direction. He slid a phone from the blazer's breast pocket and flipped it open, his thumb punching the numbers. Speaking with a feminine air, he said, "Miriam? This is ViVi Vestala. Tell your agents— what?" Pause. Surprise widened the owlish eyes. Then, "You should know I am armed." Another pause. "I have your word?" His lips curled. "I'm far too old and cynical for that . . . I see. No, we will rendezvous . . . Until then." He snapped the phone shut, his tone dipping toward the masculine again. "It seems Mr. Chen is not the only one whose vision has broadened of late. Your beloved Ezekiel took the liberty of informing the Israelis of our whereabouts. They're on the way."

"I thought you didn't trust them."

"I don't. But I trust ICARUS and Mr. Chen less. One must have a little faith at some point." Vu crossed his legs and removed the captain's hat, setting it on a side table of glass supported by fake tusks. "You're a rash young man, Carson. I like you despite myself. But this horn-blowing isn't going to work. Leave that to the angels." He nodded toward the vid.

Carson saw that it still showed his routing form. Then there was a burst of light like a camera flash and a quick static jolt. The screen was blank.

Hope you made a backup.

Chen. But only his voice.

'Cause I just wiped your mail.

The fear was cold and familiar. He yelled, "Fuck you, Harry," as if volume would carry his words to Chen. "Fuck you. We still know it. Erase all the files you want. It doesn't change anything. If I have to go deliver it myself, they're gonna find out. You can't wipe Michael."

I don't need to.

The hair prickled on Carson's neck and arms as a new projection appeared next to Vu, standing *in* the side table. Not Chen, but a tall angel with unflinching gaze. Gabriel.

The psychic raised the pistol and fired. The bullet ripped a hole in the woven grass covering of the cabin wall. He pleaded, "Michael, stop him!"

The Seraph's hand reached for the gun. His glowing fingers closed around Vu's.

The psychic screamed. "No!" He clawed at Gabriel. Their joined hands disappeared in the light. Then Carson saw the gun rising toward Vu's face. He covered his own, cowering.

The androgyne's last cry was truncated by a single shot.

Carson couldn't look. Saliva flowed into his cheeks, the wave of nausea building. In darkness, he waited for the final light.

Forget the mail, Carson, and I'll let you live until Judgment Day.

The bifold creaked open. He heard Poodle whimper and run down the stairs.

Carson bit against the nausea and opened his eyes. No projection, just—

His vomit hit the corpse slumped on its tasseled, zebra-skin cushion two meters away.

Seventeen

Carson made it through the bifold door and into the helm room before vomiting again. Half-digested remnants of his dinner splattered across the dashboard.

The bullet had left a burnt hole in Vu's temple. It was the psychic's contorted face and the ruby trickle crossing the still-open emerald eye—

He dry-heaved twice more.

Straightening, he saw that they were adrift. Poodle must have turned off the engine. Carson fumbled over the instruments, looking for the key. There it was. He got the boat in gear. The movement was rhythmic, mesmerizing. He let himself be lulled by it, swaying against the wheel, as the yacht cruised through the tunnel its lamps bored in the night. He didn't know if he would reach the airstrip. It didn't matter.

The skimmer appeared uncounted minutes later, bouncing across the water behind a cone of light. He wasn't aware of cutting the engine, or of them boarding, but then someone was there with him, at the helm.

"Carson McCullough?" The man's English was unaccented, precise.

Carson's head turned of its own accord.

The Israeli slipped his gun inside a quilted navy jacket. He wore a two-day stubble and jeans. His hair was short and dark. He glanced at the brownish splotches drying on the dashboard, then at Carson's soiled clothes. "I am Stev. Ezekiel sent me. Come, we must leave." He wrapped an arm around Carson's shoulders and shepherded him through the bifold door.

Vu hadn't gone to hell; he was still in the living room. Another man was there, older than Stev, and bald, with a clipped mustache and beard. He had Poodle by the elbow. The man-dog was whimpering.

Carson heard himself ask, "Male or female?" The voice belonged to someone else. "Which is it?"

Poodle turned, a look of outrage in his eyes. Tears streaked his gaunt, pockmarked face. He threw himself across the androgyne, sheltering it.

"Leave them," Stev said to the other. He guided Carson out onto the aft deck.

The wind brought him voices. He didn't understand their words.

"Here. Down this ladder."

Carson climbed into the skimmer's backseat. Stev and the bald man followed. Peering up through the bubble top as the vehicle came about, Carson saw Poodle dragging Vu's lifeless body from the yacht's cabin. Then they were racing over the foiled waves. Lost in the seat cushions, he tried to understand the muffled wind-voices outside.

It wasn't until Stev spoke on his phone, in Hebrew, that Carson recognized their ancient tongue.

The plane was descending. Through thin clouds he glimpsed the Mediterranean and the sprawling white metropolises of the coastal plains.

"Please, you must wear this." Stev held a wide sash of black fabric.

Carson looked from the blindfold to the man's face. His expression was reasonable, even pleasant. "Where are we going? Jerusalem?"

"An installation nearby." He added, "The trip is fairly short."

Carson let himself be interned to the solitude where phosphenes wriggled, like worms through a corpse.

There was a long ramp just before they parked the car. His ankle hurt when he got out. Something heavy thudded, causing a tremor that came up through the soles of his sneakers. He sensed they were underground.

Stev guided him into air that was faintly antiseptic. Dropping sensation. New voices when they emerged from the lift. A plastic bracelet was clasped on his wrist. Then more doors that opened with a whirring of machinery and led to silent corridors. They paused at one point in some sort of chamber. Suction, as if the air were being changed, and the smell of disinfectant grew stronger. Stev squeezed his upper arm reassuringly. "Very soon," he said.

Carson could guess what this installation was: a closed-system, self-sufficient bunker impervious to everything from radiation to airborne biological and chemical agents. Most governments, and a number of wealthy private citizens, had built comparable facilities as part of their invasion preparations. The chamber was probably an air lock where they'd undergone low-grade decontamination, a relaxed version of the entry protocol.

"Here." Stev removed the blindfold. It took a minute for Carson's eyes to adjust to the bluish fluorescence. They were in a corridor, walled and floored with a smooth, brown-specked material that absorbed the light from the ceiling grids. The bald man keyed something on a pad set next to an oval, door-sized hatch. *Whish.* It withdrew into the wall.

Stev nodded. "Go ahead."

Beyond the portal was a common room. A large wall screen showed olive groves at sunset. Zeke stood in front of it. He wore jeans and a pair of sport sandals with black rubber soles. His chest was bare; the bandages and cane were gone.

Carson took three steps into the compartment, then stopped. Behind him, the hatch slid shut. "You're alive," he blurted, realizing that he hadn't believed it until now.

The Seraph responded, "Because of Michael. I didn't want to be." Zeke crossed to him, his gait and wings even.

Carson looked into the familiar gray eyes, resentment and fear displacing his relief. "Alden isn't. Neither is Déjà Vu. If only you'd told me; if only I'd known sooner. They're dead, and I'll be next." A tear overflowed onto his cheek. He batted it away.

"No," Zeke said. "That will not happen." It was promise, prediction, or both.

He struggled for composure. "I want to believe you—"

"But that's never been your strong point, has it, Carson?" The Seraph's tone was kind. "You don't need to tell me about Chen and what Gabriel has done. I already know. I saw, and I accept the truth now. That is why I told them where to find you." Zeke gestured to a pair of modular couches, inviting, "Please, sit. You've come a long way."

Carson noticed Miriam for the first time. She gave him a tight, acknowledging smile. He limped to a seat across from her. She wore plain khaki fatigues tucked into the maroon combat boots. Her eyes were tired.

The Seraph stood between them.

"You said you know about Harry—" After Chen's warning, he wasn't about to blurt out the messiah's dirty secret.

"Yes." *But our friends here do not.*

Zeke's voice was soft in his mind. He still twitched.

Miriam said, "Ezekiel has briefed us on your activities. I'm sorry now that I left you and Vestala behind, but under the circumstances . . ."

He nodded, unsure if the apology was sincere, as Stev interrupted with a breakfast tray of coffee, bagels, and fruit. Carson hadn't felt hungry, but he ate, trying not to think of it as his last meal. Swallowing a mouthful, he asked Zeke, "So what about Harry? He's being too quiet."

"Chen and the others are in ICARUS custody. Their forces raided the Sea Station and he surrendered. Chen's body is heavily sedated. He doesn't want them to know *he* is awake."

The hatch slid open again. Two men in their fifties entered. The younger wore a tan Israeli army uniform with a general's stars. Carson didn't even try to catch their names as they all took seats at a rectangular table adjacent to the couches. Zeke remained standing.

"We've been watching over the vid," the general said without apology. His accent hinted at a Russian childhood. "Earlier you told us that for our own protection you could not explain Chen, other than to say his presence had confused you. We rescued your friend." He nodded at Carson. "Now we need to know what Chen intends to do and if it poses a threat to our country."

Zeke's gray eyes focused on the man's weathered face. "He intends to come here."

They exchanged glances. The plainclothes—Carson assumed he was Mossad—twisted his wedding ring compulsively.

The general asked, "Why?"

Carson recognized the faint amusement in Zeke's

tone. "Because he wishes to ascend his throne, and this is where it is."

"ICARUS will act if he attempts to escape," the general said. "They'll be able to stop him."

"No, they won't," Zeke said. "You don't understand."

But Carson did. The Seraph's next words impaled him as surely as nails through a cross.

"He will not come by any means they can stop. He will just *come.*"

The one with the ring quit twisting. "Why should we believe you? You won't tell us what you are or why you're here."

"I cannot yet provide the understanding you desire." Zeke shrugged. "I've told you of Michael, and you've always known about the dissection. Harry Chen is not our mistake."

The general said, "If Chen does come, ICARUS will follow. Our intent in closing our borders was to preempt that. Chen must be neutralized. How can we accomplish this?" His chair was pivoted to face Zeke. The Seraph went and stood before him, placing a hand on his shoulder. Carson saw the sudden rigidity in the man's posture.

"Do nothing." Zeke's steely gaze held the general's. "Chen is more than his body. Killing him will not solve your problem—or mine."

Carson added wearily, "You should believe him."

As Zeke released the soldier, Miriam made a little gasping sound. Carson felt it, too, the pricking of invisible needles against his skin.

Yes, you should believe him, because I'm coming, and there ain't nothing you can do. Or did you think this snake hole would hide you?

Chen stood in the grove that still showed on the wall screen. Only they were apple trees now, heavy with ripe red fruit. Sizzling light outlined his body. He stepped from the screen and crossed the room to the low table that held Carson's breakfast tray. An untouched apple lay there. Chen picked it up. *Go ahead, eat.* The messiah grinned and tossed the red fruit into the air. Miriam's brown hands came up automatically and caught it.

Soon, suckers, soon. Chen walked back into the grove. It was olive. And empty.

Miriam's nails dug into the apple's polished skin. Zeke's wings were forward, wrapping him in a protective cloak of feathers. The plainclothes was whispering a Hebraic prayer.

A hot flush marked the general's cheeks, but his tanned skin had paled. He said, "We've been prepared for this a long time. If he wants his kingdom, he'll have to take it by force."

"Do not waste more lives." Zeke fanned a wing impatiently. "I've told you: There is nothing you can do."

Miriam still held the apple. Juice dripped from the broken skin onto her hands.

The general pushed his chair back and stood, squaring his shoulders. "We appreciate your warning, Ezekiel. But you must appreciate that we have no particular reason to trust you. Two days ago, you wanted to end your life. Now you'd have us believe that this messiah of yours is immortal. Chen is still flesh and blood. False prophets have died before—and stayed dead." He turned on his heel and, with the plainclothes following, marched from the room. The hatch shut after them.

A moment later it reopened, and Stev entered. He smiled pleasantly and sat down on one of the couches, with his back to the vid screen.

Zeke was standing like a statue, his eyes focused

somewhere beyond the bulkheads. Miriam set the apple on the table's wood-grained surface. Carson watched her wipe the juice on her pant leg. Then her lips parted slightly in surprise.

Stev noticed. Looking alarmed, he asked something in Hebrew. Whatever her answer was, it made him laugh. He relaxed, crossing his legs and leaning back against the beige cushions.

Miriam casually swiveled her chair away from the other agent. Carson saw her eyes widen. Then she shut them and pressed a hand to her mouth.

It has to be Zeke communicating with her, Carson thought. He got up and whispered to the Seraph, "This Houdini trick that Chen's going to pull, can you do it? Can you get us out of here?"

"Not until he does. It seems we are bound by the limitations of his awareness."

Carson said, "I want to go with you. They didn't figure on Harry Chens when they built these things, and I'd rather die on some altar than rot in this tomb."

Zeke nodded. He was still focused on Miriam, alert, waiting. The wings extended, then settled into place.

When she made the decision, Carson saw it in her face. She opened her eyes and took a deep breath. Then she stood, saying something in Hebrew to Stev that made him smile again. She stretched and paced the length of the room and back, crossing behind the couch.

The movement was so swift, Carson almost didn't see it happen. One moment her arms were relaxed at her sides; the next, her rigid right hand chopped blade-like into Stev's neck. He grunted and keeled forward. She caught him by the collar and settled him against the cushions.

Say nothing, Carson. It was the Seraph.

Miriam continued her transit to the far corner where another couch was set near the same wall as the vid, out of its camera range. She gave Carson a look he couldn't read, then sat and removed her boots.

What on earth? Carson wondered.

Zeke's voice was gentle in his mind. *I know you are confused, but I cannot explain yet. Please stay calm; they aren't watching, but they may return.*

The Seraph went to stand before Miriam. She lifted her hands, almost in a gesture of surrender, then hesitantly undid his jeans and slid them and his white boxers to the floor. Zeke's engorging penis bobbed toward her like a dowser's wand. He stepped out of the clothes and let her pull him down onto the couch.

They're not going to, Carson thought, feeling his face flush with embarrassment and anger.

But they were.

At first, voyeuristic fascination overcame him. He watched Miriam wrap her thin brown arms around the Seraph's neck, one hand stroking the silken hair. She lifted her head and kissed the dark lips. Zeke's eyes were half-shut. As she moved under him, the virgin wings haltingly spread. Zeke raised himself up on his hands, and she unbuttoned her fatigue top. The pants she pushed down over her hips. Carson saw the smoothness of her belly, marked by a thin black trail of hair that led to the pubic triangle. Then Zeke lowered himself, and Carson could watch no more.

He turned away, but his ears lacked modesty. They listened to a sound familiar, the beat of wings, pulsing slow at first, fanning air, then quickening. Faster. And faster yet, until he thought that the angel was ascending, Miriam clasped in his profane embrace.

But a furtive glance showed him a different picture. It was all wrong: the thrusting angel, his face buried in her neck, and the brown woman, arching up to meet him, so that her braids fell over the edge of the plum-striped cushion and her head tilted back. Her expression was the only thing which fit.

He'd seen that half-veiled look of quiet ecstasy before, on the ageless face of some Renaissance Madonna.

After Zeke put his pants on, he strolled across the room to Carson. Miriam was still on her back, but she'd pulled the fatigues to her waist and closed the top.

Carson hissed, "Was that your grand plan to stop Harry? Or did you just not want to die a virgin?"

Sweat sheened Zeke's face and chest. His aspect was mild. "I need your help one more time, Carson. She will have you, but you must hurry." The Seraph adjusted his testicles.

"The world's about to end, and the best you can do is a gang bang?"

The Seraph brought a finger to his purplish lips. "Do this for me, Carson. Please."

Carson asked in an angry whisper, "Why? Why not wake up Stev and let him join in? We don't need a guard; we need a chaperone!"

An enigmatic smile played across Zeke's mouth.

"What? You find this amusing?"

"Only your assumptions, Carson. Not the situation. Very soon Harry Chen will discover the means of escape he seeks. I believe this will help us persuade my brothers, but if we are not successful, it will be too late for these matters of the flesh."

Miriam was sitting up, watching them.

Carson called, "No thanks." She gave him a hard look, then stooped to put on her boots. To Zeke, he said, "Why? What's . . . *that* got to do with Harry?"

"If I told you . . ."

"I'm not exactly in the mood, and I already know everything else, so you might as well tell me this, too."

"It was our purpose here," Zeke admitted. "A purpose subverted by the creation of Harry Chen."

Carson stared at him. "To have sex?"

He smiled faintly. "No, Carson. To procreate."

Still disbelieving, Carson said, "You're not even fertile, Zeke. You and her couldn't have a—"

No, Miriam and Zeke couldn't. And that was the reason for the ménage à trois. He took an involuntary step backward. "You don't mean that. Three gametes . . . It wouldn't work—"

"Harry Chen 'works,' as you put it, Carson."

"But you said he was a mistake."

The Seraph nodded. "Yes, he was not meant to be the only one. Nor to be before we were."

"You're not— What *are* you?"

Zeke sighed. "What are we? And what are you, Carson?"

"I'm a man."

"Yes. A child of men. And the evolutionary product of this living planet, the universe manifesting in its quest for self-knowledge, the vain creation of a wrathful god. These are your beliefs. Do any of them answer the question?" He frowned. "What you really mean is, 'Are we angels?' Yet the concepts behind that question are so poorly defined as to render it meaningless."

Miriam joined them. She was still flushed. "He's not going to stay out forever," she said, referring to Stev. "What now?"

"We wait." Zeke's fingers brushed her cheek.

Glancing away, Carson said, "I can't handle this."

They didn't wait long.

Eighteen

The messiah's return to the holy land was heralded not by angelic fanfare, but by a triumphant proclamation, *It's karma time!*

Zeke stopped pacing, his head cocked to one side. Before Carson could ask him what Chen meant, the answer materialized in the middle of the room.

Gabriel wore an orange jumpsuit pushed down around his waist, the dangling torso sporting Powell Space Base patches. He cradled a laser-targeted Kalachnikov assault rifle like a deadly infant.

Carson was on the floor without having thought about it, arms shielding his head. His vacant chair skidded on its casters and clunked into the wall.

"Get up."

Gabe wanted to do it execution-style. Well, he'd rather die cowering.

Steps came toward him, and then, as he steeled himself for the inevitable, strong hands scooped under his armpits. "Carson, please stand up." It was Zeke.

He dared to look and saw Gabriel watching him with wintry eyes. On the couch, Stev groaned. Carson got to his feet.

"You will come with me," Gabriel said. He nodded to Miriam. "You as well." Then to Zeke, "And your cooperation will ensure their safety."

Zeke gave them both a smile of reassurance and

said, "Take my hands." Miriam clasped the right without hesitation. As Carson took the left, he heard the hatch sliding open. Turning his head, he saw—

Golden light streaming through a hole in a dark wall. I can feel my body, he thought with amazement. And Zeke's hand. Then he realized that the opening was in a rough face of rock and that he stood on an uneven stone floor.

They were in a cave.

Gabriel was opposite them, in the center of the low-ceilinged chamber, flanked by Uriel and Raphael, who wore matching orange jumpsuits, but were unarmed. Beyond the Seraphim, in dimness barely penetrated by the sun rays, Carson could just make out a human form lying on the ground.

As Zeke released his hand, he felt the tiny electric shock, and Chen's projection, complete with rat tail and purple glasses, appeared in front of them. He was very bright.

Good choice back there, man. Chen gave Miriam a disdainful glance. Then to Carson, *I knew you wouldn't do it. They're not here to make no cherubs. He's just listening to Michael, and Michael's a liar; that's what I've told you all along. And when have I ever lied to you? I always call it the way I see it; you know that about me, man.*

Carson drew a deep breath of the cool cave air. It had a sharp mineral taste. Voice quavering, he said, "I know that you killed Déjà Vu because you didn't want anyone finding out what you are."

Chen's eyes narrowed until they were black slits in the glowing face. *You think that changes anything? I got news for you, man: It doesn't. You think explaining it makes it any less real? It doesn't. You think I'm worried they'll make more? I'm not.* He drifted closer.

But you should be. You want ICARUS to have this kind of power? Haven't you learned?

Holding his ground through sheer force of will, Carson asked, "Then why kill Vu?"

'Cause he was spreading lies, turning you against me. Anyway, it's not like Vu's gone. That's what I've been trying to tell you: I'm the messiah. You're all gonna live forever through me.

"No, Harry. You're not God. And Vu isn't going to live forever."

Chen smiled. *Sure, he is. I'll show you.*

The projection vanished. Chen's body still lay on the cave floor. Then the air in front of Carson shimmered, the light congealing into a new three-dimensional image, a slight figure in a white cowl girded at the waist with a tasseled cord of gold. Pale hands tipped by magenta talons emerged from the sleeves and drew back the hood. Large, luminous emerald eyes in a smooth, young face framed by short, tufted copper hair. Birdlike features that might be called pretty, but their gender was ambiguous.

"Oh no," Carson said. "I don't believe this."

Déjà Vu, at your service. The androgyne executed his trademark bow. It came off much better with the younger body.

Carson looked at Zeke. "It's a trick right? It's just Harry?"

The Seraph shook his head. "No. It is as he says."

Carson felt like he needed to sit down, but there was only the stone floor. He stared at the projection. "You're dead."

Vu nodded. *Apparently so.*

He let his gaze flit up and down the chaste cowl. "Does this mean you answered to God?"

In a manner of speaking, Vu told him. *But mostly I wanted to dress for the occasion.*

Carson didn't return his smile. "And what about Harry?"

Mr. Chen. Yes, well, I have him to thank for this state of—

Carson demanded, "What is he, Vu?"

I thought we'd been through this, Carson. He's a genetic product. Homo seraphim, *if you will.*

"You know what I'm asking."

The androgyne waggled a magenta claw. *I have told you that I will not put this in religious terms. I just won't.*

"Well, then what about Michael? Do you still believe in him?"

Believe in him? I never believed in anyone, Carson, except for myself. As for whether I believe him: Yes, he was truthful with me. That doesn't mean he's right. It just means I found his views preferable to Mr. Chen's.

The projection vanished, and Chen was back. *Heard enough?*

Next to Carson, Zeke said, "Perhaps not quite."

The air shimmered again, but this time the image that formed was a naked Seraph, youthful and, except for his wings, dark, as if carved from black marble, a statue that moved.

He and Chen stared at each other. The other Seraphim looked on, curious.

Carson whispered, "Michael?"

Hello, Carson, the projection said, turning toward him. Even without sound, the voice was melodic. The eyes burned like two stars in the night.

This is a trick, Chen said. *He never had a body.* He glared at Zeke. *Stop it.*

Michael looked at the other Seraphim. *My appearance does not matter. You know this. But our purpose here does. Why does he fear me so, if I am wrong?*

Raphael said, "But our purpose here was to herald

the coming of the messiah. To restore mankind to their god. This is almost accomplished."

Chen's projection was beside Zeke. *Stop it. Now.*

Michael remained. *What kind of god is this, that fears the devil?*

Gabriel, Chen commanded. The Seraph raised the rifle, aiming its alloy barrel at Zeke. A pair of wings rustled nervously.

Carson begged, "Harry, no!"

"Release him," Gabriel commanded.

Michael was gone.

Don't try that shit again. Chen threatened.

Gabriel addressed the messiah, "We will deal with him."

Chen nodded, appeased. *Hear that, Zeke? I could kill you, but I don't wanna have you hangin' around.* Then to Carson, *You see, man? Want me to bring back your dad?*

Carson was beyond anger, beyond fear, into a sort of numb confusion. "No! And, no, I don't see. I don't see why you're so frightened of Michael."

You just don't get it. Michael wants to control you, control me, control us all.

Zeke spoke. "This gift was not meant for you alone. We do not wish to control you, but neither should you control us."

Bullshit. Chen glared at the Seraph. *He doesn't want me to fulfill my destiny.*

"What destiny?" Carson demanded. He gestured to the cave. "This isn't a new Jerusalem. We're hiding here like criminals, and to the rest of the world, that's what we are. ICARUS already caught you once, and I know you heard that the Israelis want to stop you, too." He glanced at Miriam, who stood next to Zeke, arms crossed, expression wary. "What are you going to do, start another crusade? Kill a few million more in the name of God?"

Chen held up his hands. *Chill, man. That's not what I'm all about; you should know that. And this place is just temporary until I get ICARUS and everybody else in line.*

"In line? They're not going to obey you."

Chen laughed. *Oh yeah, they are. They're gonna do exactly what I want, 'cause I've got what they want.*

"They don't want your powers, Harry. Not that bad."

Yeah, they do. And not just my powers, man: the gates.

Carson said, "The gates? They don't care about heaven, Harry. You've been spying on everyone; you ought to know that. They don't believe the Seraphim are angels, and they've just been going along with the Party until they figured out what the aliens were up to and got a chance to steal their warp drives or something."

Right. And that's what I got.

Carson peered at him. "Warp drives?"

Chen snickered. *Shit, man, how did you get here? You didn't 'xactly walk. You think this is the only place I can go?* He grinned. *Chew on it, man. I gotta wake up.* His projection vanished.

Gabriel and the other two Seraphim stayed in front of Chen's body, guarding it. Miriam exhaled, then moved to the cave opening. Carson felt weak; he went and sat against the rock wall. Zeke came to kneel by him.

"Carson . . ."

He looked up, feeling only a coldness toward the Seraph, and met the gray gaze. "Why did you come?"

"Because it was willed that we should."

"Willed? By whom?"

Zeke sighed. "I can't answer that question."

"Can't or won't?" he demanded.

"Can't, because I can no more tell you, than you can tell an animal who it is that wills your actions."

"Is that what we are, your pets?"

The Seraph shook his head, silver strands whispering against feathers. "Have we treated you as such?"

He was tired of the vagaries, of the uncertainty, of the partial answers. He was tired to his bones. "Zeke, I've run out of opinions and I've run out of beliefs. If we just saw what I think we saw, then it doesn't matter if I'm alive or dead. Either way, I'm gonna be in Harry's world. So all I wanna know is this: What are you going to do?"

"Nothing."

Carson scrambled to his feet. *"What?"*

The Seraph straightened, his wings extending slightly as he rose. "I cannot convince my brothers, and I am outnumbered."

"Then tell the world. Do some of that telepathic shit."

Zeke tried to place a hand on his shoulder, but he slapped it aside.

"Carson, I told you once before that I don't have words to quell the fires. Do you think denouncing Chen would do this? Would those words fall like rain?"

Carson looked away.

"I'm sorry to have disappointed you, but the time for words has passed." Zeke went to join Miriam.

Carson sank down against the wall, burying his face in his hands.

Minutes later, footsteps, and the warmth of someone beside him.

She spoke softly. "I'm here because of what's inside

me. Sperm takes a few days to die. At least human sperm does."

Carson felt himself blushing, as he remembered.

"That's where the other two are," Miriam continued. "Ezekiel told me. Chen sent them to destroy all the samples ICARUS took while the Seraphim were quarantined after they rose."

He looked at her. She sat, knees pulled to her chest, arms clasped around them. "But Harry could stop them from making an embryo, or stop you—"

She nodded. "That's true. But he has a lot of other things to pay attention to. And Ezekiel said the presence might be enough, that the others would sense the child. That's why he asked me to do it."

"And why did you?"

"Because like your deceased psychic, I prefer Michael's view to Chen's. Don't you?"

Remembering Vu's comment about feeling like a puppet, he said bitterly, "We've been used."

Miriam shrugged. "It's our fault as much as theirs. Not just the dissection, either. But what we wanted them to be."

"We didn't ask them to come."

"Can you be sure?"

He stretched his legs out. "I'm not sure of anything. I had a moment of certainty ten years ago, when they rose, and I don't think I've had one since. Excuse me."

He got up and went to the cave opening, which was at chest height. Through it, he peered, squinting, at lapis, broken in the distant middle by a ridge of barren rust-colored plateaus. Above them the blue was sky; beneath them it was sea. He recognized this place, the canyon of lifeless water.

Leaning out, he saw the entrance was in the middle of a cliff at least two hundred meters high. Carson stepped up onto an outcropping of stone, unzipped his fly, and watched his urine jet into the blankness over the Dead Sea.

When he turned around, the messiah was getting groggily to his feet. Chen's hair and beard were plastered to his skin by sweat, and his white cotton pants were stiff and wrinkled from their dousing in the Atlantic. Wavering a bit, he made his way to Carson, who looked into the familiar face, almost not believing that the Harry Chen who stood in front of him, scratching at his bare chest, was the bright projection that had resurrected the dead.

Chen yawned. "Man, I think they gave me enough to put an elephant under."

"What are you going to do with us, Harry?"

Chen leaned against the cave wall. "I wouldn't hurt you, Carson."

"That's not what you said on the *Sea Safari.*"

Chen shrugged. "Yeah, but I was still adjusting then, gettin' over the shock of it. I mean, unlike these guys, I didn't always know who I was. And then when I did, I thought it was just gonna be that Herald Party scene, some ceremonial gig. Took a while for me to realize the power I had. Talk about a weird head trip, man . . . and I've done a lot of *serious* drugs." He regarded the zigzag space scars on his forearms, then looked up at Carson, dark eyes bright under the folds. His projection had worn purple shades; Chen the man had lost his magic glasses. "But now I see it all, and I'm gonna do something about the real *Freak Follies.*" He pointed to the cave entrance and the world beyond.

Carson would have choked had he allowed himself to laugh. "You're gonna save the world, is that it?"

Chen smiled. "Sure. Isn't that what you've always wanted to do?"

"Not like this."

"That's just 'cause you didn't think it through. Never thought about what you were savin' it from."

His face burned. "And you've thought things through? People are dying, Harry. You've made things worse; I wanted to make them better."

"It's gonna get better, 'cause I'm the real thing. I got the miracles, and that's what people want."

He shook his head. "You're not the messiah, Harry. You're something we made."

Chen's expression was patient. "You're still thinking about this all wrong, man. You're still thinking that God doesn't have nothin' to do with the universe. Like God and physics are two different things, like they can't be angels 'cause they're flesh and blood. Man, this is your big chance. It's what all this religious shit has been about, always tryin' to be a saint and failing. You understood that it was gonna take something more than human, and that's what I am."

The other two Seraphim appeared in the center of the cave. They wore orange jumpsuits from the space base.

Chen said, "Mission accomplished?"

They nodded.

"Good." The messiah grinned at Carson. "Now you're really gonna see the light." He gestured Gabriel over to them. "I want my brother to have a VIP seat. He's used to that." Chen snickered as the pale Seraph took hold of Carson's wrist.

"Harry, what's—"

The cave was gone. Blinking against full day, Carson saw that he and Gabriel stood outside on a high surface of bleached mortar. Chen's projection appeared next to them. Behind it, down a flight of steps, an emaciated Ethiopian monk emerged from his roof-top hovel. Seeing Carson, the armed angel, and the transparent messiah, his mouth popped open, then he fainted dead away, dropping his crossed staff. It fell, clattering.

Carson turned from the prostrate monk to look across the buff-colored buildings of the Old City to the gilt Dome of the Rock and, beyond it, the Mount of Olives. Alarmed, he said, "We're on top of Holy Sepulcher. This is Jerusalem."

Shit, man, where have you been? 'Course it is.

A breeze lifted heat from the planes of the roof and blew it at him, like a giant, hot breath. "What are we doing here, Harry?" Carson's queasiness was more than just vertigo from the sudden transport.

What do you think we're doin' here? I mean, you're the one that's been running around for eight years spreadin' the word! Chen snorted, then raised his right arm, pointing at the sky.

Blue, no clouds. The sun—

The brightness overhead wasn't the sun. The sun was still in the east. But there was another star above them, and as Carson watched, the asterisk expanded, dilating, rays bursting forth, not the blinding gold light of Sol, but the silver lambency of more distant . . .

Starburst. The phenomenon that had accompanied the eggs' arrival.

Gabriel had released his hold on Carson's arm. He staggered back into the shadow of a ridge, still staring upward. Below, in the plaza, people were shouting.

See, man? The gates of paradise. They're openin' for me.

Carson tore his gaze from the sky, to look at Chen. The messiah was grinning ear to ear. "What's happening, Harry? What does this mean?"

I told you, man—

"Our work here is done," Gabriel said, interrupting. He extended the Kalachnikov to Chen.

Nah, I don't like guns. You hold on to it.

Gabriel pressed the rifle into the projection's hands. "Our work here is done," he repeated.

Yeah, I know. Chen tried to give the gun back to the Seraph, but Gabe refused to take it.

Gabriel said, "We were sent to herald your coming. You have arrived at your potential, and Michael's efforts have been thwarted. Now we see that as was foretold, our work here is done."

The rat tail twitched. *What are you sayin', Gabe? You got plenty of stuff to do here. Shit, you think I can rule this whole planet by myself?* He laughed, forcing it.

"We did not come to rule, Harry Chen. It is not our purpose to stay. We leave now as we came, and take with us our fallen brother, Ezekiel. Farewell."

Gabriel's wings spread, and he launched himself, gaining altitude fast. Above him, Carson saw five winged shadows appear against the starburst.

Chen was shrieking, *You can't leave! Get back here! You can't leave me!* And Carson realized he heard the words with his ears *and* his mind, but he couldn't look away from the light, where the five Seraphim were no longer discernible and Gabriel was already a receding silhouette.

Chen's cries were interrupted, just for an instant, and then there was a figure dangling from the Seraph's legs.

Before Carson could understand what he was seeing, the staccato song of a machine gun rang across the Old City, and the dangling figure fell, vanishing as it did. Then Gabriel disappeared, and with him, the light.

"Carson . . ."

He looked down and saw Chen lying at his feet, face twisted with pain, blood oozing onto the white mortar from a bullet hole in his chest.

"Harry . . . Oh my God." He knelt and took the messiah's outstretched hand.

They were back in the dimness of the cave.

"Where'd they go?" Miriam came up from behind, gasping when she saw Chen, who had a death grip on Carson's hand. His eyes were closed.

"Harry! Harry, can you hear me?"

Chen appeared by his own body, kneeling over it. The projection was very dim. He lifted his gaze to meet Carson's. *I'm dying,* he said, his expression tormented. *It wasn't supposed to end like this . . . not again . . . it wasn't supposed to end—* The projection pointed an accusatory finger at Miriam. *Your people, they did this.* It stood, advancing. Miriam stepped back.

"Harry!"

The projection stopped and looked down at him.

"Harry, she didn't do this. Don't let your last moments on Earth—"

I'm dying! Chen shrieked. *And I'm not going alone!* His real fingers were still locked around Carson's.

Frantic, he said, "What about Michael?"

Chen howled the name with anguish and rage. *Michael?*

"He healed Zeke's wing!" Carson was shouting. "Maybe he can help you, Harry."

The projection shifted its gaze back and forth, considering. Then it vanished and was replaced by the image Zeke had conjured earlier, the ebony angel, rendered so faintly he was little more than a pair of bright eyes. They turned toward Chen's limp body.

Chen mouthed the words: "Heal me."

The eyes burned brighter, then the melodic voice said gently, *I cannot. Your wound is too deep.*

The shade disappeared.

Carson found he could cry for the man, if not for

what he had become. "Harry, I'm sorry," he whispered, still holding on to Chen's hand, tears trickling down his face.

I'm the messiah. Chen's voice only.

"No," Carson whispered. "But it wasn't your fault."

Yes! Chen screamed, and the cave was gone.

Nineteen

Carson had felt nothing the other times he'd been transported, but this was different. It was exactly the same fall into oblivion that presaged sleep, and at the point where he would have sunk into the abyss, something jerked him back—but not from slumber.

The force was almost spine-snapping, which made him realize that he still had body awareness, and he screamed. Then there was solid ground, and he was flat on his stomach, arms outstretched and mouth filled with the taste of chalk. He lifted his head and looked around.

The place was unfamiliar, a pale, barren land of craters and rocks. Chen was nowhere in sight.

Carson sat up, coughing, which expelled some of the terror, leaving a small space for thought. Overhead was a directionless void, blacker than night. Whatever light there was, seemed to come from the . . . *moonscape.*

"Harry?" he called out, his own voice sounding strange. He was too frightened to stand. Then, listening, he heard something which made no sense: the whir of an approaching motor. But a bright speck had appeared in the darkness. The speck grew larger, took on form.

Red, the narrator of the *Freak Follies,* alighted beside him and folded his black chrome wings.

"No—" Carson shut his eyes. When he opened them, he was still on the moon, and Red, with his crimson Mohawk and black leathers, was still there.

"Yer seein' me, all right," the Seraph told him, leering. "This ain't a dream."

"Harry?" Carson called, struggling to his feet. "Harry, where are you?" Then added, to himself, "Where am I?"

"Where do ya think ya are?" Red asked.

"I'm not in a VR show," he managed.

The Seraph nodded. "That's right. Yer in the Realm."

Carson peered at him. "The Realm?" He shook his head, trying to clear it. "No, I didn't do any space. This isn't a trip."

"It's the ultimate trip."

He demanded, "Where's Harry?"

"I'm Harry," Red told him. He waved black talons at the battered ground. "That's Harry. It's all Harry, 'cept for you."

"Harry's dying. Or dead."

Red's cheek twitched, jiggling the chain connecting his nose and ear rings. "Almost. And 'e told ya 'e wasn't goin' alone."

Comprehension dawned. "Harry transported me to . . ."

"More like stopped in transit. 'Cept this isn't really a place, not like ya think of it. What ya see is more of a . . . *interface*. And yer the user. But that'll change soon."

"Why?"

Red gave him a wicked smile. " 'Cause soon ya'll be dead."

"No." Carson shook his head. "No. This isn't real." He backed away from the Seraph, then he turned and ran, yelling, "No, this isn't real!" But the ground kept coming up to meet him, his footsteps raising puffs of lunar dust.

Red descended in front of him, hands on hips. "It's real, all right."

Carson dodged around the Seraph and kept running. "This isn't real!"

It's real, all right. Chen's voice. *As real as me. Now do you believe?*

Carson slowed, stopping, and sank to his knees. He couldn't help himself: All the anger, all the fear, had been compressed by his need to survive, pushed into some hypogeal reservoir, and now it welled up and erupted, a geyser of emotion. Shaking his fist at the void, he screamed, "No, Harry, I don't believe! You can trap me in your hell, but *you are not God!*"

The voice was ominously low. *Oh yes, I am. And eternity's about how long you're gonna have to figure that out.*

He shuddered.

You're dying, Carson, just like me. And we're gonna be together, man. Forever. I'm your god, and you're gonna believe!

Head bowed, he whispered, "Why, Harry?"

Why? Because I was cheated, man, cheated out of my destiny.

There was a calm now, inside him, where the reservoir had emptied. "You weren't cheated," Carson said quietly. "You cheated yourself."

Bullshit.

"Michael tried to tell you. I tried to tell you. Zeke tried to tell you. You had every chance, but you wouldn't listen, Harry, and that's why we're here."

Something shivered, loosening. The moonscape blurred.

You're wrong, man. I'm the messiah, and you're my first disciple.

Carson shook his head. "No. I don't believe."

And that's your whole problem.

Carson stood up. Speaking to the empty black sky, he said, "I'm here because you want me—no, *need* me—to believe. And you're right: I never had the faith. But there's one thing I'm certain of, Harry: Whatever the Seraphim were, whatever you are, you aren't God."

The ground felt like it was disintegrating under his feet; or maybe it was him. He looked down and saw that his body had blurred, too.

Feel that, man? You're slippin' away.

The calm held. "You can keep me, Harry. It won't change anything. You brought back Vu yourself, and he still had his beliefs."

Kiss it all good-bye, man. You're dying, and you never did it; you never changed one damn thing.

"You're right about that too, Harry. But I was only a man; you were something more. Less than a god, but more than us. You had the miracles, and you never used them. The only thing you left behind was confusion and fear." His vision was going. Touch, too.

You're fadin', man.

"Oh well. It doesn't matter then, does it? We're both slipping away, and the world's gonna go on without us. And the really sad part, Harry, is that you could have done so much. But now you're gone, and the DNA is gone, and Miriam probably won't make it out of that cave— What a waste."

Why, man? Why won't you believe in me? Chen's voice was faint, his speech indistinct. When Carson spoke, so was his own.

"Because you don't believe in yourself," he said, the truth of it sinking in. "That's why you need me. And if you were God, you wouldn't."

Chen's last words were a sensation as much as a sound. *But I believe in you.*

And in the fading twilight of awareness, he fell, accelerating, until everything was lost in an explosion of pain.

His body belonged to a squashed ant. He sucked in air, trying to reinflate the popped lungs, his ruptured heart splashing in its attempt to force blood through his flattened vessels.

The first breath was a battle he almost lost. The second was close. Then, inhale by exhale, beat by beat, he was restored to a body that was hurt and exhausted, but his.

He lay on cold stone, on his side.

"Carson?" Miriam's voice.

It was a while before he had enough energy to open his eyes. When he did, he saw static. It resolved, gradually, into khaki-clad legs, bent at the knee, and a pair of maroon combat boots. He managed to groan.

"Carson, what happened?"

He tried to speak, but it came out as another groan. His mouth tasted of chalk. He shut his eyes and worked at making saliva. When he had a good flow going, he opened them again. She squatted, out of reach, watching him.

"Harry—" The name was an unintelligible croak. He tried again. "Harry—"

Her expression was apprehensive. "What?"

He coughed, then worked up some more spit. "Harry." That was clear.

"Yes. Harry. Where is he?'"

"Gone."

"And what about the Seraphim?"

"Gone."

"Ezekiel too?"

She must have seen the answer in his face. "I'm sorry," she said, drawing closer. "Are you okay?"

He nodded, cheek scraping against the rough floor, too weak to cry. He needed to roll over; the pressure of the stone against his face was becoming unbearable. He shifted, falling onto his back.

It was all the energy he'd had. Closing his eyes and trying to ignore the pain, he let himself drift.

He returned to the cave and his damaged body. Opening his eyes, he saw only uneven rock walls. His voice was hoarse, but more reliable. "Miriam?"

"I'm here." Her answer came from the direction of the cave entrance. "Tell me what happened."

"I don't think I've got enough spit."

"Take your time," she said. "I'm not going anywhere."

Her bodiless voice disquieted him, and it was too much effort to sit up. "I'd rather be able to see you," he said.

He heard the crunch of footsteps, and then she came into view.

Miriam wore her maroon combat boots and not much else.

Carson stared. Her legs were strong, the thighs heavily muscled, curving out into the round of her hips, their center marked by the triangle of her black panties and the shaft of hair, like an arrow. The nipples of her small breasts were large, dark and erect.

"Uh . . ."

"We needed a banner if anyone's going to know we're in here," she said matter-of-factly, and sat cross-legged on the cave floor.

He decided the disembodied voice might be better, and looked away. "How long was I gone?" he asked, feeling the flush of his embarrassment.

"Seconds. Then you were back, and barely alive. Where are Chen and the Seraphim?"

"I'm not really sure." He recounted for her what had happened—at least, what he *thought* had happened.

"No one is going to believe you," she concluded.

"I know." He glanced at her, forgetting, then turned his face aside. Torrie's kidnapping charges were nothing compared to what he'd probably face now, even with the witnesses in Jerusalem.

"So Chen is dead?"

"That's my best guess, though in his case I'm not sure what it means." Carson speculated, "He might be where Michael is."

"The Realm?"

"That's what Vu said. But Vu's gone, too, so I guess we'll never know."

"Not unless . . ."

This time, he looked intentionally.

"Of course, if we don't get out of here, that won't matter either." She met his gaze. "Mind if I strip you?"

"Miriam . . ."

She placed a finger against his lips. "Rest." Then gently, she removed his clothes.

Thirsty, drained, he lay on the cold stone, drifting, half-aware of her getting up periodically to check the cave entrance for signs of rescue. Time became a rhythm measured in heartbeat, breath, the flow of light to dark and light again, a progression as seamless as that from good to evil, from life to death, where black and white dissolved into endless shades of gray. Continuum.

Dawn.

She was awake. Perhaps she hadn't slept. He was

one bruise, blue like the waters, and like them, heavy with salt. He needed to drink.

It was Miriam who brought it up. "I could get pregnant," she said.

"What?"

She sat against the cave wall, her brown cheeks stained with the faint trails of tears. "If we had sex, I could get pregnant."

Carson stared at her. "I can't believe you're saying this."

"Why? It's what they came for, and I'm the only one that can." She added, "Ezekiel wanted you to, at the bunker."

Anger flared, like a distant nova in empty space. "I don't need you to tell me what Zeke wanted. And I'm not going to play stud so you can have your lost love's baby."

"I wasn't in love with him, Carson."

He fell silent, rolled away. A few minutes later, he turned back to her and said, "Then why?"

She looked at him. "Why? Because it seemed like the right thing to do at the time. And it still does."

"That's it? You just feel like it? I don't think this sort of decision should be made on a whim."

"On a whim?" She frowned. "There wasn't much time to consider; you know that. And what's to consider? You've been to hell and back, and you still can't say what they were: angels, aliens, both. And so it does come down to what we believe is right or wrong, doesn't it? We're the only ones who know. We might not get out of here alive, and if we don't, then it won't matter. But there is a chance. There is a chance I could have this child."

"Maybe they were using us." The words hurt him to speak.

"Maybe. It comes down to what you believe, Carson."

He countered, "What do you believe?"

"That something went wrong a long time ago and that they came back to correct it, whatever they are."

He remembered his statement to Alden about the Seraphim being part of God's grand design. If there was a final reckoning, this choice would be weighed.

"It obviously wasn't their intent to stay," she added. "They couldn't reproduce their own kind, and their bodies were just as fragile as yours or mine." She looked at him sadly. "It's our fear that makes us want to hold on."

Sex. Sex wasn't something this body could do.

"I'm sorry."

"Don't be." She removed her boots.

He was limp. Kneeling, she took him in her mouth.

"Stop," he said.

But she didn't. She worked him a good ten minutes, sliding his flesh between her generous lips. It didn't help.

She sat up and took his hand. "You have to let go, Carson," she said. "You have to let it go."

Her hand was warm. He pressed it to his heart. "There's nothing," he told her. The reservoir of fear had emptied, and now he felt hollow, void.

"No," she said, kissing him, "there's always more."

Her tongue slid into his mouth, and he swallowed the warmth of her. It sank through his gut, wakening him. His penis hardened.

She lay prone on his body, every point of contact another connection where warmth flowed, something that could fill him, as he could fill her.

He grabbed handfuls of her ass, kneading with his fingers, and lifting a knee, he spread her legs apart.

He slid into her as she had slid into him, warmth

and wetness, moving in the dance that even angels knew, and lost himself there, in its hard, throbbing pulse, in the cry of thrust and the sigh of flesh.

At the surging moment, his aim was true.

Spent, not even salt-thickened water now.

She rolled off.

Eyes shut, he lay there, fingers entwined with hers. Time was a rhythm measured in heartbeat, breath. Continuum.

She let go of his hand.

He opened his eyes.

"Listen . . ." she said. And she was already up, moving to the cave entrance.

At first, nothing. And then, in the distance, he heard the engine whine.

Rescue.

Carson sat in the unequivocal fluorescence of the bunker, where day and night were determined by the flip of a switch. During the long hours of their debriefing, Miriam's warmth had seeped away. He smiled at her across the table of the common room and saw a brown-skinned Mossad agent smile back.

"Senator Bloom will meet us in Geneva," she said. "We testify before the Planetary Security Council tomorrow in closed hearings. It's up to you and him from there."

He nodded. They'd come to hasty agreement in the cave, while putting their clothes back on, that the nature of Miriam's pregnancy would remain a secret. In all other things, they'd been honest with the Israeli authorities, and if Carson had any say, the world would know the truth, too.

Not that it mattered, he reminded himself, now that

Chen, the Seraphim, and all traces of their DNA were gone.

A hatch whisked open, and the general entered. The man seemed to have aged. "A vehicle will be here shortly," he told them. He pulled out a chair, hesitated, then sat, giving them a tense smile. "It will be difficult to convince the PSC of your story. It's a fantastic tale, and ICARUS, in particular, will demand proof." He placed both hands flat on the table. "They know, of course, about the dissection. And there were a number of witnesses to what happened in Jerusalem. For the rest, however, there are only two corroborating items, one of which has just come to my attention."

Miriam returned his glance.

The general regarded them. "You both asked yesterday how we were able to locate you. I will answer that now. The last public announcement was of Chen's capture at the Sea Station by ICARUS forces, but we knew that he later escaped them. After your disappearance and the incident in Jerusalem, we noted something on the net, a rumor that Chen was in a cave above the Dead Sea. There were many rumors, of course, but this one seemed worth investigating, especially since a report came in from one of our MPs who believed he shot someone during the starburst effect, someone who then vanished in midair."

Stunned, Carson asked, "Where did the rumor come from?"

The general gave him an odd look. "There was a vigil for Chen after his capture, held by fans of his virtual-reality show. A lot of them were using space, and many reported a vision in which the show's narrator told them where to find the messiah. Once they posted this on the net, there were similar accounts from other space users." He cleared his throat. "Of course, we didn't find Harry Chen in a cave above the Dead Sea. We found you. Harry Chen's body was found at Powell Space Base. ICARUS has completed an autopsy. He died from a severe bullet wound to the chest."

Miriam drew in her breath.

Carson processed the information, and as he did, started to laugh.

"Why is this funny?" the general asked.

Carson shook his head. He wanted to stop, but the laughter wouldn't, it kept bubbling from some inner well.

"Give him a few minutes," Miriam said. "He'll be okay."

They left him there, helpless with laughter, tears streaking his face.

Epilogue

"There it is," Carson said, pointing to a break in the palmetto fans lining the coastal highway. Bloom's driver took a hard right, and the limo bumped off onto the rutted road. Carson glanced back for the twentieth time. No headlights followed them through the Florida night. Ahead, the Victorian loomed in silhouette.

They stopped before the arched gate.

"Wait here," Carson told the driver. He got out and let himself into the Stargate compound. The windows of the main house were lit.

Carson walked across the sand clearing to the Victorian and climbed the porch steps, sweat beading under his arms from more than just humidity. Through the screen door he saw Esmerelda the cat, asleep on her cushions.

Echo came to answer his knock, a cloud of cigar smoke preceding her. When she recognized him, the glowing red tip bobbled up and down. "Didn't expect to see you again," she said, letting him in. "Quite a circus in Geneva."

"You've been keeping up with it?"

"Course." She watched him with faded brown eyes. "And I'm sorry that things didn't work out like you'd planned."

"Me too," he said, glancing away.

"Come on back," she told him. He followed her down the hall and into the kitchen. It was hard being here, harder than he'd expected.

They sat at the old chrome-and-red-Formica dinette. She said, "Heard your speech. That was a good thing you did, trying to set the record straight."

"Yeah?" He shook his head. "I probably started as many fires as I put out."

Echo shrugged. "People believe what they want to believe." She folded her gnarled hands on the table. "So to what do I owe this pleasure, Mr. McCullough?"

He leaned in. "I want to ask you a favor."

"Shoot."

"Do you still have the feather?"

She puffed orange-scented smoke before answering, "Yes."

He sighed, relieved. "May I have it?"

"That depends on why." The crone pointed her cigar at him. " 'Zekiel gave it to me, and I gave him my word it wouldn't be misused."

Carson had to smile. "All right." Suddenly he felt sheepish. "I didn't even know if you still had it," he said, thinking of the destroyed samples. "I want to give it to someone, but before I do that, I want to use it to pray."

Echo peered at him. "You serious?"

"Yes."

She hooted with laughter. "All right, then. I think that can be arranged. But this giving it—"

He'd known that he'd have to tell her. When he did, her eyes opened wide.

"You and her and 'Zekiel? I didn't hear anything about *that* coming out of Geneva."

"And you won't," he said. "But I got word from Miriam: She had a daughter."

Echo chewed on the cigar. "Well then, I guess it's her birthright, isn't it?"

He'd thought she'd see it that way.

The crone got up and left the room. She returned with a thin, narrow box. Inside, folded between sheets of gold-flecked tissue, was one white feather.

Carson studied it, trying to connect to that reality when angels trod the Earth. He lifted Zeke's quill. "Mind if I go down to the beach?"

Echo nodded approval. "Be my guest."

It was a clear, moonless night, and that seemed appropriate somehow: He'd had his conversation with Harry already. The Planetary Security Council had officially designated the messiah MIA, but Carson and a lot of the spacers knew where Chen was. And if the projections of Vu and Michael had been real, then Harry had heard him offer thanks for the gift of his body, which someday mankind might decide to accept.

But no ghosts haunted Carson there, alone, on the starlit beach, no alien angels or androgynes. And there was one conversation he hadn't had.

He waded into the surf. The shining black waters of the Atlantic rushed over his feet.

The Party was in disarray, and Bloom was still fighting to get a full disclosure from ICARUS. Some people thought the Seraphim would return, and others expected that if they did, it would be with an invasion fleet. Everything was different and nothing was different.

Yet.

Miriam had given birth to a daughter. *Their* daughter . . .

She might work miracles, but she wouldn't save the world. Carson didn't expect her to. He could only guess at what the Seraphim had intended, but he did know one thing: Religion, technology, government, war—none of these could change the human condition. To do that required changing human nature. He and Miriam and Zeke had. Maybe that meant that they, like Harry, had appointed themselves God. Maybe it didn't. He'd have the rest of his life, and perhaps longer, to ponder that. Meanwhile, the world awaited, still rife with problems, and there was a desk in Bloom's office from which he hoped to solve a few of them.

A wave rolled in carrying the lambency from above, and for the briefest instant, he felt himself awash in the silver light of stars and angels.

It ebbed.

Raising the feather, Carson whispered, "Zeke, wherever you are, whatever you are: Thank you. And good-bye."

Watch for a
new novel by
Elisabeth DeVos
coming from
Roc in 1998.